To Justify The Wicked

DON RABON

To Justify The Wicked

ISBN 978-0-9903367-2-3

Contents

Prologue

I N 1713 BEAUFORT, North Carolina, was established. It was named for Henry Somerset, Duke of Beaufort. Subsequently in 1723, the town incorporated. One of the oldest towns in the state, it's across the Newport River from Morehead City and accessible via US 70 over the Gallants Channel Bridge, which replaced the Grayden Paul Bascule Bridge. The town is historically significant. In June of 1718, Blackbeard the pirate ran the *Queen Anne's Revenge*, his flagship, aground as well as his sloop, *Adventure*, near what's now Beaufort Inlet, North Carolina.

The well-preserved and maintained historical district provides primary and secondary homes to professionals from all over the country. Among them are found doctors, real estate investors, stockbrokers, and lawyers.

In the flow of events, our lives intersect constantly with others. In some cases, we pause and pass on as before—nothing of significance has changed. In other circumstances, however, that intersecting results in a life-course shift that can be observed and articulated. The ripple effect of a life touching a life and each in turn touching other lives and so on, is a driving force in the course of human proceedings. Nothing happens in a vacuum.

—An Endless Stream of Lies, p. 1

Woe unto them…which justify the wicked for reward and take away the righteousness of the righteous from him!

—Isaiah 5:22a, 23

CHAPTER ONE

An Espresso, a Stranger, and an Offer

W ITH THE ROLLING tide of time, it often crossed the operative's mind how all this circumstance came into being. Before that life-changing encounter, the label for all those persons under consideration for inclusion was "prospect," certainly not the hard-earned designation "operative." The journey involved an arduous transition from prospect to candidate to apprentice and ultimately to operative. But everyone started out with the label of "prospect." Everyone started out, but not everyone finished.

That particular encounter was the butterfly effect for a certainty. Up to a point, life had been as good a formative experience as any young person could ask. A comfortable, middle-class home in a stable, tree-lined, shaded neighborhood. There were friends and confidants. There were a series of teenage significant others, parties, and a senior trip. The seasons came around and, with them, the various festivities. One day, one week, one month, and one year all folded so seamlessly into one another that there was no real understanding that time changes everything. The youth had been lulled, like most, into thinking on a subconscious level, *This is how it has always been. This is how it's always going to be.*

But then, a car accident, involving a drunken driver, took away a loving mother, father, and younger sister in the blink of an eye. Having gone from a family of four to an orphaned, eighteen-year-old in an instant, it was necessary to skip the societal tendency for the delayed onset of adulthood and assume the mantle of personal responsibility immediately. And the mantle was heavy indeed.

Continued educational undertakings consisted of a blur of classes, lectures, labs, examinations, and a series of part-time jobs. There were no personal distractions. Academics became a most welcomed, all-absorbing challenge. Now, there was no time for significant others. Each course was a hill to be taken. Every semester moved the board piece closer to the finish. Finally, the arduous lectures, studies, and examinations were over. Victory.

There was a typewritten note taped to the apartment front door earlier in the day. The note was a request for a specified coffee shop meeting that same day at four in the afternoon. This meeting would be well after the graduation ceremony had concluded.

And now, perhaps something other than the butterfly effect had resulted in the luxury of sitting outside on the shaded patio of a tastefully out of the way coffee shop just off campus. The people around were not engaged in any conversations with those with whom they shared a table. Rather, each had plunged deeply into the plastic screen of a handheld device, all agreeing implicitly that whatever was on the other side of the screen was significantly more important and "real" than being in the moment directly with another person.

The prospect relaxed comfortably at a white-trimmed, orange, wrought iron table, encircled with black chairs, hoping that whoever had requested the meeting had changed their plans and would fail to show. The orange-and-black cap and gown honoring the university colors were resting comfortably in a chair on the other side of the table. The diploma, unopened, lay upon the seat of the same chair. The warm sun peeking through the dancing leaves of the large oak trees, served to offset the caffeine rush that came with the double espresso.

"What now?" was the primary question for which neither the sun, the leaves, the graduation attire, or the coffee seemed to have an answer. As if on

4

cue, a looming figure of a man stood between the pieces of the sun and the table. Now, there was even more shade. Standing at six feet, four inches, he wore an impeccable tan suit with a blue shirt and a darker blue tie. The cuffs of his shirt extended perfectly from the arms of his suit. Incongruently, on his left wrist was an inexpensive Smith & Wesson military watch. The band, however, did complement the suit. His salt-and-pepper hair, rugged facial features, and infectious smile ensured that the first critical seven seconds of impression management were positively accomplished.

Behind the stranger to the right and on the opposite side of the uneven, brick-lined street, the prospect saw a full-size, black GMC Yukon XL Denali. The windows were tinted to a degree far beyond what the law allowed.

"May I sit down for a moment?" he asked as he pulled out the chair and took a seat, not waiting for an answer. The wrought iron feet of the chair protested at having been disturbed with the four voices sounding as if fingers were being raked across a chalk board. He placed himself beside the prospect rather than the more socially acceptable position of directly across the table. Maintaining direct eye contact, smile in place, he extended his hand and said, "Hi, my name's Mike."

"Mike what?" the prospect queried.

The smile lowered by half on the man's face as his intensity doubled. He replied, "Just Mike for now."

Returning his smile, the prospect shook his hand and thought, *Well, so much for reverie.*

The interloper continued. "First, I want to congratulate you on completing your objective. I know it hasn't been easy under the circumstances."

Now, Mike had achieved the prospect's full, undivided attention.

Sitting completely upright in the chair now and leaning toward the shadow man, the prospect asked, "What do you know about my circumstances?"

"Everything. Your family was killed when you were eighteen in a car accident with an individual driving under the influence. The driver received a light sentence—probation, limited driving privileges for one year. There were minimal damages awarded in the subsequent civil case. All due to manufactured, extenuating circumstances as brought out by the driver's attorney. You worked your way through school, graduated with honors, and here you are."

"Okay, then my next question to you is *how* do you know so much about me?"

Mike's smile dropped completely, the brow furrowed, and the shadow maker leaned in closer, "It's my business *to know.* I also know you're sitting here now, wondering what your next move is going to be. Do I keep renting my room by signing the upcoming twelve-month lease? Should I go back home? Is that really home anymore? Where and how do I start looking for employment? You're at one of life's biggest crossroads, and now you either formulate a plan, or you will be part of someone else's plan. That pretty much sums it up."

He leaned back, transitioned into silence, and let his words penetrate the prospect's cognition.

"Well, you've got my attention. So how does your being here right now fit in with any decisions that I need to make?" the prospect asked, all the while establishing direct eye-to-eye with the caffeine-reverie disrupter.

"I have an option that I want to put on the table for you to consider," he answered as he tapped his right index finger on the top of the table. It dawned on the prospect that Mike's suit even matched the top of the table. The prospect had followed the movement of the hand to the table, contemplated the finger still pressing the table, reestablished eye contact, and asked simply, "What's the option?"

The man answered the question with a question. "How would you like to help make the world a better place?" Before the prospect could answer, he followed up with still another question. "Could you ever imagine being part of something bigger and more significant than yourself?" A third question followed rapidly. "Will 'normal' be an acceptable descriptor of your life or would you like for it to be 'extraordinary'?"

Mike didn't wait for an answer to any of the three inquiries. Continuing, he noted, "This is a one-time encounter. You're going to have to take it or leave it."

After reflecting, the prospect said, "Okay. I'm listening."

Leaning closer into the prospect, an even warmer smile now appeared on the man's face. "That's all I ask. Just hear me out. Then whatever decision you make, all well and good."

"And one thing more," he added, "from this point on until we get up from the table—either separately or together—you don't get to ask any questions. Does that work for you?"

The prospect looked down at the tabletop. There was a long, contemplative silence. The prospect took a deep breath, exhaled heavily, reestablished eye contact with the man, and replied, "Okay, I'll hear you out."

"Excellent," returned the man. He signaled to a waiter for two more coffees, waited till the cups were on the table and the waiter gone, and began.

One hour later, he concluded, "That's it. What do you want to do? You can stay here; I'll get up and leave and this time together was nothing more than a dream—it never happened. Or you can get up with me right now and get into that vehicle over there." Mike looked toward and pointed to the black SUV. The prospect focused on the vehicle and found it hard to look away even as Mike continued articulating the circumstances around a decision.

"If you decide to go, your apartment will be cleaned out, your furniture—such as it is—will be donated to charity. We'll hold onto your clothes, identifications, and eventually, you'll get them back. The balance of your car loan will be taken care of, and the car will be donated to a program designed to aid wounded veterans. Your laptop will be shredded. Everything will either be cleaned out or wiped out by midnight tonight." The additional information returned the prospect's focus on Mike most steadily. "You've got sixty seconds to decide," Mike added.

The prospect had often heard the term *event horizon*, the point of no return, used offhandedly. In the beginning, the term related to the dynamics of a black hole. Very quickly, it obtained an existential function. But now, the meaning, the application, and the experience took on a whole new clarity.

The thought flashed, *There really are times when we can't see beyond a certain point.* The sudden loss of family instantly came to mind. It had redefined life for the prospect. There was no looking to the past in order to navigate into the future. It was a black-swan occurrence. Only, in this case, the prospect had a degree of control—walk over to the edge, go over or walk away.

Relativity has been described as the difference between a minute sitting on a hot stove as opposed to a minute talking with someone found to be especially attractive. Whatever the frame of reference for the prospect may have been, the decision was made after only fifteen seconds.

"I'm in," was the prospect's succinct response.

The smile returned to Mike's face. "Most excellent," he affirmed as he stood up. He extended his hand, and the prospect instinctively took it. He reached into his pocket, pulled out a silver money clip, and placed a twenty-dollar bill on the table. Looking back at the prospect, he said, "Let's go."

The prospect automatically reached for the cap, gown, and diploma.

"Leave them, along with your cell phone," Mike directed as he turned toward the vehicle.

The prospect turned the phone off and placed it on the table. As the two walked in the direction of the SUV, the waiter reappeared, dutifully gathered what was left of the prospect's belongings, pocketed the twenty-dollar bill, and walked back into the coffee shop.

As the two drew closer to the SUV, the prospect thought, Well, there's my black hole. If I get in, I don't know where I'm going. If I stay here, the situation is pretty much the same. I still don't know. The lady or the tiger? Is this Schrodinger's thought experiment, and I'm the cat—simultaneously alive and dead?

They reached the SUV. Mike opened the door and turned to the prospect with a *what-are-you-going-to-do-now?* expression on his face.

The prospect answered by getting into the vehicle. "Oh, well," the prospect decided while settling into the seat, "No turning back now."

Having entered the SUV, Mike and the prospect settled into the back seat. Mike was behind the front passenger seat and the prospect behind the driver. There was a large leather arm rest separating the two. The driver had the front of the SUV to herself. The prospect could see that she had dark-brown hair and was wearing a white cotton shirt and the top of what looked to be the coat of a woman's business suit. What the prospect couldn't see was the matching vested, pants suit or her holstered 45-caliber handgun. Looking up, into the rearview mirror, the prospect saw that she had on dark sunglasses even though the vehicle remained in the shade. She never turned around or spoke.

The SUV still had the alluring new car smell. There were no indications that the vehicle had ever been driven before. The prospect thought, *This seat is much more comfortable than anything in my apartment. I could have lived back here while I was in school.*

Trying to maintain a level of levity to mask a growing sense of *what-in-the-world-have-I-gotten-myself-into?* related anxiety, the prospect said laughingly, "Well, I guess this is where you blindfold me."

Mike displayed a degree of surprise and answered, "Look at you. You're exactly right, very perceptive. That's good. It's necessary," he said. Glancing and pointing as he spoke, Mike continued. "The blindfold is right there in the pocket on the back of the driver's seat right in front of you. Would you reach in there and get it out for me, please?"

The prospect leaned forward, pulled the top of the pocket back with the right hand, and stuck the left hand deeply into the pocket to search for the blindfold. At that point, Mike jabbed a needle into the right thigh of the prospect. The solution instantaneously entered the body and accomplished what it was designed to do. Immediately, the prospect slumped over to the left, hard against the door. Mike reached over, took the prospect's left hand—still in position to continue searching for the nonexistent blindfold—out of the pocket and pulled the prospect back up to a more comfortable resting position.

The driver turned the front headlights on and off twice. One hundred feet ahead, a full-faced helmeted rider sitting on a motorcycle cruiser, facing the SUV, returned the signal by turning the headlights on and off one time. Then the rider fired up the bike, looked into the left rearview mirror for any oncoming cars, and pulled away.

After the motorcycle had left, the driver started the SUV and pulled into traffic. Reaching to turn on the radio, she glanced into the rearview mirror and asked, "You care if I listen to some music?"

"That's fine," Mike answered.

"Got any preferences?"

"I don't care just as long as it's not too loud," he said emphatically.

After a few moments, she found the genre for which she was looking. A segment featuring the works of Vivaldi had just commenced. Mike immediately regretted that he had forgotten that he didn't like classical music in the least.

Why didn't I just say light jazz? Oh, well, he thought as he sat back into his seat. No channel changing now. It isn't a long ride. I guess I can live with it.

Harnett Regional Jetport is two and a half miles south of Buies Creek, home of Campbell University—the Fighting Camels and the Lady Camels. It sits just off Highway 421 on Airport Road in Erwin, North Carolina. The driver turned off Airport Road and continued forward to a guarded gate. Bringing the vehicle to a stop, the driver blinked the lights up to high beam and back. The vehicle was waved through by a uniformed Harnett County deputy sheriff. Straight ahead was a parked Ember Phenom 300.

The SUV was parked with the driver's side across from the cabin door of the plane. One of the two pilots hurried down the steps to assist the driver and Mike to quickly deposit the unconscious prospect into the plane. Coming back down the steps, the driver tossed the keys to Mike, grabbed her go bag from the vehicle, and returned to the plane. The cabin door closed immediately behind her just as the engines began to get louder.

Mike closed the vehicle doors, got in the driver's side, adjusted the seat back to a comfortable position, and waited for the plane to leave for the runway. At the point the plane began moving, he drove back to the gate where the deputy waved him out. After exiting the compound, he stopped—engine running—got out of the car, watched, and waited for the plane to take off.

Inside the plane, the prospect was strapped into a fully reclined seat. There was a pillow and a blanket placed accordingly. The former driver sat directly across in the aisle seat. In her go bag, she had an ample supply of hypodermic needles in the event the prospect began to wake up earlier than anticipated. She sipped dark-brown diet soda from a large, clear, ice-filled plastic cup. There was a large slice of lime floating leisurely at the top. This was not her first rodeo. At this point, it always reminded her of her own, initial "meeting." She took out her dated, though highly coveted, musical technological device, turned it on, placed the earpieces comfortably into her ears, and dialed into a selection by Vivaldi. Though desperately wishing to let the chair back and close her eyes, she didn't.

The plane made its way to the end of the runway, turned, set the engines, released the brakes, and headed out, its speed increasing accordingly. Gently, the plane lifted higher and higher, turned to the northwest, and continued to climb. The plane became a dot in the sky and then disappeared. Mike turned on his phone, made a thirty-second call, turned his phone off, got back in the vehicle, and drove off the airport compound.

Although unknown to the abeyant prospect, it was going to be a long night. There would be several changing of planes and a final, long ride into the wooded night. Lastly, they were in a four-wheel drive that deceptively appeared to be an older, well-used, crudely painted, camouflaged Jeep. Fishing rods were sticking out of the partially opened rear window. The muffler sounded as if it had seen better days and was merely along for the ride. In fact, the vehicle was highly tuned with a motor that far exceeded factory stock.

At this final leg of the journey, the prospect was accompanied by three other men, one of whom, just like the prospect, had no idea they were in this world. As the ride continued, the road transitioned from bad to worse to appearing to have given up the idea of being a road altogether. It didn't matter. Both the driver and the other conscious passenger, who was riding shotgun, knew the way by heart.

Next, Mike turned back onto Airport Road and headed for Highway 421. When he got there, he headed north until he got to Greensboro. There he picked up I-85 South. Having made it to Lexington via I-85 Business South, he stopped at Lexington Barbeque. He placed a to-go order for a chopped barbeque sandwich, onion rings, a slice of pecan pie, and a large, sweet tea.

Easing back onto the south bound lane of I-85 Business South, he took an immediate right on Highway 64 West. From there, he was only minutes away from the Holiday Inn Express and Suites next to Vineyard Crossing. He checked in, using a name other than Mike, paid in advance with cash, went to his room on the first floor, made one last phone call, turned on the television, laid back on the bed, and started in on his still-warm, aromatic barbecue sandwich. Tomorrow, he had a similar meeting on the far western end of the state. He would need to get an early start.

CHAPTER TWO

Does It Take a Monster to Fight a Monster?

O N HIS ANTIQUE, mahogany desk there resided a reminder from Friedrich Nietzsche, "Whoever fights monsters should see to it that in the process he does not become a monster—If you gaze long enough into an abyss, the abyss will gaze back into you." The prompt sat in a matted frame and was positioned so that only he could see it. Even though he knew the quote by heart, he glanced at it from time to time whenever he was seated at the desk.

Over time, the quote had become a major point for contemplation. He knew that in his twenty-plus-years investigative career, he had dealt continually with monsters. He had experienced the abyss of the depths of human depravity in combat and in professional inquiries involving everything one person could do to another but shouldn't. And that's why the admonishment served as a point of reflection. Had he become a secret monster because of his experience? Was he a monster from the start, allowing for him to experience all that he had, with no apparent, emotional effect? In the end, he had concluded that the truth of the matter was positioned somewhere in the middle of the two extremes—two extremes for a certainty. He was someone who could *keep* a secret. But he was also someone who *had* many secrets. Some of those secrets were dark indeed.

His one-hundred-fifty-year-old desk had the smell of "old." And to him, it was a comforting smell. His nineteenth century, crinkled, brown-leather, oak, swivel-desk armchair creaked and protested at the slightest turn or movement. He wondered if, over a hundred years ago, someone sitting in this chair had heard the same sounds. In his mind, adding a little oil here and there to dispel the noise was not something he would ever do. He liked the sound and the comfort it provided.

The matching grandfather clock in the corner, served as an audible sands of time. The quarter hour, the half hour, three-quarter hour, and the hour all served to remind him time moves on. The built-in bookshelves that took up a quarter of the room were filled with the classics. Dickens, Shakespeare, Bacon, Poe and a host of others all waited patiently to be taken down again to fellowship with the reader. Some were valuable first editions. Others were dog-eared, used paperbacks rescued from bookstores. There were multiple copies of the same book. There was no order to the books. Wherever they could find a vacant home in the stacks would serve purposefully, until they were taken out again. Currently, he had five investigative/interviewing-related texts he had written, in publication. He had been casually working on the sixth.

As his specialties were investigations and the interviewing process—questioning for quality information, detecting deception, and gaining compliance—constituting a central element of an investigation, these classics served as his procedural and psychology books, sans footnotes and with no hidden attempt at social engineering. The writers were wonderful observers of human behavior, motivations, and strategic actions. There was, he believed, nothing new under the sun when it came to human constructs. There were just different environments and different actors.

He glanced over at the shadow box on the wooden stand beside his desk. Displayed in the box were the patches and name tags he wore as a uniformed officer. Each tag read T. Spence.

Tim Spence wore early middle age like a Tom Ford suit. It fit him as if it were tailor-made. Experienced and enthusiasm had coalesced into a productive and enjoyable life. At six feet, he was taller than average height, solid build, weight appropriate with age and height. He had noticed the ever-increasing flecks of gray starting to present on each side of his head, just above the ears. It was only his sea-green eyes that set him apart. They reflected his intense interest in people—people on both sides of the criminal justice table. Whenever he interacted with someone, they immediately became the most important person in the room. He epitomized the advice he gave to those in his interviewing classes: "Be interested not interesting. Always make the 'other' the center of attention." Consequently, most people with whom he interacted found him to be most engaging and perceptive, having never realized that, from his subtle questions, they'd contributed the bulk of the conversation.

All of this "averageness" served him well as an investigator. He could easily get lost in a crowd, fade into the woodwork, operate hidden in plain sight, and most of all, interviewees had a ruinous tendency to underestimate him. He offhandedly attributed his interviewing success to his "melodic, sweet-tea, North Carolina, Southern accent."

Most people—those in the public space—knew of and referred to him as Tim. Some, in his social space, utilized his initials—K. T, his first name being Kenneth. Only those in his personal space referred to him as Spence. Shared adversity and trust built over time were the only means of admission to that position. His intimate space was reserved for a special, few others. They called him by the name he had inherited from his paternal grandfather, Kenneth. Lastly, only his mother and sister called him Timmy.

The number of people in his personal space far exceeded the average. He genuinely liked people, and more often than not, people liked him reciprocally. If he had time to kill in an airport, someone was going to have somebody to talk to. He referred to the encounter as his "fourth-and-one rule." They were within one yard of him, and he had this one chance to learn something about them: he would undertake to make it happen. Someone who, when they parted for their gates, had both his card and an impression of having met a most interesting conversationalist. It just never occurred to them that they had spent most of the time talking about themselves, their families, occupations, and problems. Always, the questions they had posed to him somehow resulted in their continued revelations about themselves.

A lot of people in his social space thought of themselves as being one zone closer. To him, the public space was reserved for those for whom he had just not had the opportunity to meet yet and, subsequently, bring them into the closer zone. As a result of his time in the Army National Guard, local law enforcement, and the North Carolina Department of Justice, he had learned there were all kinds of people on both sides of the law. No, it wasn't so much a criminal record or the lack thereof that located someone in the outer zone as much as it was the display of an elevated personal impression of the self.

Comfortably, at this stage in his life, his self-assessment was as "the Goldilocks' mean." He was neither too young nor too old. He was not too tall or short. His face was neither ruggedly handsome nor one that would frighten small children. He had found that his everyman persona served him well in his investigative and interviewing undertakings. It allowed him to relate to others and to rapidly breach barriers of distrust and suspicion. He was comfortable being who he was. If others liked him, great. He liked them back proportionally. If someone didn't like him, it no more mattered to him than a falling leaf.

He had often wondered about his inability to be adversely affected by another's opinion of him. *Maybe*, he thought, *I have a touch of psychopathy when it comes to certain dynamics.* If that were to prove to be the case, he was comfortable with that attribute just as well. For one thing, it kept him from becoming a sheeple in an ever-increasing population of societal sheep following blindly where they were led. For another, it allowed him to stay focused.

In his mind, group thinking and the inability to stay in the moment for a protracted period combined to become the death knoll of an inquiry. He always ended this internal deliberation. "I ought to get tested sometime." By that possibility, he meant the Hare Psychopathy Checklist. But even as he considered it, he knew it would never happen— "If it isn't broken, don't try to fix it. Sometime 'broke' is just what's needed."

That's not to say that there weren't some attributes that he possessed, or vice versa, that could well undergo some modifications. At the top of the list, and the one he had worked most arduously to ultimately master, was his temper. Whether from genetics, combat, the cynicism that can develop from looking at life through the windshield of a patrol car, or a contentious patriarchal relationship, he had a temper. Not a temper that could increase incrementally with the passing of time and circumstance, but rather one that could go from zero to one hundred in a New York second. He knew that explosiveness all too well and endeavored mightily to control it. He understood, at the point the dial registered one hundred, he was no longer in control. Cause and effect as well as consequences were noncognitive factors.

Within an investigation or the subsequent interviews, his temper was never a factor. He understood the actions of the guilty and deceptive interviewees. To him, these verbal, vocal, and nonverbal indicators were tells that he utilized to carry the interview to its productive outcome. The interview was never personal. The interview was a challenge involving moves, countermoves, and strategic interaction. He had long since discovered the interview to be "the theater of life." The interview was a most invigorating undertaking. He was more than happy to take on a role.

Rather, issues that have the potential to compromise his self-control involved specific circumstances. There was, he believed, an implicit fairness dictating the interactions of people. A violation of one of those propositions had, in the past, served to turn the dial. There had been an incident when he had been a patrol officer in Salisbury and he'd arrested an individual for public drunk and disorderly. It was a hot and humid July night. Having cuffed the individual and placed him in the backseat of the patrol car, he turned on the air, opened the window of the plexiglass shield, and directed the cool air to the back of the car to provide a degree of comfort to the man he had arrested. As he drove to the magistrate's office, the arrestee kicked him in the back of the head through the open window.

Immediately, he turned down an alley and killed the lights of the patrol car. The trailing patrol car followed. Getting out of the patrol car, he told the trailing officer in the car behind not to let any vehicles into the alley. Opening the backdoor of the patrol car, he pulled the man out, turned him around, took the handcuffs off, and told him, "Now, hit me face-to-face." At that, the arrestee took a swing. When they arrived at the magistrate's office, the magistrate looked at the individual, who now was also charged with assault on an officer, and asked, "What happened to him?"

"He fell going up the steps," he replied.

"Going up the steps?" the magistrate queried. "I've never known of someone falling up the steps."

"You had to be there," was his terse return. He turned to the arrestee and commanded, "Tell her what happened."

"I fell going up the steps," he replied in a low voice.

"Oh," answered the magistrate, having decided she didn't want to inquire further.

Sometime later, he transitioned to the High Point Police Department. Before administering the polygraph examination, prerequisite for employment, he was asked, "Have you ever utilized more force than necessary when effecting an arrest?"

Immediately, he replied, "Yes," and conveyed the entire episode, leaving nothing out.

After a few moments of contemplation, the polygrapher replied, "I don't blame you. I would have done the same thing. Let's get you wired up here." That was that.

He often shared the episode in his interviewing classes, telling the participants it was not his finest hour and that they should strive to be better than him. Try as he may, however, he knew, in his heart of hearts, that were it to happen again, there was a high probability he would most likely respond in the same manner.

He had opted, after twenty years, for early retirement from the North Carolina Department of Justice. At that point, primarily to stay busy, he, along with a number of his friends—also professionally related contacts who called him "Spence"—formed a partnership to provide investigative support services and training. It was at a backyard cookout where it was decided the partnership would be known as the AIR Federation.

AIR stood for Academy of Investigative Resources. Rumor had it that, in the formation of the partnership and the agreement on a name, alcohol may have been involved.

In its conception, it was assumed that the bulk of the partnership's activities would take place in North Carolina and be directed toward the one hundred sheriffs' offices, four-hundred-plus police departments, and the score of state law enforcement agencies. In fact, due to the law of unintended consequences, over sixty percent of their collective time and talent would involve the private sector, especially within the area of fraud. What began as an undertaking to remain active and engaged transitioned into a most lucrative and challenging enterprise far beyond anything the influence of the fifteen-percent alcohol content of the beer at the cookout could have ever been imagined by the tight-knit inebriants.

He stood up, producing a cacophony of protestations from his chair, picked up his coffee cup, and headed to the kitchen. *This Sunday is going to be a good day,* he thought as he rinsed out the cup and placed it in the drainer. He knew that because today he was going to ride—ride a lot. Turning off the kitchen light, he walked through the mudroom, opened the door, and stepped into the garage. Immediately, his eyes focused on his pride and joy.

Grabbing the chrome handlebar grips, he threw his right leg over the saddle of his 2004, dark-emerald custom motorcycle. Immediately, the molecules from leather, oil, metal, and gasoline made their way to his nasal passages, into his bloodstream and ultimately to his brain. As a result of the symbiotic, molecular special recipe, the instantaneous sensation washing over him was so stimulating that he reflected it must be the same as a drug-induced euphoria. The aroma and the effect were unmistakable and, in their own ways, just as addictive. He knew riding a motorcycle was an activity that one was either passionate about or wouldn't do for love or money. It was the same with military service and law enforcement. Ambiguity never rode a motorcycle for any length of time. Anytime it was possible to get where he needed to go via his motorcycle, that was his preferred mode of travel—rain or shine.

What clothes he would need immediately were packed carefully in the saddlebags and the black backpack strapped securely to the sissy bar. Earlier, he had sent his diving gear, computer, and other clothing ahead. Whatever additional toiletry he might need, he could purchase after he arrived. He was good to go.

As he settled into the saddle and straightened up the bike, he thought, *This is* really *going to be a good day.* And he was right. The day itself *was* good. How could he have known that the day would lead to a series of ghoulish homicides, an attempted homicide, a covert organization that made the deep state appear to be children on the playground, an intrigue that would prove to be a three-pipe problem even for Sherlock Holmes, and a connection with someone who would redefine what constituted his innermost circle? Later, someone asked, if he had known what he was riding into, would he have left anyway? "Without a doubt. I would have just left a lot earlier," was his only reply.

Ahead of him lay a 3,200-foot drop in altitude, over four hundred miles of road, and a time frame that was dependent on which route he took and how much he decided to stop along the way. From mountainous Jump Off Rock in Laurel Park to the coastal town of Atlantic Beach—each at the extreme ends of North Carolina—was a "ride." This ride was the beginning of what he wrongfully anticipated would be an extended break.

First, he would attend the annual meeting of the North Carolina Public Safety Divers' Conference. The conference would include updates on diving safety measures, legal considerations, and current challenges. Additionally, he would make new friends, reconnect with seasoned friends, swap tall tales, chill, and take advantage of the opportunity to do some fishing and diving. Lastly, he would get the annual required hours in as a reserve officer with the Carteret County Sheriff's Office. As circumstances would dictate, some of these goals would be realized fully, and others not so much. In any case, his three-month reservation at the Atlantic Beach DoubleTree would prove to be most fortuitous.

Atlantic Beach is a valued part of North Carolina's crystal coast—North Carolina's southern Outer Banks. Located in Carteret County, it's one of the five communities located on Bogue Banks. He had attended high school in Rocky Mount, which is one hundred thirty miles north of Atlantic Beach. As a result, Atlantic Beach was "the" gathering place, spring, summer, and fall, for those who pooled their money for gas and were even willing to sleep on the beach. There was eating-and-beer money to be made by shoveling the sand off the walkways of the houses that, at one time, lined the beach. Everyone made sure no one went hungry. Other than beer, everyone poured all the liquor and wine they possessed into a bathtub for an unholy if not unhealthy communion they referred to as "purple passion." Sometimes, there would be as many as ten people to a room. Damaging furniture or the room was never a consideration amid the revelry. He had packed away a trunkful of good memories. His only wistful regret was that, at the time, he hadn't realized that was the most carefree life would ever be. Had he done so, would have more knowingly savored the experience.

As he left home in Laurel Park, he jumped onto I-26 East from Upward Road. Near Columbus, he turned onto 74 East and kept going until he got to Shelby. There, he stopped at Red Bridges Barbecue Lodge for the mandatory barbecue, slaw, baked beans, and sweet tea. He topped the feast off with a serving of banana pudding.

He followed 74 until he hit 85 North. From there it was past Gastonia and Belmont then crossing the Catawba river, he skirted to the south of Charlotte using 485. From there, he caught 74 East again and followed it all the way to Rockingham. At that point, he turned onto historic Highway 1 until he made it to Cameron. From there, Highway 24 East would take him all the way to Jacksonville, past Camp Lejeune, Swansboro, across the bridge over the White Oak River to Cedar Point and ultimately to Cape Carteret. There he took a right on 58 and crossed the intercoastal waterway via the Cameron Langston Bridge to Emerald Isle. From there, it was a leisure ride north to Atlantic Beach. He had arrived! While the four-hundred-plus-mile trip could have been accomplished in seven hours, his time was a little over ten hours. If he saw something interesting, he stopped. The bike attracted people like a puppy. The bike was the great leveler. Judges, those whom they had sentenced, bankers, and inked-up others, all found commonality through the bike. Consequently, along the way, he had a number of conversations with some most unique and interesting people.

He was right. This had been a good day. What he hadn't known was that, like his high school experiences, he would have done well to especially savor the moment.

Slowly making his way up the coast, he reached his destination, the DoubleTree, Hilton at Atlantic Beach. From May until the last of July, this hotel was his home away from home. With the amenities available, he could relax as much as he wanted and work as much as he needed. Good food and drink, indoor and outdoor pools, expansive exercise facilities, a beautiful stretch of beach upon which to run and close enough to wherever he would need to go.

When he checked in, the desk clerk knew him well. "You've got your door app on your phone, so you're ready to go. All that you sent ahead is already in your room," she said as she handed him a warm chocolate chip cookie. "Want another one?"

"No thank you," he answered, "one's a-plenty."

She followed up with a voice as warm as the cookie. "I hope you have a wonderful stay."

He picked up his motorcycle bag, turned right, walked to the elevators, entered, and pushed the button for the fifth floor.

Opening his door, the first thing he saw was the diving equipment, clothes, and work-related necessities he had forwarded. His room had a king-size bed with a bright, white cover and a light-brown wooden head-board. There was a gray-blue couch that made into a double bed. By the double sliding glass doors, there was a comfortable, brown-cloth chair on the right with a floor lamp placed in the perfect location for reading. On the left, was the workstation comprised of desk that matched the headboard, a desk lamp, plenty of electrical outlets, and a cushioned, adjustable work chair.

Sliding the glass door open, he saw the pier leading out well past the breaking waves, the blue beach house, the large, white beach umbrellas, and the Carolina-blue outdoor pool.

Closing the door and returning into the room, he thought, "Home sweet home."

Stiff from the long ride on the Harley, he decided, Just enough time for a short run up the beach to loosen sore muscles, lubricate aching joints and get ready to attend the meet and greet.

CHAPTER THREE

Up from the Grave, Clear the Fog, Make Yourself at Home

S LOWLY, EVER SO slowly, the fog began to clear from the candidate's—no longer the short-lived prospect—brain and body. As the concept of self-awareness was made manifest, the candidate's mind endeavored to sort things out and gain a sense of reality.

The last thing I remember was being in a back seat, looking for a blindfold. Now, I'm lying on a hard surface, most likely a floor. My mouth and throat are bone dry, and I'm about to starve. There's hair stubble on my skin.

The fog lifted just a bit more, and the perception continued to increase. Finding it difficult but possible, with the head lifted slightly, the candidate looked around the room as more details came into focus. Taking inventory, the candidate's awareness level progressed.

This is some kind of a cabin, and I'm lying on a rug. There's a wooden table and two chairs. The sun is shining through the windows. I can smell cedar. Glancing to the right, the candidate thought offhandedly, And there's a dead guy lying on his back beside me on my right. That revelation served to clear the fog considerably. The candidate was now, aided by the elbows, able to prop up and gain an even better perspective.

Like Lazarus, but less dramatically so, the dead guy sluggishly returned to life. He buried his face in the palms of his hands and made a washing motion as if he had the restorative waters of Bethesda. After a few moments, the dead guy spoke.

"Oh, I hate this part more than anything." Turning slightly toward the candidate but deigning not to raise himself up just yet, he advised, "Let's just continue to lie here for a few more minutes. The grogginess will pass, but you've got to give it time. And just so you'll know, that humming sound you hear is not in your head. That's the generator that runs the cabin and the well pump. It only kicks in when the batteries, charged by the solar panels on the roof, need a boost. After a while, you won't even notice it."

The candidate, sensing that the dead guy had a level of knowledge based upon prior experience, took him at his word and laid back down. For a considerable time, the two remained there, not speaking and seemingly contemplating the roughhewed, wooden beams that spanned below the A-frame ceiling. Eventually, the dead guy, made it to a sitting position, he turned to his left to speak directly to the candidate, whose back still maintained a relationship with the floor. Extending his right hand and flashing a smile, he said, "Hi, my name's Mike."

The candidate's next thought was, *I never realized there were so many people named Mike.* Implicitly placing concepts into convenient cubicles, for easy retrieval, the candidate would now and forever more think in terms of "Coffee Shop Mike" and "Dead Guy Mike."

Dead Guy Mike appeared to be just on the other side of fifty, in excellent shape, with salt-and-pepper gray hair that had been styled, not cut.

While making an effort to shake Mike's hand, the candidate said, "My name's—"

Before the candidate could make this disclosure, Mike tightened his grip and cut the candidate off. "Don't tell me your name," he said emphatically. "I don't have a *need* to know your name. And you don't have a need to give it to me. Until I tell you differently, your 'name' is *Candidate.*" Mike pronounced it dramatically, articulating each of the three syllables as if the name was comprised of three different words. He placed a heightened emphasis on the middle syllable. It came out, "Can—*Di*—Date."

The smile returned to Mike's face. "Look, I know you have a lot of questions—some I'll be able to answer, and others I either cannot or will not answer. But I also know that like me, you're bound to have a profound need to hit the head and be about to starve. Let's take care of first things first. What say, we first, take care of business, fix us something to eat, and then we'll talk?" He pointed. "Your bathroom is in that direction."

With that, Mike got to his feet with the help of a table chair and reached down to assist Candidate in becoming bipedal. Both headed to their respective bathrooms. When they each had returned to the place of their resurrection, Mike continued. "Now, here's the deal. When it comes to meals, one of us will prepare and the other will clean up. We'll alternate. And since I'm more familiar with the layout here, I'll cook first, and you clean up. What about a big, hearty breakfast with an endless pot of coffee? Does that sound okay to you?"

"Works for me," Candidate replied.

As his hands were busily making preparation, Mike turned to Candidate and pointed his left foot toward a large, green duffel bag that had been placed in a corner. "That's your stuff in that bag right there." Never taking his hands out of the white porcelain farmhouse sink and with a slight nod of his head, Mike directed Candidate's gaze to an open door. "You'll be in that room there. Why don't you take the bag into your room, get your stuff squared away, and I'll have this meal on the table in two shakes of a lamb's tail?"

Candidate walked over to pick up the bag. The bag was large, and Candidate expected it to be heavy. Nevertheless, there was surprise at just how heavy it really was. Candidate's right arm made its way between the strap and the bag. As Candidate hefted the bag behind the right shoulder, a muffled humph served to vocalize just how dead weight heavy the bag was. Leaning well to the left to offset the weight of the bag, Candidate entered the room, all the while thinking, *I hope there are no forced marches with all of this.*

In the room, Candidate was pleased with the arrangements. The room was more than large enough. The walls consisted of knotty pine boards running horizontally. A built-in bookcase was packed with dog-eared paperback books with a variety of subject matter. In time, the books would be most appreciated as there were no electronic devices or connections within the cabin.

Burgundy gingham curtains framed each of the two windows—one window behind the single bed and the other on the wall to the right as Candidate faced the foot of the bed. The bedspread—a multicolored woven blanket—blended well with the burgundy curtains. Candidate reached over, pulled back the blanket, and saw that the bed was already neatly made with high-quality, white cotton sheets. Gently, pressing the fingers of the right hand into the matching pillowcase, Candidate could tell it was, indeed, a feather pillow.

How cool is that? Candidate thought. Looking closer, Candidate saw the bed was comprised of a mattress on flat metal webbing. Sitting on the bed, Candidate heard the wonderful chorus of the protestations of the metal webbing connections. *Music to my ears. I'll be sleeping like a baby.*

As Candidate stood up from the bed, the metal webbing commenced the second chorus of its song of lamentation. Candidate concluded, *Probably not gonna be any silent, midnight trips to the bathroom for some time to come.* It was at that point that Candidate saw again the door to the small, private bath. Inside the room, Candidate, now less urgent than the initial trip, noticed that the knotty pine pattern had made its way into the bathroom as well. The room was comprised of a single stand, porcelain sink with dark copper towel racks on each side. Each rack held a large, white cotton towel. The rubber, sink stopper that rested in the basin of the sink was connected to the faucet by a nickel-plated chain. Left of the sink, a similarly plated metal wicker basket was attached to the wall at eye level. In the basket were white hand towels folded neatly under matching washcloths and crowned with a large, unopened bar of soap. To the right of the sink, six inches out and six inches up, was a toothbrush holder with spaces for six toothbrushes— two on each of the three sides, not attached to the wall. Lastly, there was a matching, empty soap dish sitting patiently on the back of the sink.

There was a medicine cabinet with a mirrored door. Candidate opened the door only to find that the three shelves of the cabinet were empty. *I don't know what it was that I expected to find*, Candidate reflected silently. *Still if you don't look, you'll never know, right?*

Right as rain, answered Candidate's internal whoever.

The remaining functionalities of the facility, to include the shower, were decoratively in line. The shower consisted of black-and-white subway tile, a dark-gray plastic shower curtain, and a black drain in the middle of the shower floor.

Eventually, opening the door and walking out of the bathroom, Candidate placed the heavy bag upon the ever-complaining bed. Within the opened bag, there was all that one person, in this circumstance, would require. The solid-blue work shirts and pants were all the right size and length. The blue flip-flops, black running shoes, and work shoes all fit perfectly. Candidate noted with a wary eye the vast array of exercise clothing. *Those have to be in there for a reason*, Candidate concluded. Also included in the toiletries were requisite personal products.

There was a chest of drawers by the wall on the left of the bed. Candidate carefully folded and put away the clothing—pants in one drawer, shirts in another, undergarments in still another. The shoes were placed neatly at the foot of the bed and the flip-flops at the side of the bed. Just as all had been put into place, the aroma of food took control of the totality of Candidate's attention.

Next came Mike's most welcomed herald, "Come and get it. Breakfast is ready!"

"You won't have to call me twice," Candidate answered, walking out of the bedroom. Candidate looked at the table and understood completely what had gone through the mind of Pavlov's dogs upon hearing the sweet sound of the bell. Candidate walked over, pulled out a chair, and sat down to feast.

CHAPTER FOUR

Retrain, Refrain, and Regain

S PENCE'S FIRST SEVEN days proved to be everything that he wished for and more. It began with the Sunday night meet and greet, which included an expansive buffet and an open bar. He ordered a ginger ale with a lemon twist and nursed that drink the entire evening. In public settings, he preferred a clear head allowing him to process attentively what others had to share at the point alcohol had provided the password to whatever was on their mind. It was in settings such as these that elicitation techniques proved to be most advantageous. Gaining information without asking questions was a vital part of his stock in trade. He practiced whenever he had the opportunity. He viewed paying attention to the speaker as a sign of respect, a form of self-discipline, and an opportunity to learn.

Many of those in the setting were vendors who had set up their booths in the adjoining room. Each vendor paid a fee for a table based upon table size and location. Those fees helped to offset the conference costs and aid in the administration of the association. Vendor-booth subjects ranged from diving equipment, law enforcement tactical equipment and clothing, and the North Carolina Police Benevolent Association to private sector intelligence agencies. It went without saying that each member would visit all the tables, review the merchandise, engage the vendors, and take a card. Additionally, each table had a variety of "giveaways" making the visit worthwhile. For the vendors, the new contacts and the post conference sales more than made up for the display costs incurred. Although it was never stated publicly, some of the vendors used the opportunity to entice participants from the public sector into the private sector. And sometimes they were successful in their undertakings. Some of the vendors themselves were previously sworn participants at the conference. Each vendor knew commonality could serve to open a number of doors.

Spence had no sooner taken his drink in hand and turned away from the bar than his first opportunity to practice presented itself. Standing in front of him was a six-foot, four-inch wall of a man. He was just beyond middle-aged, wearing light-brown pants and a navy blue, short-sleeved knit shirt that could have served as a sail on a small boat. He had a blue-and-gold vendor lanyard around his tree-stump neck. His full head of impeccably combed silver-gray hair topped it off. He was big, but there didn't appear to be an ounce of fat on him. He extended his massive right hand and introduced himself.

"Mr. Spence, my name is William—Bill—Bill Dockery."

Taking Bill's ham of a hand, Spence said, "Please, call me Tim."

"Tim, I wonder if I might take up a moment of your time?"

At the socially appropriate moment, the two men disengaged their hands, and each stepped back one step.

Not wanting to stand in the middle of an active crowded room, continually staring up while conversing, Spence spotted an empty table over in a far corner of the room. Spence knew having both conversationalists seated would serve to take away the implicit advantage of the differences in height. Pointing toward the table with his hand holding the drink, Spence looked directly at Bill and asked, "How about we sit at that table over in the corner? That'll give us a little bit of quiet so we can hear."

"That's great. Thank you for your time."

Seated across from Bill at the table, Spence placed his drink to his right, locked eyes on Bill, and asked, "What can I do for you, Bill?"

Bill sat back in his seat and began. "Tim, I need for this conversation to remain strictly confidential."

"I can assure you that whatever you share with me goes no further. I wouldn't be in business for any length of time if I couldn't maintain the confidence of others."

Satisfied, Bill began. "I'm the owner and president of a private intelligence agency—a PIA. We are involved in the collection, analysis, and exploitation of information that we evaluate from open-source intelligence—OSINT."

"Yes, I visited your booth. It was quite impressive."

"Thank you."

"I read an interesting article regarding the growth in electronics within the PIA industry. It's fascinating to see the enhancements that have been made in such a short period of time."

"Indeed. As a matter of fact, in my company, we recently spent over a million dollars in electronics expansion and upgrades that put us on an equal footing with any federal agency you would care to name."

"That speaks well of you and your company."

While Spence was knowledgeable, from his own experience, of the scope and operation of private intelligence agencies, by raising his eyebrows and turning over his right hand, he encouraged Bill to continue as he knew that the more people tell you about things or circumstances, the more they tell you about themselves.

As Bill continued, Spence slowly and minimally nodded his head, indicating rapt attention and involvement. At the same time, he provided vocal feedback with encouraging, periodic mm-hmms. From the question he asked, to his verbal and nonverbal communication, all that he did was designed to encourage Bill to continue talking.

"I would describe us as a nongovernmental or a quasi-nongovernmental entity. We often work in conjunction with other private and public sector organizations. Also, when the situation arises, we do contract work for individuals. We have thirty full-time staff and about the same number of entities to which we outsource for specific services and support."

Spence said nothing while maintaining comfortable eye contact.

After an awkward three seconds, Bill filled in the vacuum of silence. "While businesswise everything is going well, I have an issue."

Spence echoed, "You have an issue."

"Yes, I'm concerned that one of my top operators has been compromised by a counterintelligence undertaking. I'm walking a tightrope here because, truth be told, even if he has been compromised, I don't want to take any adverse, reactive action, and I don't want to lose him."

Spence continued to remain silent and flashed a facial display of puzzlement.

"First off, I can't take the adverse publicity if this issue were to become public. High-end intelligence agencies don't succumb to counterintelligence attacks and maintain the confidence of their past, present, and future clients. So, that option is completely off the table. Secondly, this guy is so good that if I just let him go, my competition will scoop him up in a heartbeat, and he'll cost me painfully, working for someone else."

"So, let me make sure I understand this situation, and you correct me where I'm wrong. You have a high producer that may have been compromised by counterintelligence undertakings. You want to keep the inquiry under the wire to avoid adverse publicity. You want to keep the individual on the payroll because of his efficacy and the fact that his working for a competitor would result in a financial loss for your organization."

"Exactly."

"Explain to me just how you suspect this individual has been compromised."

"He has been outsourcing specific, service-topic contracts to a single source. For example, all his surveillance needs contracts have gone to this one entity. Additionally, under the excuse of time-sensitive urgency, he has repeatedly bypassed the outsource bidding process. And lastly, contracts awarded to this vendor sometimes were for services outside of this company's wheelhouse. My suspicions are that he has developed a relationship with the woman who owns the company that goes beyond a professional association, or he has placed himself in a compromising position and is being coerced into driving business to this one entity. Because he has knowledge of classified information from our other undertakings, I'm concerned that information may be compromised. If that's the case and it were to come out, that would be the death knell for my company."

"Is this employee married?"

"Divorced with two young kids."

"Got it. I need the names of the company, the owner, and your employee."

Bill reached into his shirt pocket, pulled out his business card, wrote the information on the back, and handed it to Spence, who took it, looked at the back of the card, and placed it in his wallet. At that point, Spence drew a leather card holder from his right pants pocket. He took one card and handed it to Bill. The card was of expensive stock. On the card, the raised lettering contained only *Tim Spence* and a phone number. Bill looked at the card and placed it into his right front pocket.

Before he got up from the table, Bill asked, "How much do you think this will cost me?"

Spence used the act of picking up his drink, slowly taking a sip, placing the plastic cup back on the table, and reestablishing eye contact as a dramatic effect.

"Bill, if you have to ask…"

After a contemplative silence, Bill sighed heavily, threw in the negotiating towel, and concluded. "Okay."

Then to seal the deal, Spence added, "Keep in mind, if we don't solve your problem, the entire operation costs you nothing."

With that assurance, Bill's face lit up like a kid in a candy store. "I can't ask more than that."

Spence reached across the table with his right hand. Bill engulfed it with his, shook it to the point of nerve damage, and they closed the conversation and the deal. Bill left the reception. Spence reached for his phone, hit a speed-dial number for an experienced employee who had recently been promoted to junior partner, and waited.

When the call was answered, Spence said, "Hey, Mary. I'm sorry to call you at home. Before I lay this out, how are your kids?"

After listening to the rundown from the oldest to the middle to the youngest, Bill offered, "Listen, if you need anything while Jack is away, all you have to do is let me know." Mary assured Spence that everything was covered.

"I've got four names I need for you to assign someone to perform comprehensive research on each."

After going through the list, he closed out. "Thank you. If you would, please have someone brief me when you've got something." With that, Spence got up from the table, walked over to the bar, had his ginger ale replenished, turned, and continued to enjoy the evening.

From Monday until the end of the day on Friday, he continued to connect with old friends, made new acquaintances, and relaxed. He lateraled every inquiry from the communication center to another appropriate agency member. He kept his smartphone on silent and, unless it was family, let every communication go to voicemail and stay there. Other than that, he waited until evening to return any requisite phone calls and emails.

Each weekday morning included a breakfast buffet, set up in the back of the conference room, comprised of all that would be expected in the South. Walking into the room involved walking into a curtain of olfactory delight, scrambled eggs, bacon, sausage, grits, cantaloupe, honeydew melon, toast, butter, orange juice, and a never-ending supply of the hottest, freshest coffee anyone could want. Each element made its own contribution to the enjoyable link between smell and taste. Each member first compiled a breakfast plate. Then they would make their way to one of the round tables, find a spot, take a seat, dig in, and fellowship. Spence ate, listened, and occasionally employed one of a multitude of subtle techniques to encourage the interlocutor to share even more.

Each morning session addressed a conference-related topic. For the week, those topics included underwater evidence-recovery techniques, the legal elements related to underwater evidence recovery, underwater crime scene diagraming, underwater crime scene photography, and most importantly, diver safety.

The afternoons provided a variety of options from which the participants could choose. There were diving trips, diving practical exercises, and short, topical webinars conducted by diving experts from the federal level, military, and other states. Each year, Spence chose to retake a PADI—Professional Association of Diving Instructors—foundational, open-water-diving class. Even though he had long held his certification and was an experienced diver, he regarded reviewing the basics as anything but a waste of time. This undertaking of constantly reviewing the fundamentals mindset had a place as well in his assessment of investigations and interviewing. In all cases, the highly capable were those who had mastered the fundamentals. When diving, neglecting the fundamentals could prove to be fatal. In an inquiry, neglecting the fundamentals could result in focusing wrongly on the innocent and letting the guilty go free. Neither of the last two were acceptable in Spence's view of the world.

Friday night when his head hit the pillow, he thought, *This has been an exceptionally, good week—all enjoyment with no bumps in the road. I couldn't have asked for better.* Little did he know it would prove to be the last exceptionally good week for some time. In a very short time, typical bumps in the road would have proven to be a welcomed reprieve from that which was about to transpire.

CHAPTER FIVE

Candidate's First Briefing

T
HE TABLE WAS laid out to uniformed perfection—each setting was the same. At each of the two place settings, there was a dark-green cloth placemat with string tassels at each end. There was a pewter plate centered exactly on each of the placemats. Diagonally, across each plate from ten to four—as numbered on the face of a clock—was a folded cloth napkin of the exact color as the placemats. Lying patiently on each napkin were silver-plated knives, forks, and spoons all in exact and duplicating position. A thick, tall mug brimming with steaming coffee was placed precisely at two o'clock and a small glass filled with orange juice had taken its place precisely at nine o'clock.

Mike noticed Candidate taking in the consistency of the table placements. "I'm a little OCD," Mike confessed sheepishly. "I may not know exactly where everything is supposed to go, but I'm good to go as long as everything is the same."

"Works for me." Candidate returned an understanding smile, reaching eagerly for the scrambled eggs from which the visible aroma was rising. Next on the plate came the country ham, followed by an ample serving of grits. The grits were perfect—not too runny and not too dry. Immediately, a large pat of butter crowned the grits. Adding color to the plate, sliced tomatoes joined the feast. Grabbing two biscuits from a basket nested by a matching napkin, Candidate introduced the butter to the biscuits. The preparation ritual was topped off by a rounding application of salt and pepper to the eggs, grits, and tomatoes.

As the two enjoyed the food, their conversation was limited to their shared level of hunger and the wonderful taste of each item on the plate. The only time either would break from eating was when one got up, brought over the coffee pot, filled their respective mugs, returned the pot to its rightful place, took their seat, and continued to devour everything in sight. One serving satiated neither participant. Round two came and went. Only then did things begin to slow down. Mike, reached for one more biscuit, opened it adroitly, placed a healthy portion of apple butter in the middle, closed it, grabbed his coffee mug with the other hand, and settled contentedly back in his chair. "Now, that's what I call a meal," he proclaimed as he slightly raised his mug and biscuit in salute.

"I'll never eat again," Candidate returned in agreement.

At that point, they both settled into a reverie, each lost in thought and finishing the last of the coffee. Time passed. Finally, Candidate broke the silence, remembering Mike's admission regarding his slight case of OCD. "Well, time for me to do my part. I'll wash, dry, and put everything in its rightful place."

As if reading Candidate's thoughts, Mike declared, "Since this is your first time, I'll help you out, show you where everything is supposed to go, but from then on, you're on your own. Okay?"

"Okay," Candidate answered agreeably.

It was only at this point that Candidate began to take in just what comprised the large interior room of the house. There were two large windows that went down to the floor in the front of the cabin—one on each side of the door. The third smaller window was above the sink. Each of the three windows looked out onto a deep forest.

Next, Candidate noticed that all of the furniture, including the bedroom, was mission style. The kitchen area had ample counter, working, and storage space. There was a large, forest-green refrigerator and matching stove. Countertops were light-tan granite with dark flakes of brown and black.

Sadly, Candidate noticed there was no dishwasher. There was, however, a medium-sized, stacked washer and dryer, each forest green in keeping with the color scheme.

Well, at least, I'll not be beating my clothes on some rock by a stream, Candidate reflected gratefully. A ceiling-high, well-stocked open pantry served as a sentinel next to the back door.

What was taken to be Mike's room was directly across the room from Candidate's own. In the front left corner of the main room was a large stone fireplace. The front door led onto a covered porch whereon waited two big rocking chairs. In the center of the room facing the fireplace was a large, cranberry-red leather couch framed on each side by two large, matching leather chairs. The coffee table in front of the couch had been made from an old door. Glass panels had replaced the wooden panels. The black metal doorknob and square lock remained on the door. A key rested comfortably in the lock.

Candidate, began to fill the sink with hot water while adding dish detergent.

Mike suggested, "Why don't we wash the table implements first, then refill the sink, and wash the pots and pans next?"

Boy, Dead Guy Mike really is OCD, Candidate reflected. "Sure, that sounds like a good idea to me," Candidate said.

Mike seemed to be more than pleased with Candidate's acquiesce.

Thus began the first of a number of rituals that would continue for some time to come. In this particular ceremonial process, the first round was washed, dried, and put away. Mike pointed out carefully several times to Candidate where each implement resided. Then round two—the pots and pans had their turn in the pageant and were housed in like manner. Next, the napkins, dishcloth, and dishtowels were washed, dried, folded, and neatly placed in respective drawers to the left of the sink. The dish detergent was placed under the sink just to the left of the curved drainpipe. Having taken one last evaluative look at the detergent bottle's placement, Mike reached back in and moved it one millimeter to the left. Now, satisfied, he took a deep breath, sighed heavily, gently closed the door, and glanced around the kitchen area with an expression not unlike a young boy coming down the stairs on Christmas morning. The declaration "Perfect" served as his summation.

At that point, Mike's whole demeanor changed from an obsessive single-mindedness regarding order and placement. Mike now shifted to the topic that had gone unmentioned for the last two hours. Taking his place at the same seat he had occupied during the meal, he fixed his gaze on Candidate and pointed to the other chair. "Let's get down to brass tacks."

Still keeping thoughts under tight lock and key, Candidate concurred, ruminating, *Forget brass tacks, I could use some brass nails.* Instead of speaking, Candidate chose to acknowledge the transition with a slight nod of the head and a look of rapt attentiveness. Candidate retuned to the chair, settled in, and waited.

Now Mike's voice was somewhat lower than it had been during and after the meal. His words were more purposely pronounced, and his voice had lowered still more as he came to the end of the sentence. He sat with his elbows on the table. His hands were clasped with fingers entwined. His chin rested comfortably in the crook formed by his thumbs and index fingers. His eye contact with Candidate was well above the forty to sixty percent for normal, Western interpersonal communication.

Mike started in. "Keep in mind, as I told you previously, there's knowledge that I *can* give to you, information that I *won't* reveal to you at this time, and information that I *can't* share with you. As strange as it may sound to you, starting at this point, you're going to have to learn how to become comfortable, even take comfort from, not knowing. If there ever was a time when the adage 'What you don't know can't hurt you' holds true, this is it.

"There are going to be questions that you can ask and questions that you can't ask. If you ask a wrong question, I'm going to tell you just that, but more importantly, I'm going to let you know why that's a wrong question to ask.

"In that same vein, know this, before we go any further: if at any time, you determine that you want out of this pursuit, this endeavor, and that this circumstance is not for you, all you have to do is tell me, and it all ends. No questions asked. That being the case, you need to stop now and reflect on your assessment of all that has transpired so far. Because if you imagine circumstances have been too convoluted for you up to this point, then I have to tell we haven't even scratched the surface.

"You take a few minutes and reflect on all of this. I'm going to step outside and give you some time to think this all over. Decide what you really want to do. Ask yourself, 'Am I really willing to sacrifice for a greater good?' When I come back in, you tell me, at this time, are you in or out?"

Mike walked out the front door. Candidate could hear the rocking chair slowly, going back and forth, making a comforting repetitive sound on the wooden porch flooring. Candidate looked down at the table and processed.

Eventually, Mike returned and sat down at the table. Reestablishing his focus on Candidate, he asked, "Well, what's it gonna be?"

Candidate replied simply, "I'm in."

He fixed his gaze upon Candidate even more intently. "Okay, we'll start. What's your first question?"

Candidate came back at him with no hesitation. "Where are we?" he asked, never taking eyes from returning Mike's stare.

"I have no earthly idea." Mike's reply was candid and. "If you remember, I was laid out on the floor as unceremoniously as you were. I have no idea where we are or how we got here. Remember: what you don't know can't hurt you."

"Well, then, *what* are we doing here?"

"That question I *can* answer. We are here to get you up to code—informationally and capability-wise. We are here to prepare you to take on an awesome task. We are here to prepare you to do something you've never done before and to be able to emotionally prevail in the undertaking."

Then Mike slowly and methodically began to explain the purpose and scope of the mission. At each point where he went deeper and deeper into specifics, he gauged Candidate's reactions.

Having previously been in this circumstance time and time again, he could determine if he had reached a point where going further would accomplish nothing. In those cases, he terminated the briefing and explained to the individual that there was no need to go on. There just wasn't a fit. In those cases, the relief shown on the individual's face was palpable. The individual was strongly advised to forget all that had happened and all that had been said.

That night, while the now-rejected prospect was sleeping, Mike would go for walk into the woods and lay out the communication signal for an extraction in twenty-four hours. One hour prior to the extraction time, both would take a pill with a glass of water, lie down on the floor, and wait for their cerebral lights to go out. After a time, Mike would wake up in a hotel room, take the time to regain his sea legs, and then by a countersurveillance circuitous route return home.

Similarly, the rejected would wake to find themselves in familiar surroundings with all possessions previously taken now returned. It was as if nothing had ever happened. What the individual hadn't known was that for the next several weeks they would be under physical and electronic surveillance.

Those wise enough to get on with their lives were eventually released. Those displaying an alternate course would meet with an "accident" that left no doubt as to its purpose. At that point, the vast majority of those rejected would see the error of their ways and change course. The others would quickly learn their last life lesson: lightning most certainly does strike twice in the same place.

By the time Mike had concluded his briefing, all the air had escaped from Candidate's body. The eyes widened, the mouth fell open, and the head, neck, and shoulders moved forward three inches.

Mike continued by way of support. "Maybe, if you thought of it as making the world a better place, it would make it a bit more palatable. Maybe if you framed it as making life better for a whole lot of people that would help—a sheepdog protecting the sheep."

"Maybe," Candidate said weakly. "Just need a minute to get my head around it."

"Take all the time you need. While you're thinking, know this: what we are and what we are doing is all directed at making the world a better place—a much better place. You can choose to be a part of making that happen. Also, you can choose to pull the pin, and we'll close it out. No pressure from me. It's your decision."

"Well, can you tell the name of the organization?"

"There's no name. Having a name would make it a thing. 'Things' can be defined, discovered, picked apart, and ultimately revealed. Things can leave traces. While it may sound frivolous, nothing leaves nothing."

Candidate rose from the table, looked at Mike, and asked, "Can I go sit on the porch for a few minutes?"

"Certainly."

Candidate made it through the door to the edge of the porch just in time to deposit what had been a wonderful breakfast on the ground. Candidate then fell into one of the two wooden rocking chairs. Soon it was Mike who could hear the chair slowly rocking back and forth. After about twenty minutes, the rocking stopped, Candidate came back in, returned to the table, looked Mike in the eye, and confirmed, "I'm still in."

CHAPTER SIX

The Calm before the Storm

SATURDAY MORNING BROKE bright and beautiful. With a cup of coffee in hand, Spence was up in time to see the fingers of light from the still-hidden sun reach out and paint the clouds that were placed far out to the visual point where the eastern sky met the ocean. From its palette, the sky painted some layers of clouds dark gray. Between those layers, there were thin brush strokes of brilliant orange-pink. The scattering of clouds closer to the shore were cotton white.

The ocean was calm with ripples, not waves, lapping the sandy beach. Then the sun lifted itself up from the horizon. For a moment, there was a dramatic contrast between the dark and light. But the distinction was there only for a moment. Quickly, the sun took over, pushing back the dark and sprinkling diamonded stars twinkling on the top of the water.

Now, he could see a spattering of people walking on the beach. From time to time, someone would stop, look down, pick up a shell, and place it either in a plastic bag or in their pocket. Some were standing as still as statues as they stared out at the breaking of the day. Runners from the left and right would wave as they passed by one another and travel on. Some walked with their dogs who ran in ever-widening explorations until they were called back to begin the adventure again.

There was one fisherman with his rods placed into pieces of PVC pipes that were stuck into the sand. The rods nodded gently and in unison to the energy of the ripples making their way to the shore. He had a large cooler in anticipation of a respectable catch and a folding chair that would allow him to sit, look to the east, and keep a guarded eye for the more dramatic tilting of a rod that was not a result of the mechanics of the ocean.

A solitary treasure hunter with a metal detector was slowly working his way up and down the beach. He was sweeping the coil back and forth as if searching for a landmine. From time to time, he would stop, dig in the sand with a metal scoop, examine, and secure his find and move on—the personification of hope springs eternal.

Various seabirds flew across the water. Some were skimming the surface. Others were diving into the water, emerging with a meal, and flying away. Other birds would endeavor to filch that meal—sometimes successfully and sometimes not. What Spence couldn't see at this point were the sandpipers in their perfectly timed feeding patterns that kept them always just out of reach of the lapping ripples. There are a good number of circumstances—not just for sandpipers—where timing is everything.

Having finished his coffee, Spence decided to take a shower, get dressed, and have breakfast. Thirty minutes later, he was riding down the elevator to the hotel restaurant, Prime 1079.

On his way to the restaurant, he had stopped by the lobby desk and picked up what he thought of as a "real" newspaper—as opposed to a blue-dotted national publication flopped outside of the doors of hotel rooms with the biased depth of coverage just below the level of an elementary school *Weekly Reader*. While eating, he habitually would peruse the headlines, and if one caught his attention, he quickly read the article. If, in his mind, the article was useful, he tore it out, folded it up, and placed it in the right back pocket of his blue jeans. In this case, there was only one article that merited being torn out and secured.

Now seated and while waiting to order his breakfast, he used his phone to return text messages, review his email, and forward to the appropriate personnel any messages needing a more immediate response.

After a short time, a member of the waitstaff quickly appeared at the table.

With a pen in her right hand in the ready position on the order pad which she held in her left hand and looking directly at the pad, she declared, "Good morning. My name is Ann, and I'll be your server."

Spence locked his eyes directly at her, smiled, and replied, "Good morning, Ann. How are you this morning?"

Slightly taken aback at a question she was seldom asked, she took her eyes away from the pad, returned Spence's eye contact, smiled, and said, "I'm doing pretty good this morning. How about you?"

"I can't complain. You said you were doing pretty good. What could be doing better?"

Still holding the pad in one hand and the pen in the other, her arms dropped down to her side. Her smile dropped slightly when she said, "Well, I could use some help raising two kids."

He noticed that there was no ring on her left finger. "It can't be easy raising two kids as a single parent."

"Do you have any kids?"

"No, but I have friends who do. I've not been where you are, but I have some idea. Listen, I can tell from your accent that you're not originally from around here. What brings you to Atlantic Beach?"

Her shoulders dropped, and her facial expression changed to grief. "I married my husband while he was stationed at Camp Lejeune. We quickly had two kids. He got sent overseas and didn't make it back. Living near the base makes it better, cost wise, with medical and groceries and all. But money is always tight. To make matters even worse, my husband's parents tried to take my kids away from me. Their lawyer kept delaying and delaying, costing me more and more. When I finally won the case, I was cleaned out and head over heels in debt."

By this time, her eyes had welled with tears.

"I'm sorry for your loss. What is it that you need the most right now?"

Without a thought, she responded, "A reliable means of transportation. I'm working two jobs, and I never know if my car is going to start or not. It was a used car when I bought it. It's ten years old now, and the mechanic said it's not worth the money it would cost to fix it right."

Spence pulled one of his cards out of his right shirt pocket. On the back, he wrote a name and number. "You call this guy." He pointed to the front of the card. "There's my name. Tell him I told you to call and tell him the situation you're dealing with exactly as you told me. Tell him I said to give you the deal. I'm going to be here for the next three months, so I'll be checking to make sure he's got you squared away."

She took the card and started to speak, but Spence jumped ahead. "Now, tell me: What kind of breakfast would you recommend for a hungry guy from the mountains of North Carolina?"

The breakfast she served was more than Spence could have eaten in two meals. Before leaving, he signed the room charge for the meal and placed a twenty-dollar bill on the table. Returning to his room, he looked out the sliding glass door to a much more active panorama—more shell collectors, runners, fishing rods, metal-detecting treasure hunters, and those leisurely strolling. A young man was setting up the rental chairs and large, blue beach umbrellas. Spence could see some were already planted in and around the area.

Spence made a decision. *There's only one thing left to do for today: ride.* In the parking lot, he took five of his business cards out of his shirt pocket. On the back, he wrote, "Call me," and placed the cards under the windshield wiper of five cars scattered around the parking lot. Next, he and the motor-cycle set a course for Swansboro. *They*—Spence and the bike—decided on the scenic, beach route. The twenty-nine-mile trek served to clear his head and soothe his spirit.

He spent the day visiting the multitude of shops offering everything from candy to antiques. For a goodly amount of time in the afternoon, he sat in the green-paint-chipped bench in front of the Front Street Grocery, just watching and greeting people as they walked by. In a few instances, a passerby sat down and provided the opportunity to experience the enjoy-ment of making a connection with another human being.

Twice his nearly perfect day was interrupted by operational-related phone calls that required answering and processing. Skipping lunch, he had an early dinner at the Boro Low Country Kitchen restaurant. There he feasted upon a low-country boil consisting of potatoes, corn on the cob, crawfish, clams, and shrimp. Just as the sun was beginning to set, he made his way back to Atlantic Beach by the same picturesque route he had taken earlier in the day.

Sunday, he was blessed with no phone calls. He spent the first half of the day fishing on the Oceana pier at the hotel. The fishing was good. Whatever he caught, he either threw back or gave away so that the fish could make its way onto a table.

Investigating is a lot like fishing. When fishing, one must be patient and know the patterns of the fish. In an investigation, one too must be patient and endeavor to figure out the patterns of the doer of the wrongful deed. The other commonality is that, in both cases, it was never pleasant when the big one gets away.

His plan for supper that night involved eating at one of his most favorite restaurants, the Sanitary Fish Market and Restaurant on Evans Street in Morehead City. Walking into the door transported him back to his time at Rocky Mount Senior High. He was reminded that the beach was *the* place to go for the Blackbirds—the school mascot at that time. While at the beach, the restaurant was *the* place to eat. To top it off, joining him would be his good friend Detective Jesse David Rollins. Although separated age-wise by a number of years, the connection had been made, and it stuck.

Jesse David Rollins had been with the Carteret County Sheriff's Department for just over eight years. He had joined the department on the day he was eligible and had attended basic law enforcement training at Carteret County Community College, graduating first in his class. His father, a local Baptist minister who had married later in life and then had children, pinned the badge on him on his day of graduation.

His mother had endeavored to ensure that, biblically, he was on the right path from the very start. The names Jesse and David were both found in the Old Testament, and she wanted for him to be reminded continually of his spiritual foundation.

At five foot and ten inches, he was rock solid. Solid enough to play fullback in high school and wise enough to turn down a scholarship to focus upon academics. He graduated with honors with a degree in criminal justice.

After working in patrol for four years, he was promoted to detective and had served in that capacity since then. Spence was conducting a five-day foundational interviewing class for North Carolina law enforcement officers when he first met Jesse. In that class, Jesse distinguished himself by asking a number of insightful questions and displaying the rare capability to stay off his cell phone while class was in session. From then on, Spence had assisted in making sure that Jesse—known as J. D. to his associates—had access to the more advanced interviewing classes he facilitated, to the point of covering his travel expenses when the training was being conducted outside of Carteret County.

Jesse had put forth the determined effort to become an excellent investigator, not only within the interviewing tradecraft, but also having an enhanced capacity for critical thinking. When taking on a case, he could form a hypothesis from the information available and then proceed to develop alternative lines of inquiry. Just as importantly, he could objectify the various aspects of the process of inquiry so that confirmation bias was not a rabbit hole into which he fell as so often was the case. When he testified in court, he had the respect of the attorneys sitting behind each of the two tables and the judge sitting behind the bench.

He had been recruited by state and federal agencies to make a transition. But Carteret County was home. Spence, too, had told him that, should he ever wish to make a change, the door to the AIR was always open.

On the desk within his work cubicle, there were three framed pictures: his wife Jacqueline and two daughters, Starletta and Shemesa; his mom with his late father; and Dr. M. L. King. Hanging from his bookcase above his computer was a cross on a silver chain given to him by his maternal grandmother.

Exactly at six p.m., the two converged at the restaurant's front door. Spence spoke first. Smiling, with arms open, he said, "Bring it in, young man."

Rollins returned both the smile and the gesture and stepped forward into the hug.

Spence asked, "Why in the world are you sweating?"

"Just finished my run and a quick shower."

"When I was your age, I never sweated."

"When you were my age, they hadn't invented sweat."

"Listen. If I had looked as worn-out as you when I was your age, I'd have thrown in the towel right then and there."

After the catching-up laughter had stopped, Spence reached for the door. "Let's get something to eat."

Inside, the aroma of a variety of foods instantly made it past the nose and to the brain. A scrapbook of visual memories opened up in Spence's mind's eye. The wooden walls and straight-back chairs were just as they should be. On the walls were pictures showing decades of people, service, and exceptional food. The picture timeline ranged from the restaurant's opening in 1938 until now. He noticed the dark-blue vinyl tablecloths had been replaced with a deep red.

Red's okay, he thought.

The Tall Tales Bar with the arching swordfish on the wall had been added since the time when Spence would walk in knowing exactly how much, and no more, he could spend for a meal.

Immediately, a smiling hostess appeared, two menus in hand. "Dining inside or out?"

Still wanting to absorb all the memories the circumstances provided, Spence jumped in. "Let's eat inside."

Rollins offered, "Works for me."

Still smiling, the hostess said, "Great. Follow me." She led them to a table by a window, placed the two menus and napkin-wrapped utensils on the table. "Someone will be with you shortly," she advised and walked away.

From his position, Spence could see the water, the boats, and the painted sky.

Dinner, good company, and a show, he thought, *what could be better than this?*

In a short time, a waitress appeared. "What would you two like to drink?"

Spence answered, "Hey, we'll give you the whole order, if that's okay?"

Realizing that he had saved her at least one trip in a night of endless trips, her face brightened, and she replied, "Sure."

Without looking at the menu, Spence said, "I'll have fried popcorn shrimp and flounder, unsweet tea, and a piece of bourbon pecan pie."

She shifted her gaze to Rollins.

"I'll have the same except I want sweet tea."

"Got it," she said, turned, and walked away to place the order.

Rollins smiled and jokingly said, "Unsweet tea! And you call yourself a Southerner." That was the opening gambit for a leisurely time of catching up and filling in the personal blanks that the passing of time had opened. Only after desert and coffee did Spence turn to business.

"If you can, let's meet tomorrow at lunch and see if we can get this project moving forward."

"Let me see what's on my desk when I get to work. I'll text you right after that."

"Perfect."

At that moment, the waitress brought the bill on a black plastic tray and laid it on the table between two. Spence quickly grabbed the tray with his right hand, showed Rollins the palm of his left hand, "I got it. You can pay next time when I'll order steak and lobster."

Rollins acquiesced.

Spence laid a credit card in the tray and handed it back to the waitress.

"Back in minute," she said.

When she returned, Spence added a generous tip, signed his name, and placed his copy along with the credit card back into his wallet.

On the way out, they stopped at the shop, and Spence purchased two small shirts advertising the restaurant. Handing the bag containing the shirts to Rollins, Spence said, "Tell the girls I was thinking about them and I'll see them as soon as you invite me over for a cookout."

Having made their way past those now waiting for a table to the much quieter outside, they agreed on tentative plans for tomorrow and called it a night, neither knowing that the project they wished to develop wouldn't make it from the back burner to the front for some time.

Back in his hotel room, Spence read for a while, called it a day, and hit the sack.

CHAPTER SEVEN

Candidate's Second Briefing

HE REMAINDER OF the first full day at the cabin served to allow Candidate to decompress. After silent periods of contemplation, Candidate would pose a question to fill in the cognitive holes, clear the fog, and achieve some degree of balance.

"I can't get my head around the fact that you have no earthly idea where we are." Candidate reflected with an emphasis on the pronoun *you* and the verb *are* climbing upwardly at the end of the sentence.

"None whatsoever," Mike replied. "As I said, you're going to have to get comfortable with not knowing. There's an important reason for the restriction on the dissemination of information. Not knowing is a primary safeguard for you as well as the entirety. It's an operational strength. What's not known can't be disclosed. Whatever the big picture that's going on and wherever it will happen to be will be oblivious to you. In like manner, you and your functioning will be self-contained. There can be no link analysis to be made if there are no links. Compartmentalization is a strategic directive. Understood?"

"I think so," Candidate responded weakly.

Seeing that he needed to undergird this concept more before he moved on, Mike added, "Think of it in this manner. I know you play chess. What are the pieces on a chessboard?"

Candidate answered automatically, "The king, queen, two rooks, two bishops, two knights, and eight pawns—sixteen pieces for each player— thirty-two pieces in all."

"Right. Now each piece has purpose and range of movement. Together, under the direction of the player, they work in unison—commonality of purpose. But no one piece 'knows' what the other pieces have done, are doing, or will do. If a chess piece were to be captured, it can't disclose anything about the other pieces or reveal the strategy of the game.

"Each piece is an isolated unit working in oblivious concert with the other pieces on the board. But the determination of the individual piece movements and overall game strategy is determined by an element that's *not* on the board.

"The board itself is made up of sixty-four squares set up in an eight-by-eight grid. There are eight rows on the board called 'ranks,' and they're numbered one through eight. There are eight columns on the board referred to as 'files' and they're delineated by the letters *A* through *H*.

"Think about the complexity of the board with the pieces in play. After each player only makes one move, there are four hundred positions that could manifest on the board. After each player makes two moves there are over seventy-two thousand positions. Three moves each gives over nine million positions. And four moves each results in over two hundred and eighty-eight billion different positions.

"You and I are just two pieces on the board. Strategically, we make no decisions. Operationally, we *do* come into play. And there are the occasions wherein two chess pieces will work in alliance. But other than that, I don't have to know what you're doing and you don't need to know what I'm doing. Think of yourself as having the possibility of becoming a pawn. You would be on the board but you wouldn't be determining the moves."

"Are you a pawn?" Candidate wondered out loud.

"I don't know that either," Mike answered after a moment's reflection. In any case, does the chess analogy make for a clearer picture?"

"It does," Candidate replied with a nod of the head and more conviction in the voice.

"So let's move forward—first things, first. You're going to be here with me in an orientation—training capacity for a while. How long we will be here will be determined by my assessment of the progress you're making, or not. When and if I determine that you're ready to transition that's exactly when it will happen—not a day sooner or a day later."

"Should I make the determination that you're not viable, you will be returned to from whence you came, none the worse for wear, perhaps in a bit better physical shape, compensated adequately for your time and effort and none the wiser than if this entire escapade had been nothing more than a dream. Still with me?"

"Yes." The answer came forth with still more resolve.

"Excellent. There will be *no* written training materials. Everything you learn will be as a result of direct communication between you and me." Mike smiled and added, "By the time we are finished, I'm sure you will be tired of me, the sound of my voice and my face. And that's okay, but just keep in mind that all I say, do and require of you, is for you and ultimately, the operation."

"At the conclusion of our time together, you will be ready to go. There are no lesser degrees of achievement regarding the cognitive or the skill levels. Everything is pass or fail. You either know that which is essential or you don't. You can either perform at the optimal level or you can't. If I make the determination in either domain it's just not going to happen, I don't want you to feel badly. You will not be the first to phase out and you will not be the last. It just is, what it is."

Mike's last assertion only served to steel Candidate's resolution. Mike saw that increase to be the case.

Candidate's ruminations continued, In for a penny—in for a pound. It's settled. I'm going to see this unknown wrapped in anonymity through to the end.

Having rapidly completed the private contemplations, Candidate returned Mike's smile and resumed the dialog. "Let's do it."

Satisfied, that he had articulated the operational concept adequately, Mike continued. "In conjunction with compartmentalization, there are no attempts to communicate by any type of electronic means. Cell phones, computers, handheld devices or the like are never in play. Communication will only be conducted via codes, signs, symbols, signals or WOMO."

"WOMO?" Candidate echoed.

"Word of Mouth Only. You will be taught an extensive series of communication methodologies and their subsequent purpose. Additionally, as it does occasionally happen, should all communication modes change, you will be contacted directly and briefed on the new practices."

"How will I be contacted?" Candidate asked, endeavoring to take in all of the information.

"If everything works out, that knowledge will be provided to you at a later point," Mike replied in a manner that indicated to Candidate that a good amount of personal accomplishment and character demonstration would precede the disclosure of that information. Trust was not to be easily conferred. It had to be earned step-by-step.

"You're to never write or record a sign, signal or other modality whereby any form of communication would take place. Don't develop, write and try to conceal mnemonics. You have to commit all of the alert, initiation and directional modes to memory and believe you, me, I'll be testing you time and time again. I'll wake you up in the middle of the night and make you run through them all. When you're the most fatigued and brain-dead, I'll require you to recite them back and forth, in and out, up and down, and around and around.

"You'll be required to demonstrate that you can physically set up signals and alerts for others. If I use an alert word or phrase within the course of our normal conversation, you're required to respond with the alternate and describe what actions you would initiate from that point. I'll expect you to spontaneously articulate a code in your part of a conversation and tell me what actions I would need to take after you've spoken the communication."

Rather than serving to overwhelm, these few insights, complexities, and future tests Mike had presented resulted in an adrenaline rush that Candidate had not experienced in sometime. College had required concentration, effort, and presentation but lacked a real challenge.

Before his death, Candidate's father had often advised that a trial provides an opportunity for one to discover a previously undisclosed personal dynamic. That dynamic, he asserted, could either be an asset or a liability. If the dynamic was an asset, capitalize upon it. If the dynamic was a liability, endeavor to overcome it. Never before had Candidate's father's words taken on more meaning.

"Can I ask a question?"

"You can give it a shot. I'll answer it if I can," Mike answered.

"Can you tell me what all of this covert complexity and subsequent actions are ultimately endeavoring to accomplish?"

Mike answered the question with a question. "What's the object of a game of chess?"

CHAPTER EIGHT

Candidate Takes the
Final Assessment

S IXTEEN ARDUOUS WEEKS had passed. There were one hundred and twelve days of long, cross-country runs. Candidate had observed that after especially long runs, the refrigerator and pantry had been magically restocked. Additional activities included physical exercise, defensive tactics, and verbal instruction. These were weeks wherein Candidate had been required to perform, recite and respond; weeks involving a three-in-the-morning wakeup call followed immediately by a verbal or performance test. Should the results of the test fail to meet Mike's expectation, it was immediately repeated until an appropriate level of performance had been achieved. Candidate had no trouble sleeping at night, and the sound of the compressing bedsprings served as the siren's song leading to blissful slumber.

It was early morning. Breakfast had been served. The dishes and cookware were washed, dried, and put away. The aroma of sausage, scrambled eggs, buttered toast, and grits draped the air with the last vestige of what had been an enjoyable meal, including a heaping side order of conversation and joviality. The two had come to know each other as much as circumstances would allow. The candidate had learned it's not always necessary to know a great deal of specifics about someone in order to make a connection. Sometimes just the personal qualities of each were enough to allow for a positive linkage.

The rays of the sun were just beginning to make their way to the curtains that framed the kitchen window. The cabin itself had grown quiet. The only sounds now were the birds in the forest calling in expectation for the bread and other leftovers Mike dutifully threw out the backdoor each morning.

Candidate and Mike sat at the kitchen table, which was covered with an oilcloth covering that matched the curtains. Coffee cups were full, steaming, and at the ready. As they faced each other, Mike's cup was near his right hand. The candidate's left index and middle fingers were through the handle of the cup with the thumb resting comfortably on the top. The candidate sensed that the time had come for additional instruction and accordingly transitioned from active conversation participant to pupil.

Mike took a deep breath, grew serious, and opened the assessment session. "Explain to me the way communication functions on the operational level as it applies to texting, phones, computers, social media, and the like."

"Okay," the candidate responded and then waited. The silence grew uncomfortably heavy and long. The candidate found it necessary to adjust to a more comfortable position in the chair, yet, all the while, waiting. Finally, a sip of coffee allowed the candidate to do something to dissipate the anxiety generated by the prolonged silence.

"It doesn't," Candidate responded. "It doesn't operate in any manner electronically."

"Then how will you ever know what you're supposed to do?" Mike sked.

"All communication on the base level is made by signs, symbols or WOMO."

"WOMO," Candidate Mike echoed.

"Word of mouth only. At the point I'm operational, any instructions or directives I receive will be delivered primarily by word of mouth, visual notifications, or both. Nothing, absolutely nothing, is ever conveyed by any electronic capable of being copied or traceable means."

My placement is as in a honeycomb. I'm to be positioned in a hexagon. All around me are others in exacting dimensional hexagons. In most cases,

I have no knowledge of them, and they have no knowledge of me. In the event of an adverse outcome, only one hexagon is affected with no collateral damage to any other hexagon."

"Adverse outcome?" countered Mike, continuing with the pattern of repetitive responses.

"In the event that there's an issue involving one hexagon, the individual will have no information to disclose. In this manner, the only element comproised is the one hexagon."

Continuing with the metaphor, Candidate added, "No other elements will be impacted as the result of a negative consequence. When it comes to a compromised individual, contingencies are in place for extraction. I'll not be left hanging in the breeze."

"What contingencies?" countered Mike, wishing to delve deeper.

"In the event of a situation where I find myself compromised, I'll not forcefully resist. I'll maintain absolute silence and wait. I'll never talk. Even if I'm viewed to be only on the peripheral of someone's inquiry, I'll never, ever talk."

"What is it that you wait on?"

"Extraction."

Mike continued. "What about higher levels of functioning? Are computers and electronics communications utilized there?"

"I have no idea."

"Excellent," Mike replied with the satisfaction, having completed a job well done.

"You see, in my position, I'm in a hexagon too. When you and I finish here, our paths, in all probability, will never cross again. I have no idea as to from where my directives emanate or what comprises the overall plan. I have no idea who you are, what your real world, skill set comprises or what you will be doing after we complete this agenda. I only know that which involves me directly. Think of it this way: You and I are looking through an electron microscope. We see very little. I can only assume others are looking through a magnifying glass, viewing a much bigger picture. And, again, that's only supposition on my part. Simply stated, the only thing you need to do is to attend to that, for which you're tasked."

"Got it."

Picking up where he left off, Mike asked, "After we have finished here, what are you to do?"

"Get a job at the location wherein I'm deposited, self-sustain, and wait for a directive."

"Wait how long?"

"Undetermined."

"Exactly. A record will be kept regarding your time in service. Upon your expiration term of service, you'll be compensated via hard assets to include, gold, silver, platinum, and palladium."

With that, Mike reached his hand across the table. "Well done. That's all she wrote.

Let's go for one last, enjoyable run. When we get back, get your stuff together, and we'll get them to beam us up."

During the run, Candidate was continually quizzed. Mike stopped at a small clearing, placed a fist-sized rock upon a larger stone. On top of the smaller rock, he placed a quarter, facedown.

"That ought to do it," he said as he picked up his run. Candidate fell into stride.

The next morning, Mike informed Candidate there would be no breakfast, only coffee.

"Trust me: you don't want to begin this return with a full stomach. Here's your pill."

With their packed bags beside them, the two sat down on the floor, took their pills, drank their coffees, placed their cups on the floor beside them. In unison, they laid down. Mike turned his head, looked at Candidate, and said, "Sweet dreams." Shortly thereafter, the curtain fell.

Time doesn't pass when one has no awareness of time. Slowly, very slowly, the cobwebs began to clear from the brain. While the room was dark, the light that shone through the vertical shaft between the two thick curtains was enough to help to bring objects into an ever-clarifying focus.

I'm in a hotel room was the first lucid thought. The second was *And the room is spinning around like the house in* The Wizard of Oz. Remembering an old hack from college, the left foot laboriously made its way from under the bed cover and onto the floor. While the spinning didn't immediately stop, it did begin to slow down.

"I'm just going to lie here until the ride is over and I land on the witch." A few more cobwebs disappeared. The spinning slowed to a stop.

Tentatively lifting up onto the elbows and looking around, there came still more awareness. Now noticing that the room had two double beds, a flat-screen TV, and a coffee maker. Beside the coffee maker were two energy bars. While hunger trumps cobwebs, nature trumps hunger. Gingerly, the apprentice—no longer a candidate—made it from the bed to the bathroom. Habit is a powerful factor in the human equation. Even though the apprentice was alone in the room, the gentle closing of the bathroom door, ended with a notable click.

Afterward, one energy bar was consumed in a flash. The next goal was to make coffee. Having accomplished that, the apprentice sat in the gray-green, upholstered chair, positioned precisely in the corner. While the white, lamp shade from the floor lamp glanced perfectly over the left shoulder, the apprentice slowly savored the coffee and the remaining energy bar. It was at that point that the apprentice became aware of the fact the still-worn clothes had achieved the ultimate degree of wrinkled.

After the second cup of coffee, the cobwebs were gone, and equilibrium had been restored, allowing for the apprentice to take stock of all that had been placed in the room. Walking over to the wall table between the two double beds, the apprentice looked at the tan telephone to see the area code in front of the phone number.

"That helps a little bit."

The next step was to open the drawer and take out the phone book placed next to the Gideon Bible. Looking at the front of the phone book provided the apprentice with the next piece of requisite information. It was time for the third cup of coffee.

With coffee in hand, the apprentice began to examine the contents on the other bed. There was the driver's license taken at the initial meeting with the first "Mike." The three debit cards were stacked neatly one upon the other. Next to the cards, the apprentice saw a stack of cash in various denominations totaling one thousand dollars.

To the right of the case was a vehicle title for a seven-year-old Camry. Resting on the top of the title was a set of keys. Last in formation was a burner phone with an inexpensive charger.

Hanging in the hotel open closet was a complete set of the correct-sized, used clothing from casual to business.

Thank goodness the shoes look new, thought the apprentice, looking at the floor below the hanging clothes.

Having noticed the filled toiletry bag in the bathroom, the apprentice wondered, *How much time do I have to stay here?*

Picking up the phone, dialing zero, and posing the same question to the front desk clerk, the apprentice heard, "You're scheduled to check out tomorrow at eleven a.m."

Gently hanging up the phone, the apprentice fell back onto the bed and resolved, "Well, I guess I had better get my act together and go find myself a job."

CHAPTER NINE

What Is It They Say about Monday?

ONDAY MORNING WAS perfect. Watching the fiery sunrise and the blue-gray water provided Spence with the equivalent of a shot of vitamin B-12. Breakfast had consisted of a cup of coffee and an energy bar. Knowing that he was scheduled to meet his friend Detective Rollins for lunch, he opted for "light," knowing full well that lunch would be "heavy."

From sunrise until eleven a.m., he stepped out of his retreat and into the work mode. He reviewed a backlog of emails and text messages. There were three phone calls that had to be made. One of the returned calls was a direct result of one of the call-me cards that he'd placed under a windshield wiper in the hotel parking lot.

"Hello. This is Scott Wiggins."

"Mr. Wiggins, this is Tim Spence, and I'm returning your call. Thank you for calling me."

"Well, I found you card under the wiper of my truck with a note to call you."

"Was your vehicle a black Ford F250?"

"Yes."

"I apologize. I thought that was my friend's truck who was also staying at the hotel during the public-safety-officer diving conference. By the way, that's a really nice truck."

"Thank you. No problem for the card or the call."

"Good. Scott, I'm just curious. What do you do for a living?"

"I'm a forensic auditor."

"Interesting. What do you do as a forensic auditor?"

"I do system procedures and financial assessments for client entities and present reports with my conclusions and recommendations. I work mostly in and around the Piedmont area—Winston-Salem, Greensboro, High Point. But from time to time, I do have to travel."

"Oh. Of course. Are there times when you need more information on one or more of the stakeholders involved when doing an audit?"

"Often."

"How about that? Listen, in my work, we often have the need for an operational or financial assessment. Would it be okay with you if I kept your name and number for a contact in the future?"

"Sure. That would be great."

"All right then. And if you would be so kind as to keep my card. Part of our wheelhouse is conducting comprehensive background examinations on individuals and organizations upon request. By the way, our company's name is the Academy of Investigative Resources. In the meantime, you can check us out."

"I'll do just that."

"Well, this has proven to be most fortuitous, but I won't keep you any longer. I've enjoyed talking with you, Scott and I hope we get the opportunity to collaborate in the future."

"Same here. It has been nice talking with you as well."

Spence ended the call. In a well-worn, six-and-a-half-by-five-inch leather journal he wrote the date, Wiggins's name, number, occupation parameters, and a brief description of the conversation, including when and where the card had been planted. He didn't believe in waiting for opportunities to appear as low-hanging fruit. He was dedicated to working the business like a garden—till, plant, and harvest. Fully knowing that, businesswise, the company was operating at full capacity, he operated under the axiom that *today* was not a promise of tomorrow. Little did he know how right he was.

He and Rollins had planned to meet for lunch at the Beaufort Grocery Company on Queen Street. When Rollins arrived exactly on time, Spence was seated at an outside green table under a matching green, retractable awning. Several surrounding identical tables were occupied by others in various forms of activities. Some were engaged in casual conversations. Others were reading while they waited for their order. Other tables were empty, waiting patiently for the rush to soon arrive.

Spence opened the conversation. "I don't know about you, but I'm still full from last night's supper."

Rollins, who had, prior to going to work, completed a five-mile run, countered, "I'm starving."

In just a short time, Spence had ordered a cobb salad with chicken, and Rollins went for the Queen's Club. When Rollins's sandwich arrived, Spence enviously eyed the generous helping of ham, turkey, bacon, cheddar, Swiss cheese, honey mustard, and basil mayo on toasted sourdough with lettuce and roasted tomatoes. But upon reflection, Spence reminded himself, *The last thing I need is a middle-aged spread.* Pleased with his advanced degree of self-control, he prepared to dig into his salad.

The purpose of the lunch meeting was for he and Rollins to discuss an idea for an investigative, training-related project they had been casually bantering around for some time. Just as Spence was prepared to get the subject into the conversation, a chair was stolen from an empty table, pulled over next to Rollins, and down sat Assistant District Attorney Bob Russell, who then made himself part of the conversation.

Though their plan had been shot for the time being, both Spence and Rollins were more than happy to place it on the back burner and spend time with a true character.

ADA Bob Russell was, indeed, a Son of the South. Bo, with a long O, was not his given name, though perhaps it should have been. That's what the majority of his friends and associates called him. While his first and middle names were Robert and Andrew respectively, Bo defined him more accurately. He was definitely not a Robbie or an Andy. He often related the story of the origin of his name, citing that his younger sibling, unable to say "Bob" clearly, settled on "Bo." The designation stuck and permeated to all who knew him.

Three years into his career as an assistant district attorney, his uniform of the day was comprised of khaki pants, madras shirt, a light-weight blue sport coat, blue-cloth braded belt, and brown Bass Weejuns penny loafers.

Additionally, and most Southern-like, for eastern North Carolina, he wore no socks—year-round—no socks. Having on more than one occasion, by district and superior court judges, been threatened with contempt of court for exposing his naked ankles, he continually maintained a pair of either gray or blue socks in his left inside coat pocket and a neatly folded, solid-colored tie in the right-side pocket.

Like his English counterpart who donned a white wig prior to entering the court, he would dutifully stop and sit down on the Carteret County courthouse steps. He would then wait for a knowing crowd to gather before putting on his socks. That undertaking would, more often than not, result in a smattering of applause. Having basked in the warmth of being able to laugh at himself along with affable others, he would stand and secure his tie loosely around his neck using the simple knot pattern and carefully leaving the portion of his shirt under the knot of the tie unbuttoned. Thus, dutifully clothed in the minimum that the Carteret County judicial fashion police would allow, he entered the courthouse and commenced to advocate for the people.

His entrance into the courtroom itself generated a flourish of attention. Standing around, waiting for court to start, were uniformed officers and defense attorneys. As soon as he walked in, everyone looked at his feet to see if he had remembered to put on his socks. On his face was a smile described by one of the officers as "looking like a mule eating briars."

Wishing to never miss a moment, he stopped, turned, and faced all four sides of the courtroom, in turn, and pointed to his socks. Having saluted one and all, he bowed slightly and, like a bride walking slowly down the aisle to the altar, he proceeded to the prosecutor's table and ceremoniously took his seat. He was wise enough to confine his performance to the period prior to the judge's entrance into the courtroom. After the judge entered the room and pounded the gavel, it was game on.

While Bo didn't take himself, organizations, or systems seriously, he was most earnest about the responsibilities that his job entailed. In district court, he could move the myriad cases along quickly. In this area, at least, he endeared himself to most district court judges. Moving cases quickly and efficiently served to cover a multitude of his eccentric "sins."

He was adroit at working with most defense attorneys, especially with first-time offenders. Often, case deposition arrangements were "worked through" in advance of the opening of court. There were, however, some areas that were infrangible, assault on an officer being one, child and domestic abuse being two others at the top of the list. His willingness to confer and, when possible, accommodate resulted in an understanding on the part of the defense attorneys as to when to expect an adjustment in the charge and when to know that asking was nothing more than a futile exercise that had to be undertaken as a duty to the client.

During a superior court trial, Bo was a bear. He was prepared and good on his feet. The claws came out. He knew the facts of the circumstance, and he knew the law. He keyed onto the flaws and discrepancies of the defense. He could, if it were to his advantage, make a hostile witness even more hostile. With his portrayal of naivete, he would lead an expert witness for the defense down a primrose lane and quickly box him in, like the last checker on the board, trapped into one of the four corners. No matter which way the expert moved, they were jumped. Game over.

In his closing remarks to the jury, he would adroitly utilize logic if facts in evidence were his strongest suit. He would make the complex, simple. Without articulating it, he would convey, "This and this, this and that. It's so obvious anyone can see it, can't we?" Bo, an astute observer of nonverbal behavior in addition to verbal and vocal, could read the jury thoroughly. He would note the jury members nodding almost imperceptibly—almost imperceptibly, but not quite.

Additionally, Bo was quite skillful at sleight of hand. Through the use of misdirection, a steady banter, and being able to grab the gaze of the observer, he could make something, as Shakespeare noted in *Macbeth*, to have "made themselves air, into which they vanish'd." His skill at leger-demain converged on professional. He could remove a watch from a wrist and make a card appear in the inside pocket of a coat. When asked about the level of his talent, he shared that learning and mastering new illusions was his way of relaxing. It was a break, different from anything else with which he had to deal.

Very quickly in the genesis of his legal undertakings, both district and superior court judges put an end to his—as noted by one judge— "carnival theatrics" within the conduct of trial proceedings.

If an emotional summary was necessitated, he became as a Southern Baptist preacher who was preaching to the choir. Like two tuning forks in the key of C, he would activate a moral, emotive chord, and it would resonate sympathetically in the hearts of each of those twelve persons who had previously failed to figure a way to get out of jury duty. The crescendo would build, build, and build some more. There were times, if he were to have asked, "Can I get an amen?" there would have been those in the jury box and those sitting in the courtroom gallery who would have responded loudly, in unison, "Amen!" All that would have remained, would have been to take up an offering. But in these cases, it appeared that the defendant would serve well enough as the offering.

There was no doubt that when the current district attorney retired, Bo would stand for the job and be voted in by a significant majority.

After court, he would reverse the clothing process, again on the steps, with even greater fanfare returning socks and tie to their rightful places until the next act.

He was also active in the nonjudicial activities of Carteret County. He had joined the Beaufort Historical Association and volunteered a good amount of time to their undertakings.

Another activity that occupied his time was working with law enforce-ment officers. He taught classes through Carteret Community College. He donated whatever the college paid him for the classes to the Beaufort Historical Association. Using the text *Arrest, Search, and Investigation in North Carolina*, he taught them the elements of offense along with the explicit and implicit parameters that were involved. Just as importantly, he conducted mock court utilizing the facts of a case. In these scenarios, he would take on the role of the defense attorney. An officer would be selected to testify. He would demonstrate and then explain the tactics the defense could employ to anger, misdirect, or make them appear to be inept or biased while testifying.

He would explain to the class, "I'm now the defense attorney, and here is where I'm going after you." Then he would provide the countermeasures the officer could take. He emphasized the point to not take the antics of the defense personally, not to succumb to their tactics and most importantly not to respond in kind. He reminded them constantly that if an officer understood why the defense was doing what they were doing, the officer was more likely to walk onto the testifying arena and prevail.

He reminded them continually, "Remember the defense attorney 'triple crown': If the evidence is strong, attack the testimony. If the testimony is strong, attack the evidence. If the evidence and testimony are strong, give someone down the country. And that someone is you. When all else fails, they will endeavor to make you look incompetent, biased, or both.

"Their first principle is to win at all costs. Keep in mind, when they're coming after you in this manner, it's a desperate ploy of someone who's running out of ammo. If they can make you angry, they gain the advantage. Stay calm. Stay the course. Rise above it. Eventually, the jury will begin to see what's going on, and it will play out to your advantage."

As a result of his efforts, those officers committed enough to take his class were capable of walking through the valley of the machinations of the defense and coming out even more capable on the other side.

Along with everything else, Bo was a technophile. With no small amount of pride, he referred to himself as a "fruit-centered mega-techie." He had it all—Air, Pro, Watch, Phone, and Pad. All his devices were synchronized with his rented apartment and his seen-better-days car.

Having secured his place at the table, he took out a deck of cards and turned to Rollins.

Spreading them face down on the table, he told Rollins, "Pick a card and don't show it to me."

Rollins did as directed.

Handing Rollins a pen, Bo said, "Now write your name on the face of the card. But again, don't show it to me."

Again, Rollins followed directions.

"Now, put the card back into the deck and shuffle the deck as much as you want. Then just place the deck here on the table."

After all the steps had been accomplished, Russell tapped the deck with his middle finger and said, "We'll just let things simmer while we enjoy our meal."

Then he smiled and grabbed half of Rollins's sandwich that had been resting patiently on the side of the plate in a bed of potato chips. Just then a waitress walked by, and he caught her eye. With his mule-like smile, he asked, "Hey, darling, would you mind bringing me a glass of sweet tea with some lemon?"

Returning his smile just as broadly, she answered, "You got it, Bo. Just let me know if you decide you want something else to eat." Before she did anything else for anyone else, Bo's tea with enough lemon to make lemonade was on the table.

Having taken a healthy bite of the commandeered half of Rollins's sandwich, Bo queried Spence and Rollins at the same time. "What are you two ne'er-do-wells up to?"

Not ready to put the idea for the project on the table, Spence answered, "Solving the problems of the world while we eat. And wouldn't you know it, just when we thought we had all of the problems solved, up walks another problem and sits down at our table?"

Taking another bite, Bo explained, "I wish I could help you out, but I have to be back in court at one thirty." He turned to Rollins. "Say aren't you scheduled to testify this afternoon?"

Picking up the remaining crumbs of his potato chips with his moistened, right index finger, he answered by picking up the conversation in the very middle of the unfolding of the case. "Yep. After we executed the search warrant, I found a powdered substance in a one-by-one plastic baggie. Lab results showed it to be GHB—gamma hydroxybutyric acid. This is certainly not the first case we've had involving the drug. Russell has successfully prosecuted no small number of cases such as this. It's a growing problem."

Backing up to the beginning of the story, Rollins explained to Spence, "We had series of rapes throughout the county. We suspected that a predatory drug, Rohypnol, ketamine, GHB, or the like was being utilized. The problem is these drugs are metabolized quickly, so there was little physical evidence claim that drugs were used to facilitate the assaults."

"How did you come up with a suspect?"

"We got an anonymous call on crime stoppers that gave us a name. His description matched that which we had pieced together from our interviews with the victims. We surveilled him until we were able to recover a cigarette he had discarded. The DNA from the cigarette matched the suspect's DNA taken from the victims."

Spence looked at Russell. "Search warrant good?"

Patting Rollins on the back with his right hand, he replied, "Textbook perfect."

With the serious topic aside, the three spent the next thirty minutes engaged in small talk and good-natured banter. From time to time, from those passing by, someone would stop and shoot the breeze with Russel, Rollins, or both.

Spence never took the friendliness of Southerners for granted. He thought, It wasn't that people from other parts of the country weren't cordial. They were. It's just that they're not...well, Southern friendly. He was always mindful of the fact that one could legally come to America and become an American. It was not possible, however, for one to move to the South and become a Southerner.

As if to prove the point, an elderly lady sitting near them who had been working a crossword puzzle as she enjoyed her soup, named in the menu as Damn Fine Gumbo, along with water and some crackers, called to them as they stood to leave.

"Would you gentlemen please try and help me?"

In unison, they replied, "Yes, ma'am."

"I'm almost finished with this crossword puzzle, but there *is* one answer I just can't get. What's a nine-lettered word that begins with *S* for 'terrestrial'?" What followed was a profoundly heavy silence with all three looking up as if the answer was to be found somewhere in the Carolina-blue sky.

Finally, Rollins looked at her, smiled, and said, "Sublunary—spelled s-u-b-l-u-n-a-r-y."

"Bless your heart. I would have never come up with that."

"You're more than welcome, ma'am." Noticing the walker beside her chair, he added, "You have a good day."

Turning back in his seat toward Spence and Russell, Rollins extended his arms out to his side, palms facing forward, and with an incredulous look on his face, he asked, "Don't you two ever read?"

That question merited a healthy round of laughter which the elderly lady shared.

Russell., turned to find the waitress. Catching her eye, he asked, "Hey! Would you mind bringing me a small paper bag so I can take what's left of this sandwich with me?"

"You got it, Bo," was the automatic reply.

Having paid the two bills, the three stood up.

Speaking directly to Rollins, Russell said, "Oh. By the way, check that top card."

Rollins turned over the top card and there was the card with his signature.

"It's true. It's all true, my standing-in-amazement friend. The hand *is* quicker than the eye."

With that, they made their goodbyes, turned and started walking their respective ways.

Spence was going to Front Street where he had parked his motorcycle. Rollins and Russell were walking quickly toward Broad Street, where they would turn left and make straight for the courthouse. The very last thing they wanted was to be late for court. Russell demonstrated to Rollins how a man could walk quickly while at the same time putting on his socks and tie. It was a lot of effort with very little return. After only one hour of cross-examination, the judge called it a day and scheduled the trial to resume on Wednesday.

Spence made his way back to the hotel, changed clothes, grabbed his fishing gear, and headed to the pier. Ultimately, he had nothing to show for an afternoon's worth of fishing but a profound sense of relaxation. The sun, the ocean view, and the wind had drained all motivation from him. Dinner involved an in-room steak, salad, and a beer. After a little mindless television, it was time to call it a day. Sleep fell upon him like a weighted blanket.

Elsewhere, within the area, a signaling knock was made on a front door. Shortly, an answering knock was made on the door from the inside. Lastly, a confirming knock was made by the first. The door was subsequently unlocked and opened.

CHAPTER TEN

The Old Burying Ground:
The Last Tour of the Day

S TEPPING THROUGH THE portal of the Old Burying Ground on Ann Street
was a dimensional transport back in time. The iron gates and stately
white columns—one on each side of the walkway entrance—comprise
the bridge between the past and the present. The thick canopy of ancient
live oak trees stretched out their branches to shelter those slumbering there
as well as those visiting.

Constant contrasts of slightly shifting shadow and light painted by the
gentle movement of the leaves softened the hallowed ground. Azaleas and
wisteria added depth and feature along the sandy paths. Over six hundred
markers, most facing east in anticipation of the Day of Judgment, waited
patiently. And then, there were the unmarked graves extending forward
from the time of the battles with Native Americans. Marked or unmarked,
each grave held the story of a life lived and was no more.

A reading of the some of the markers revealed a life lived well into
dotage while others experienced a life lived only in hours, days, or months.

The Beaufort Historical Association provided guided tours, through
the cemetery, with enthusiastic, knowledgeable tour guides who could

make the stories of those resting there come alive. The tour served to remind the group members, young and old, that these markers represented someone who had walked the earth and, to a better or worse degree, made a difference.

This group was made up of twelve adults of various ages and half that number of children. Speaking as they walked through the gate, the tour guide said, "Nathanael Taylor deeded the land to the town in 1731. Three sides of the land are protected by churches, Purvis Chapel, Ann Street Methodist Church, and the First Baptist Church."

The tour guide continued. "What we'll do is go through the numbered burial sites, and I'll add some commentary about the person, and then I'll be glad to answer any questions you might have. After the tour, you can stay as long as you wish, but the gates close at five." After just a few steps in, the tour guide went on speaking. "On our right is the first site that we'll visit, that of Susanna Thomas, marker number two. Susanna lived from 1771 to 1808. Observe that her stone design is flat on both sides with straight edges. The stone's shape is designed to represent a gate. That gate is meant to symbolize the gateway to heaven. We see how, in the inscription, it utilizes the letter *F* for an *S* describing Susanna as a consort, meaning that she was the wife of Captain Thomas."

The tour group next moved forward to marker number twenty-five. "Now we visit Captain Christian Wolf, who lived from 1810 to 1856. His stone was sent from Denmark by his loving sister in order to mark his grave. He was a member of the Royal Danish Navy. In 1856, he became sick and died of yellow fever while in Beaufort. The kind women of the town had tended to him as well as corresponded with his sister. Tragically, when she traveled from Copenhagen on the ship *Austria* to visit his grave, her ship was burned at sea, and she was lost."

Next was marker twenty-four, one of the most visited sites in the entire cemetery. It's here that people pause for longer than at most other graves. It's a place for contemplation and reflection. Even an excited child will pause, look, and wonder.

"This is known as the girl in the barrel of rum," spoke the tour guide, breaking the silence of the introspection experienced by all the group members from the oldest to the youngest. "Her English family moved to Beaufort. She always wanted to see her 'home across the sea.' Finally, she persuaded her mother to allow her to travel with her father for a visit. She went to London and had a joyful experience. Tragically, then she died on the voyage home. Because her father had promised her mother that he would bring her back safely, he couldn't bear to have her buried at sea. He bought a barrel of rum from the captain and put her body in it and returned her to Beaufort for burial. Many people often leave toys, coins. or trinkets as playthings for the young girl."

The tour guide pointed to the flat, gray stone that covered her grave. "See all of the colorful beaded necklaces, the stuffed animals, the brown-and-white stones and the small, plastic toys?"

A little girl, who was saddled upon her father's shoulders, asked, "Where is the little girl, Daddy?"

"She's sleeping, Anna."

"When will she wake up?"

"Sometime."

"Then will she get to play with her toys?"

"She certainly will."

"Will she share her toys?'

"I would think so. Don't you think it's nice to share?"

Nodding her head, she answered, "Uh-huh," her eyes fixed upon the bright and shiny pieces.

After a few more moments for collective contemplation, the tour guide spoke softly, saying, "We'll continue on." But as the group moved on, one individual delayed for a moment, took a card carefully from their pocket, and placed it with items left by the compassionate on the little girl's grave. But this item was not a toy, trinket, or coin. This was an item, for which the young girl would have had no use at all.

They stopped as the tour guide picked up the narrative at the Gabriel plot, number twenty-three. "Notice how the wording addresses the death of a young mother who died following childbirth." The tour guide respectfully quoted the inscription as the others read silently along.

Leaves have their time to fall
And flowers to wither at the
North wind's breath
And stars to set … but all,
Thou has all season, for thine own,
O Death

The tour guide concluded with the fact that the baby had died soon after the mother's passing.

Not wishing for the atmosphere to become too maudlin, even for a cemetery, the tour guide, shifted gears, saying, "We're now going to visit the burial site of a North Carolina naval hero from the War of 1812. There rests a man who was given a license to steal! Come on, we'll move on to the grave of Captain Otway Burns, who lived from 1775 to 1850. This is a most notable site for visitors. He was granted letters of marque and reprisal from the United States. In essence, as I said, he was given a license to steal. How cool is that? At that time, the United States only had a small navy. He sailed from Nova Scotia to South America preying upon British ships. It has been said that, on one trip alone, he captured over $2,000,000. What you see on the top of his tomb is a cannon from his ship, the privateer *Snap Dragon*. It was placed there by his grandsons in 1902. After the war, he served in the North Carolina legislature. After his death, he was brought to Beaufort for burial. In the western part of North Carolina, the town of Burnsville was named after him. His statue is in the center of the town square."

From there, the tour continued its way, past a 1700 British naval officer who was buried standing up facing England as a way of saluting King George the Third. Next came the grave of Sergeant George Johnson, a black soldier who fought for the Union during the Civil War.

Here was the grave of Captain Josiah Pender. He led a group of fifty men that seized Fort Macon. This siege preceded North Carolina's succession from the Union by one month.

The Old Burying Ground, where former enemies, for whom Death had put aside all grievances and animosities, no longer study war. A place provided where husbands and wives, mothers and their children, lay peacefully side by side in the quiet under the canopy of the shadow-dancing live oak trees. A port of haven where, at the end of life's voyage, a restful harbor had been found.

The Old Burying Ground was meant to be a place where those who *had* died come to life's journey's end. It was not meant to be a place where the living came *to* die. But sometimes things weren't always as they were supposed to be. As was written at the Gabriel plot on the grave of the young mother, "Thou has all season, for thine own, O Death."

O Death, indeed. And now *was* the season—blown in like a "North wind's breath" from off the North Carolina coast.

CHAPTER ELEVEN

A Late-Night Visit, a Drink or Two, and a One-Way Stroll

S OME TIME HAD passed since transitioning from an apprentice to an operative. Operative kept the current operational-status name for self-reflection. Somehow it made it easier to draw a distinction between the two roles—what was presented as true and what *was* true—that must be accommodated.

While not profoundly consequential, there had been previous functioning mistakes made and, subsequently, lessons learned. As applicable as the training in and around the cabin had been, it required boots-on-the-ground experience to link training with the tactical elements of the real world.

There had been a number of *assignments*—none requiring an extended period of time. For the most part, things had gone as planned. The periods between the assignments had proven to be the most difficult accommodation to make. It was, Operative thought, *Like waiting for the axe to fall.*

In the dark of night, walking up Craven Street and turning onto Ann Street was not a problem. It was late but not that late, and the destination was well in mind. All that remained was a short saunter, up the steps to the dark-green, wood-floored porch and the single-story second home of Mr.

Duke Kacmar, JD. His primary home being well north of the Mason-Dixon Line. Duke was a survivor of three highly combative divorces. After the last, he had sworn off marriage forever. It never occurred to him—it *couldn't* occur to him—that the one constant in each of his three imploded marriages was himself. In his last divorce settlement, Duke had utilized all his considerable legal expertise to, as he put it, "Pull this house away from her grasping, covetous, well-manicured fingers."

The home, restored by a previous owner, in full compliance with the regulations of the Beaufort Historic Preservation Commission was perfectly "period" for its considerable age on the outside, including the landscaping. On the front porch were two light-green wicker chairs on one side and, on the other side, a matching three-cushioned wicker couch. Operative knew the now-gray sides of the house were, in the light of day, cream colored with white trim. The small lot was well shaded. The bushes on each side of the front steps served to enhance the curb appeal, as if any were needed.

Holding a gift in the right arm, Operative knocked gently on the door with the knuckles of the left hand. After a moment, the door opened, and there stood Mr. Duke Kacmar, JD, in all of his five-foot, seven-inch glory.

"Well, as I live and breathe rapidly. What are *you* doing here?"

"I was hoping that I could trade this single-malt scotch for a bit of legal advice."

"If it involves me having to think to any degree at all, it will cost you more than that. But it's a start," he said as he took the bottle. Opening the door a little wider, he added, "Come on in."

Walking into the entrance, Operative noticed the rich wooden floors. "Are these original?"

"Absolutely. When the house was restored, they kept everything original that they possibly could."

Above the front door was a glass transom window. On the right side of the hallway stood a wooden dresser cabinet. On the left was a long, rectangular glass-top table with two tall, identical lamps—one at each end.

"Can I see the rest of your home?"

"Sure. Follow me."

The kitchen was painted forest green, which served to highlight the wooden cabinets with the glass doors. There was a granite center island with three black bar stools. A glass-top breakfast table with four wooden seats was placed over in a corner. All the appliances were black and blended perfectly against the green walls and warm wooden cabinets. A hammered-copper farmhouse sink served to tie all elements of the kitchen together.

Operative summed it up in one word. "Beautiful."

"Let me show you the rest of the house."

There were two tastefully decorated bedrooms, a bath and a half, and a study.

"When you bought the house, you didn't decorate this yourself, did you?"

"Not hardly. I hired a decorator from here in Beaufort, showed them around the house, and told them what I liked and what I didn't like. I went home for the season, and when I came back, this is what I found."

"Well, whoever it was, they did a great job."

"I think so too. Worth every penny. I don't know about you, but I could use a drink. Let's crack open that bottle."

Reaching up and opening the glass door of a cabinet, Kacmar pulled out two Dorset double old-fashioned glasses. "We'll go into the den. It's my favorite room in the house."

When they were settled, drinks in hand, each in a deep, cranberry leather chair, Kacmar opened the conversation. "So what can I do for you?"

For twenty minutes, Operative presented a fanciful tale wrapped around a contested will and the maneuverings of a disinherited sibling. Kacmar listened carefully, taking multiple sips from the glass to Operative's one. Noticing that Kacmar's class was nearly empty, Operative jumped up. "Let me fix the next drink."

Kacmar nodded his head and surrendered his glass.

In a few moments, he was armed with a much fuller glass than his original. Operative's glass was now more water than single malt.

"So, what do you think I should do?"

After a moment's reflection, "Well, while wills are not my wheelhouse, I do know there are four basic criteria for a contested will." He began to lay out the four points one by one. "The will wasn't signed in accordance with applicable state laws. The testator lacked testamentary capacity to sign a will. The testator was unduly influenced, and lastly, the will was procured by fraud."

By the time Kacmar had elucidated upon the four points, his words were becoming slurred and holding his head up had become much more effortful.

Operative stood up, put on a pair of rubber gloves taken from a pocket, took the two glasses and the bottle, and placed them in a small plastic bag. The bag had been taken from the wastepaper receptacle positioned by the wooden desk in the den. Next, taking Kacmar by the arm and lifting him up from the chair, Operative said, "I think we need to go out and take a little walk to clear our heads."

Swinging his head around to make eye contact with Operative, Kacmar slurred, "Walk?"

"Sure. Just down the street and back. I think these drinks have crept up on us."

"K," was all Kacmar had by way of answering.

With that, the two slowly made their way out of the den, down the hallway, and out the front door. The walk to their destination, while not that far, was laboriously time consuming. For every two steps Kacmar took forward, there was at least one step wherein he veered to the left or right. Holding onto the bag, holding up Kacmar, and endeavoring to move forward was no easy task for Operative.

After they made their way to Craven Street, they turned at Ann Street Methodist Church. Just a few more steps and they were at the black wrought iron fence and anchored into the white wall. They came to a white column crowned with a large globe. Operative was eager to get off street. "Here's where we'll go over the fence."

"Ver the fence?" echoed Kacmar.

"Here, I'll help you. Step up on the wall with your right foot. Grab the ball on the top and swing your left leg over the fence. I'll help hold you up."

Kacmar slowly did as directed, aided by no small effort on the part of Operative. First, his left leg made it over the fence. Next the remainder of Kacmar's body followed. He landed into the Old Burying Ground with the thud of a bag of rocks forcing the air out of his lungs. Operative followed quickly and climbed down the other side of the fence, landing on the ground without a sound.

Lifting Kacmar up, Operative noted, "Come on. Just a little further and we'll be there."

"Be where?" Kacmar asked.

"I'll show you."

Now, the live oaks had covered the cemetery with a blanket of darkness.

Stumbling with one step right after another, Kacmar observed, "Can't see in the dark."

Operative stopped, turned to Kacmar, and said, "You don't want to see *in* the dark. What you want to do is *see the dark*. When get to the point you can see the dark, then you can go about bringing in the light."

Stumbling forward, Kacmar answer, "Oh," as if he understood.

In a moment, they had arrived.

Helping Kacmar to the ground, Operative noted, "Let's just sit down here, and we'll catch our breath. We can rest for a while so that things can work their way out of the system."

"Catch breath," repeated Kacmar as he settled to the ground and nodded off.

A requisite amount of time had passed.

Reaching behind a time-stained white block, Operative withdrew a large instrument wrapped in a brown piece of towel. Taking the instrument by the black handle, Operative reached down and forcefully thrust the narrowed end directly into and through Kacmar's heart. Operative's immediate thought was, *I'm betting that was the first time his heart ever felt anything.*

The last tasks involved making sure the bag with the glasses, the bottle, and now the piece of towel were all in hand; taking a stick and wiping away all footprints; jumping back over the fence; placing the blue plastic gloves in the plastic bag; and leaving the scene in the guise of a jogger on an early, early morning run. The Beaufort area had proven to be a much easier "run" than the rolling hills surrounding the cabin.

CHAPTER TWELVE

It Was Fun While It Lasted

TUESDAY MORNING, SPENCE'S feet hit the floor at five a.m. He immediately dressed, grabbed his flashlight, and headed out the door for a run down the beach. Ninety minutes later, he was back in his room and in the shower. After the shower, he placed his workout clothes along with various other clothing into the hotel's white paper laundry bag. Finding a pen, he wrote his name and room number on the appointed lines and placed the bag outside of his door.

With a cup of coffee and a protein bar at the ready, he turned on his computer and began to answer emails. He had positioned himself and his computer so that he could watch the sunrise and get some work done at the same time. On a yellow legal pad beside his computer, he made a prioritized list of the phone calls he needed to return sometime during the day. Beside each name and number, he included a one-sentence summary of the topic at hand.

In his mind, the only important decisions he would have to make today involved whether to fish some more, to ride or both. Meals would be left to the whim of the moment. Upon reflection, he considered the best option would be that he could do some pier fishing that morning *and* return phone calls at the same time. Then, in the afternoon, he could ride. Maybe he would make his way over to Harkers Island to the Fish Hook Grill on Island Road for a late lunch. He immediately thought of fried flounder, lima beans, beets, French fries, hush puppies, and iced tea. That image turned what had been, up to that point, a pleasant-tasting protein bar into cardboard. Nevertheless, he managed to finish it off.

There he had it. He would fish and phone in the morning and ride and feast in the afternoon. He had a plan—a very good plan—so it seemed to him.

Years ago, Spence had read a poem titled *To a Mouse* by the Scottish poet Robert Burns. In the poem, one line had been of particular note to him—"The best laid schemes o' Mice an' Men Gang aft agley." It was not a common occurrence that Spence's plans would go *aft agley*. It just so happened that today was going to prove to be one of those days. There would be no fishing and no ride to Harkers Island. They would have to wait.

At this same time an older volunteer from the Beaufort Historical Association was opening the gate to the Old Burying Ground. He had long, since retired from the United States Postal Service having spent his career delivering mail door to door. His delivery responsibilities had kept him walking and climbing steps, which had proven to be most beneficial to him health wise, dogs notwithstanding.

After retirement, he didn't want to sit down and become inactive. He wanted to keep moving. So, joining the association had proven to be just the thing. It was his service—not a job—to give the cemetery a "walkthrough" early each morning, making sure everything was as it should be, straightening up a numbered wooden marker, and picking up the odd bit of trash here and there.

He made his way to the gravesite of the little girl buried in a keg of rum. He wanted to satisfy himself that all that had been left for her had not become too voluminous, consequently, becoming distracting. Satisfying himself that what was there was appropriate for another day or two, he continued down the path.

Next, was the Gabriel gamily plot. Everything there was as it should be. Continuing, he came to the gravesite of Captain Otway Burns. And there, everything was most assuredly not as it should be—not at all.

Certainly, the Old Burying Ground served as a final resting place for the dead, but not like this. The last thing this retired postal carrier expected to find in the cemetery was death. Yet there it was! There were two things the volunteer realized that morning that he hadn't known before: one, he had one more message to deliver, and two, old guys, when they have a need to, have the capacity to run faster than they ever imagined.

A glance at his phone tore Spence away from his speculation on a morning multitasking fishing while conducting business over the phone undertaking. He knew it was serious when he heard Rollins, on the recording, call him "Tim," followed. "I'm sending a car over to pick you up."

Spence looked at his fishing rods and then at his motorcycle helmet. His gut told him, Not today. He immediately sent an acknowledgement text to Rollins. Phone still in hand, he took a picture of the callback list. Next, he sent a copy of the picture with a text to Leigh, the company's office manager. He, along with everyone else, knew she was the operational glue that held everything together. His message read, "Please get one or more of the guys to return these calls with my apologies. Also, if they don't mind, text me a summary of what was discussed and agreed upon. Something has come up."

He quickly finished getting dressed—blue jeans and light-blue knit shirt with the company logo. Outside, he saw the marked unit that was waiting for him. On the way to Beaufort, the uniformed officer shared with him what he knew.

In record time, they arrived at the iron gate of the Old Burying Ground. Getting out of the car, he thanked the officer for the ride and the information.

"No problem. Glad to do it."

Another uniformed officer was positioned at the gate. In his hand was a clipboard. He recorded the name and time of all who entered and left the cemetery.

Spence hurried up the path. He stopped momentarily at the gravesite of the girl in the keg. Within the array of small favors left for her, an incongruent gift caught his eye. Kneeling and looking at it closely, he saw that it was a yellow, heavy-stock, business-sized handwritten card. The card authorized the holder to take money from others.

Why in the world would someone go to the trouble to make and leave a card like this for a little girl? Spence wondered. Just then he heard Rollins calling his name. He stood up, turned, and began walking in the direction of Rollins's voice.

Quickly, he came upon a secured crime scene. Yellow "Police Crime Scene—Do Not Cross" tape encircled the gravesite of Captain Otway Burns at a radius of twenty feet. Two ends of the tape were tied to the iron fence that separated the cemetery from Craven Street. Rollins stood just outside of the tape as he observed the workings of the crime scene technicians. Their mission included photographing and diagraming the scene and collecting all possible evidence. Each piece of possible evidence was secured in an evidence bag with the requisite information written on the bag with a permanent pen.

Center stage of the scene was an obviously deceased, middle-aged man. He was propped so that he was leaning against a large rectangular stone that held the cannon from the Snap Dragon. His legs were placed at a forty-five-degree angle, and his hands were resting on his legs palms up. His head was turned to the left, resting upon his shoulder. His eyes were closed.

Foregoing any greeting, Spence asked, "What's that black thing sticking out of his chest?"

"I'm just guessing at this point, but I think it's the back end of a screw-driver. We'll leave it to the medical examiner to remove it at the autopsy."

As if on cue, one of the crime scene technicians walked up to the yellow-taped boundary and advised Rollins, "It looks to me like he was stabbed right through the heart. Apparently, somebody knew what they were doing."

Spence turned to Rollins. "Who is he?"

"We haven't searched him yet, but one of the uniformed officers that helped secure the scene earlier said he thought his name was Kacmar. He had served some divorce papers on him previously. He wasn't sure, but he thinks he's a lawyer. Apparently, he lives somewhere on Ann Street. I've got someone checking."

Getting past that, Spence asked, "Why are *you* here? This is in the city—you're county."

"The city, like everyone else, is shorthanded. Between that, other cases, and the annual mandatory training, they're backed up against the wall. The relationship between the city and the county is really good. The chief asked the sheriff for help, the sheriff agreed, tagged me, and here I am." Looking Spence in the eye, he smiled. "And here *you* are." Rollins knew without asking that Spence was onboard.

"You know it's going to cost you. I'm thinking at the very least a backyard grilled steak with all the fixings."

"I'll check and see if the budget can handle it. You might have to settle for a fast-food hamburger and some fries."

How was Rollins to know that hamburgers and fries would prove to be most instrumental in addressing a most complicated case?

"I'll take what I can get."

Just then, Rollins heard his name called over his handheld radio. "Go ahead," he answered.

"Bob Russell is out here and wants to know if he can come in."

"Ten four. Log him in." Immediately, Rollins's phone rang.

"Rollins." Then silence as he listened for several minutes.

"Okay. Thank you."

By that time, Russell had made his way to them, multitasking by walking, carrying on a phone conversation via his watch, and returning one text after another with his phone. Pausing only for a moment, he looked up and asked, "I got pulled out of bed by the district attorney and told to be here. Whatchu got?"

Rollins turned and told them what he had learned.

"His name is Duke Kacmar, and he has a second home somewhere on Ann Street. They're doing a background on him. In the meantime, they checked him out on social media. Apparently, he *is* a lawyer. They said he was a patent troll. What's a patent troll?"

To answer his own question, he did a quick search and shared the following, "*Patent troll* is a derogatory term for someone who utilizes patent infringements to obtain money from the courts. They'll do it either for money or to wipe out an organization. They file patent claims never having any intent to deliver anything. It isn't illegal. They are sometimes called *patent sharks* or *pirates*."

At the word *pirate*, Rollins paused and all three looked at the deceased and at the cannon.

Rollins continued reading. "When considering a corporate setup in this area, they may be referred to as a *patent-assertion establishment* or a *nonproducing patentee*."

Rollins looked at the two, smiled, and observed, "Just like old Otway, resting peacefully here beneath the cannon, the late lawyer Kacmar had a license to steal."

Getting no reply from the two, he countered, "And I ask you for the second time, don't you two ever read?"

Rather than answering, Russell returned to his text messaging in earnest. Spence remained silent, allowing himself to process the information. Eventually, the three turned their attentions back to the crime scene and those working inside the yellow tape. They grew silent in their individual contemplations. At length, Russell asked, "What do you think this is?"

From directly behind them, they heard an emphatic, voice declare, "A good start."

The three responded by turning around with an exactness that would have been the envy of a synchronized water ballet ensemble. They turned, and there she stood, Beaufort Police Department Sergeant Dixie Bell Lee.

CHAPTER THIRTEEN

Dixie Bell Lee

YES, THERE SHE WAS—Police Sergeant Dixie Bell Lee— "D" to most people who knew her to any degree at all. She had parked her patrol car a short way back on Craven Street, easily made it over the iron fence, and walked up behind the three, having never made a sound.

Years ago, when she had been going through basic law enforcement training, Spence had taught the class on interviewing. Even then, the intensity in her brown eyes signaled a determination to make a place for herself within the law enforcement community. After graduation, she had continued to take classes sometimes taking vacation from work to be able to attend.

Between her initial training and now, she and Spence had crossed paths enough for a friendship and familiarity to develop between the two. When it came to kidding, she could take as well as she could give.

If there ever was a classic, living law enforcement recruitment poster representative, she was it. Five nine, distractingly attractive, and rough as a rusty chainsaw. Even though, she was coming off a challenging third shift, her dark uniform was impeccable. Her sandy-blond hair was pulled back into a ponytail that hung to the base of her neck. It was as if the brown of her uniform was designed to complement the color of her hair.

From time to time, when she was effecting an arrest, an uninformed suspect would attempt to grab a handful of her hair to pull her down. That individual learned a lesson and then paid the price. There were a variety of healing times for fractured wrists, depending on the manner and the gravity of the break.

Throughout the department, it was generally accepted that she wore that ponytail purposely as an enticement to those who would dare to try her. She could write the narrative for the justification of the use of force in her sleep.

Sergeant Lee was the whole package—bachelor's degree in psychology and working to get her master's in forensic psychology via online classes. She was certified by the North Carolina Criminal Justice Training and Standards Commission as a driving, firearms, PT, and defensive tactics instructor. She ran marathons and what she referenced as "iron-woman" triathlons throughout the year. An avid skier, she took the entirety of her annual vacation and built-up compensatory time in the dead of winter at a variety of New England ski resorts.

Her ten years of experience with the police department had earned her a reputation as a stand-up officer. Unlike some who always managed to be the trailing officer to a dangerous call, more often than not, she was the first on the scene. Her interactions with the citizens—good and bad—was such that when she spoke, people listened.

It was common knowledge throughout Carteret County that one day she would stand for the office of high sheriff and win. But while the current sheriff, upon whom she thought the sun rose and set, maintained that office, her political undertaking was placed well upon the back burner.

A salient attribute of officer Lee was that she had no filter. She would speak her mind no matter the circumstance. Be it supervisor, peer, or subordinate, one shouldn't ask her what she thought if one didn't want to know. Her values and opinions were *there* for the asking, but more often than not, she wouldn't wait for someone to ask. She shared freely and without reservation.

Inside of that tough reputation, she had a good heart. When her days off would allow, she would serve meals to the destitute at her church's weekly

"Love's Kitchen." In cold weather, she carried blankets and coats she had purchased in the trunk of her patrol car for those who, for whatever reason, chose not to take advantage of the social service resources in the county. If there was a departmental collection being take up for someone in need, she readily made a generous (for her resources) contribution.

But there was one other distinguishing characteristic regarding Sergeant Lee—she detested most representatives from the legal profession. Russell was a notable exception. For no small number of law enforcement officers, opinions regarding attorneys can range from apathy to disdain. But not so for Sergeant Lee. She despised most of them with an undisguised vehemence. And to her way of thinking, there were a number of justifiable reasons as to why.

First, in her mind, she had been screwed over by a lawyer when undergoing a divorce from a philandering husband. The divorce proceedings had resulted in her having to buy out her ex-husband's claim to his share of her retirement to the tune of $25,000. She was still paying that loan off. Her mother, who had been injured in a vehicle accident while riding her bicycle, through no fault of her own, was denied compensation by the machinations of an attorney who twisted the circumstances to imply that her mother was partly culpable. Lastly, she had seen a number of guilty walk as a result of legal maneuverings and obfuscation by what to her were pettifoggers—pettifoggers from the defense table to the judge's bench.

Having caught the three by surprise, she was finding it difficult to keep the smug smile from her face.

"Dispatch called me on my phone and told me something was going on over here. I called the recording officer at the gate, and he filled me in. Who do you think shot him?"

Rollins filled in the blank. "He wasn't shot. He was speared with what looks to be a screwdriver."

Dixie processed the information. "So, you're telling me lawyer Kacmar was spiked with a screwdriver?"

"That's what it looks like. We don't know for sure."

Transitioning into the investigative mode, Rollins asked, "Do you know him?"

"Yes." Clarifying herself, she added, "I don't *know* him. I know *of* him. I answered a disturbance call at his house on Ann Street a while back."

"What was it about?"

"Something to do with some civil litigation. I can have records pull the report if you want." With a quick phone call, she got the search underway.

"Thanks."

Stepping into the inquiry, Spence asked Russell, "Do you know him?"

"I've seen him in the courthouse."

Just then a black, oversized SUV with darkened windows pulled up. There was a short tap on the horn. The passenger side window came down a quarter of the way, and a female voice called, "Spence."

Spence walked over in the direction of the SUV to the fence. The window came down a few inches lower, and a burst of black, curly hair appeared just above the tinted windows. For the next few minutes, a discussion ensued well below the hearing range of the three. As Spence turned and walked back to the group, the vehicle was gone. Dixie noted how quiet the engine was, for such a big vehicle.

Having returned to the three, Spence placed his hand on Rollins's left shoulder and commiserated. "Well, my friend, one thing is for certain. The calvary is not coming to help *you*."

Rollins's expression turned to quizzical. Though he never spoke, non-verbally, he asked the question *Why?*

"Apparently, the demise of this lawyer is not an isolated event. There have been a number of identical episodes across the country—even got a number of prosecutors—state and federal. And get this: apparently, all were taken out with screwdrivers."

"How much better can this day get?" Dixie marveled. When the three locked their eyes on her, she smiled and said, "Did I say that out loud?" Before, they could answer she was saved by the bell. Answering her phone, she said, "Hold on a second. Let me get something to write on."

Having pulled a small notepad from her left leg uniform pants pocket, she made a writing gesture to Russell, who handed to her his silver pen. As she wrote, she cradled the phone between the right side of her head and her right shoulder.

After a few minutes, she said, "Thanks." Before she hung up, she told dispatch to place a marked car at Kacmar's house on Ann Street, to not let anyone in or out of the house, and to not answer any questions from the curious, including the media.

Rollins signaled a thumbs-up in appreciation.

Reading from the paper, she told Rollins, "The disturbance at Kacmar's house involved a Mr. Robert O'Neill. Apparently, Kacmar had brought a suit against O'Neill's sister—Eimear—and something about that suit was the point of contention. O'Neill was told to leave the premises and that if he returned, he would be charged with trespassing."

Rollins articulated his thought process. "We'll need to search Kacmar's house." Turning to Russell, he asked, "You think I should get a search warrant?"

"I do. This is no doubt going to be a high-profile case. Everybody is going to be looking at this investigation—and you—through a microscope. In each and every step, go the extra mile—check all of the boxes twice. Write up the affidavit, and I'll look it over before you take it to the judge."

Rollins continued his verbalization of the steps to be undertaken. "Okay. I'll stay here until the crime scene techs finish. Then, I'll send them to Kacmar's house to standby until I get there with the warrant. Then we'll process and search the house. I want to get a printout on Kacmar's phone records as quickly as possible."

"Turning to Spence, he said, "You meet me there. What else?"

"At some point soon, you will want to interview O'Neill and his sister," Spence added.

"Turning to Russell, Spence added, "If all of this matter is involving attorneys, *you* might want to take some extra precautions. In fact, the entire Carteret County Bar had better be extra careful."

"I have a concealed-carry permit. I guess I'm going to have to use it."

"Another thing, Bob, as much as I know you'd like to, don't you think you shouldn't become too involved directly in this investigation? More than likely, you'll be prosecuting this case and it could open the door to a conflict-of-interest allegation. Best, stay on the sideline and help with any legal questions. Okay?"

"Okay."

Having decided that there was nothing left here to see, Dixie said, "I'm going to ride down Ann Street and make sure that marked car is in position and the area is locked down. Spence, why don't you come with me until Jesse gets the warrant to search the house? I'll make it worth your while. I'll put something on you bleach won't take out."

"How can I refuse an offer like that?" Spence countered jokingly.

They had both turned toward the fence when Rollins stopped them in their tracks.

"Would you both *please* go out the gate so that I'll have a righteous record of who was at the scene?"

Like Dorothy, the Scarecrow, and the Tin Man, the three headed toward the cemetery entrance. Midway to the gate, Spence asked the two to hold on for a second. He ran over to the gravesite of the girl in the keg, paused for a brief moment in reflective respect, reached down, placed his hand on the stone, took a picture with his phone, turned, and ran back to Rollins.

"At the little girl's grave, there's a handwritten card on the stone slab. If you don't mind, recover that card carefully yourself, bag it, and keep it. It may or may not be relevant. But I'd rather have it and not need it than to need it and not have it."

"I'll take care of it."

In a few minutes, Spence was back with the duo.

"I wanted to pay my respects, and then I thought of something I needed to tell Jesse."

The three resumed their walk to the gate.

"Virtue is now in the middle," laughed Dixie as she walked between Spence and Russell to the gate.

"I'll tell you what, Ms. Virtue. Gimme back my pen," demanded Russell.

She returned the pen. He placed it in the open palm of his left hand and covered it with his right hand. After rubbing his hands together in a forward motion, he opened them, and the pen was gone.

"Ta-da!" he exclaimed. "Disappeared quicker than my public servant's inadequate paycheck."

CHAPTER FOURTEEN

A New Responsibility, a Briefing, a Plan

S PENCE AND DIXIE sat in her patrol car parked on Ann Street near Kacmar's house, waiting patiently for Rollins to arrive with the search warrant. They turned the wait time into an opportunity to catch up. Spence learned that she was giving consideration, post master's degree, to pursuing a doctorate. He shared with her how the company was expanding its activities in open-source intelligence—OSINT—and that would involve several additional hires. While on the subject of hiring and even though he knew of her career aspirations, he, nevertheless, made his often-repeated offer to come and work with him. The latest offer included an upgrade based upon her consideration for continuing her education. The company would pay for her studies and provide any time needed. Perfunctorily, she told him she would think about it. He knew that, unless there was a dramatic change in plans, she wasn't coming on board any time soon.

The uniformed officer initially assigned to the location had, with the help of some squad members, effectively cordoned off the area around the house up to the sidewalk. Apparently, word of the scope of these incidences on the national level and the related local occurrence had made its way to the media. There was a horde of coiffured media personnel, microphones, and cameras pressed tightly against the yellow barrier tape like barnacles on the bow of a ship.

Second only to lawyers, Dixie despised the media.

"I'm so sick and tired of hearing, 'Team coverage' and 'We're on your side.' You'd think someone somewhere would be able to come up with a new tagline."

Dixie thought for a minute.

"How about these for a tagline options? 'We'll say or do anything to keep you from turning to another channel, or we promise to never let the truth or the facts stand between us and a story.' Now, those are a taglines I could respect. I'd still turn the channel, but at least, they would be momentarily honest."

"You've missed your calling," Spence replied sarcastically.

But Dixie was smart enough to know that, should she ever run for sheriff, the media could play an important role—or not—in her success. That being the case, whenever she was on camera, she gritted her teeth, plastered on her most pleasing smile, and with an ingratiating demeanor, played the game.

Just then, Lieutenant Bob Brown rode up in an unmarked unit. A younger Bob had a most productive career as a narcotics officer. But with the passing years and the promotion to lieutenant, he had transitioned to uniform. Nevertheless, his talent for vehicle drug interdiction was such that he was making more cases than filling out administrative paperwork. The chief didn't seem to have any problem with it.

The first thing the lieutenant noticed was Spence in the front passenger seat. "Spence. I heard you were in town. How have you been?"

"Just barely making it from one day to the next," he replied lightheartedly.

"That makes two of us. How long are you planning on being with us?"

"The goal is for three months unless something changes."

"Great. Carve out some time for me. We'll go out on my boat and do some deep water fishing."

"You can count on that. I have your number. Are you working shifts?"

"Yes, but I have more time built up than Methuselah. Just call me. If I don't answer, leave a message, and I'll call you back. We'll set up a time and make it happen."

The lieutenant shifted his attention to Dixie.

"Sergeant. Isn't your shift over?"

"Yes, sir. But since we're shorthanded and this case fell into our lap, I figured I'd hang around and see if I could be of assistance. I'm not looking to get any comp time out of it."

"Well, as you're well aware, no good deed goes unpunished. I've got some good news and some bad news. Which do you want first?"

Dixie had been around long enough to know whenever anyone sang the good news–bad news song, the good news was not ever that good, and the bad news was disproportionally bad.

"Give me the bad news first."

"The chief has directed you to be the media liaison in this case for the time being. You'll be on day shift until further notice."

Her head and shoulders mirrored her sinking feelings. "Okay. What's the good news?"

"The chief said you would get comp time for staying over this morning."

"Be still, my beating heart."

"Say. I heard this guy was one of a number of lawyers that have been taken out."

"That's the *good* word," Dixie confirmed.

After a moment of inward reflection, the lieutenant laughed, pointed to the media mob, and ordered, "There they are. Go tell them something." And then he drove away.

Spence observed, "Well, it looks like we've both had a change of plans. Let's just make the best of it."

As if on cue, Rollins pulled up behind them and exited his car, warrant in hand. The three walked toward the walkway leading to the house.

Rollins wondered, "What's going on?"

Spence told him, "The good lieutenant just made Dixie's day. Let's search the house."

"Okay. The sheriff is sending over a couple of officers to conduct knock and talks in the area. D, would you please coordinate that when they get here?"

"You've got it."

They left Dixie to fend for herself with the pack and walked up the steps. Rollins signaled for the crime scene techs to follow. He and Spence both put on blue plastic booties and gloves. The front door was slightly ajar. Rollins pushed the unlocked door open fully, and the ensemble walked in. Out of habit, Spence and Rollins both put their gloved hands behind their backs. "Look, but don't touch" was their paramount directive.

The house was immaculate. Nothing was out of place. There were no indications that a struggle had ensued or that the house had been ransacked in a search for valuables. When they entered the den, Rollins did find one thing out of the ordinary sitting on a side table.

"Look here, Spence."

Spence walked over and saw a card similar in size to the one that he had recovered from the little girl's gravesite. The difference was this card, also handwritten, allowed for someone to freely get out of jail.

Rollins advised, "I bagged and tagged the card we found at the grave-yard. Also, I took a picture of it on the stone before it had been recovered. I'll do the same with this one as well."

"Good. We know that in an investigation there are *no* coincidences. There's no doubt these two cards are definitely linked. If it's okay with you, let's keep the details about the cards to ourselves. It's always good to have some pieces of information to which only you have access. No one is going to be reading your report or looking at an evidence inventory log immediately. You can always file a supplemental. What do you think?"

"Works for me," Rollins replied accompanied with a slight nod of his head.

Both men waited until the house was fully processed and secured before they left. When they walked out, Dixie was facing them with her back to the media. Her facial expression reflected her *someone-help-me-please* assessment of her predicament. She directed an officer to remain on the scene until he was relieved.

The media with their microphones extended and mouths opened asking endless, nonsensical questions reminded Rollins of a *troubling* of Koi fish, packed together competing to be fed pellets of information. Spence got into Rollins's car, and they left. Dixie took the cue and returned to her car. She waited for the additional officers to arrive and gave to them a short briefing along with their instructions. Then she drove home and went to bed. She knew it would be a short respite.

After all information sources had left, the cameras were broken down, the microphones were returned to the boxes, and the media dispersed in different directions. All went searching for something else—sensational-istic—to *digest*.

Rollins took a right on Turner Street. At that point, his stomach had an idea. "Let's go get a late breakfast or an early lunch."

"Works for me. Where do you want to go?"

"Let's go to the Cox Family Restaurant over in Morehead City."

When they arrived, Spence saw the large neon sign with Cox in big letters at the top. On the billboard was written, "Smile. God Loves You."

Spence and Rollins both ordered the Big Man's Large Steak and Eggs with grits and toast. While they were waiting for their food, a bevy of people coming in and going out stopped to greet Rollins and exchange pleasantries.

Spence noted, "Being with you is like being with the pope. I'm surprised they don't kiss your ring."

"I've got something *you* can kiss," Rollins parried.

Spence had nothing to top that, so he kept his mouth focused upon eating.

They agreed to not talk about the case in this public setting. So, for the most part, they each ate in silence. Spence couldn't eat all his meal. Rollins didn't seem to have a problem.

After the meal, they drove to the Carteret County Sheriff's Office on Craven Street. It was time to put their heads together, conceptualize what information they had at hand, and lay out a strategy to move forward.

Before he did anything else, Rollins rounded up the investigative chain of command—sergeant, lieutenant, and captain—all into the captain's office and provided a briefing. He then answered the few questions they had. Spence took advantage of the break to return some text messages and phone calls.

After Rollins had answered the questions from the three-tiered chain of command, he asked, "Do you have any suggestions, recommendations or cautions for me?"

Between the three, there was well over fifty years of law enforcement experience—much of it within the investigative arena. That which they said, Rollins readily wrote down. Finishing that, he called the Beaufort chief and read him in. It remained for the captain to brief the major and the sheriff.

After the briefing, Spence and Rollins grabbed a half-dozen, yellow legal pads, commandeered a small conference room and, with each carrying a hot cup of coffee, sequestered themselves. Rollins had obtained permission for it to serve as their war room for the foreseeable future. For the next three hours, they surveyed the written-in-stone, protocol of the initial stages of an inquiry. They undertook to formalize: "What is it that we know that we know? What is it that we know that we don't know? What is it that we don't know that we don't know?"

The only interruptions Rollins allowed for himself were calls from the sheriff and the Beaufort chief of police. Everything else went to voicemail. Spence took several calls from a source that provided more information regarding the situation as it stood on a national level.

Spence made one phone call to the office and got the ball rolling on one line of inquiry. All information, not directly related to the late lawyer Kacmar's case was secured on a separate legal pad. They satisfied themselves that they had processed the known and unknown information to the limit and then set upon developing a strategy as to how to proceed.

Rollins got the ball rolling, speaking out loud to himself as much as to Spence.

"I'll have the electronic tech folks process Kacmar's computer and cell phone recovered from his house. We'll have to wait and see what they come up with. That's gonna take some time. The same holds true for the results of the postmortem from the medical examiner's office."

Looking directly at Spence, Rollins added, "With your resources, you're having a deep-dive background conducted on Kacmar." Spence showed Rollins a thumbs-up by way of affirmation.

Rollins went silent, and Spence jumped in to fill the void.

"While we're waiting for some additional information to come in, is there anyone you think we could talk to?"

"Right off the bat, I would like to talk with the O'Neills, but first, I want to get my hands on Dixie's report of that disturbance call. I want to read the assessment of what was going on and get his phone number."

"After you get that report, how do you want to proceed?"

"If possible, I would like to have them interviewed at the same time. I don't want the interviews possibly contaminated by sequencing them. The second person to be interviewed could pick the brain of the first and prepare. If they'll agree to talk with us, I'll take one and you take the other."

"Works for me."

By this time, it was late afternoon, and the copy of Dixie's report had yet not arrived. Unless another piece of information came forth, there was nothing else to be done that day.

Handing all the neatly stacked legal pads to Rollins, Spence asked, "Are you going to run me back to the hotel or are you going to make me walk?"

"You really think you could really walk that far?" Rollins asked as he picked up his car keys.

"With my eyes closed."

On the way back to the hotel, they agreed to meet at the sheriff's office the next morning at nine.

CHAPTER FIFTEEN

An Interview, a Riddle, and an Assessment

WEDNESDAY, SPENCE AND Rollins arrived at the sheriff's office exactly at nine. Inside, each grabbed an essential cup of coffee and went back to the conference room, yesterday's legal pads in hand.

Now, seated at the table, Rollins kicked off the collaboration. "Okay. Where do we stand at this point?"

Spence noted, "I thought you had court today?"

"Bo contacted me and said, with what was going on, he'd talked to the judge and would call ahead of time if I needed to be in court."

Spence read from the top page of one of the legal pads.

"We're waiting on the autopsy report, phone records, Kacmar's computer contents, and a listing of whatever was recovered at the crime scene and the house. We want to set up the simultaneous interviews with the O'Neills. Patrol officers are continuing to conduct knock and talk to neighbors in the surrounding areas. What have we missed?"

"I think that's it. I'm going to try right now and see if I can get a picture of the screwdriver in advance of the complete autopsy report."

Having said that, Rollins stood up and left the room, closing the door behind him. Spence took advantage of the time to return emails and call Leigh to check in and see if there was anything pressing that needed his attention—there wasn't. Leigh reminded him that today was the birthday of one of the founding partners.

Before he hung up, he offered, "Thanks, Leigh. I'll call him right now." Then he pressed the partner's name in speed dial. After two rings, there was an answer.

Spence went straight to the point, "Listen, I want you to know, you're not getting old. You *are* old. Happy birthday, brother." After a duet of laughter and the implicit manner in which a conversation is concluded among friends, the two hung up.

Rollins had returned to the room in time to hear the birthday greeting.

"You really know how to make someone's birthday a happy occasion, don't you?"

"Isn't it true that for my last birthday, you sent to me a bouquet of dead flowers?"

"You know what they say, 'Send flowers to someone you care about, now—don't wait until their funeral.'"

"Well, if that's the case, in lieu of flowers, send money."

Having got *their* sparring out of the way, the two settled down to the task at hand.

Spence made the first move. "What would you like for me to do?"

"First thing, let's see about setting up some interviews with the O'Neills. Which one would you like to interview?"

"Jesse, you call it. You're the boss. I'm just carrying water here. I'll do whatever you need for me to do."

"I'll interview Robert, and you interview Eimear."

"Works for me. You gonna call them now to try and set it up?"

"Yep. I'm going to go back to my desk and call Robert. I'll get Eimear's phone number from him. By calling from my desk, I can have a recording of the conversations. In the meantime, if you will, lay out the objectives as to what we want to accomplish in the interviews along with what you see as viable strategy along with the salient questions."

"Ten four."

Rollins left the room and Spence began to fill up a blank sheet on the legal pad. Just about the time he had filled up the sheet, Rollins returned.

"Mr. O'Neill has agreed to meet me here at one p.m. this afternoon."

"What about her?"

"Oh, she's agreed to talk, but she wants the interview to take place at her house—same time—one p.m. Here's her address. You can take my car."

They reviewed and discussed the interview plan until the agreed that they both shared an understanding of the conduct of the interviews.

Taking the planning process one step further, Spence added, "Let's explore what could go wrong at each step of our plan and identify the options we could employ to keep the interview going in the right direction. We have to take the position that this may be the only opportunity we would have to talk with them. If we ask for a follow-up, they may clam up or lawyer up."

Having speculated as to what could go wrong within the conduct of the interview and identified viable responsive options, it was time for a quick lunch at the closest fast-food restaurant on Live Oak Street.

After lunch, Spence dropped Rollins off, and twenty minutes later, he had found his way to his destination on Jade Street. Parking the car, he walked to the front door by the immaculately trimmed lawn. Just as he started to reach for the doorbell, the door opened and there, waiting to greet him, stood Eimear O'Neill.

Spence was very seldom caught on his back foot, but this was one of those times—one of those times indeed. There's beauty and then again, there's *beauty.*

She gave the immediate impression of having stepped out of a scene from an Irish movie—the stunningly, leading lady. Standing at five feet, eight inches with dark-red hair feathered down her neck, she smiled, glanced from him to the car in the driveway, and asked, "Are you the detective?"

Immediately, extending his right hand, Spence replied, "Tim Spence, Ms. O'Neill. Thank you for taking the time to talk with me."

Shaking his hand, she opened the door wider, stepped back, and invited him in. The smile never left her face. Stepping into the foyer, Spence looked around and noted, "You have a beautiful home."

"Thank you. I'll tell you what: I can't take any credit for the house. This is just the way it was when I bought it. I did, however, furnish it."

"It's perfect."

"Again, thank you. Come on, let's go into the den. I'll set out some tea. We can talk in there. You like iced tea?"

"Iced tea works for me."

"Great."

In the den, she pointed to several chairs. "Make yourself at home."

Spence took the brown leather chair closest to the table with the tea. She sat down on the forest-green couch on the other side of the table and poured herself a glass. She waited while Spence filled his glass and leaned back in his chair.

From an adjoining room, Spence could hear the tapping of an animal's claws walking back and forth on the other side of the door. From time to time a soft, frustrated whimpering would signal a yearning to join the conversation. Spence speculated that it was a dog breed along the lines of a Biewer terrier or at most a beagle.

Glancing toward the room from where the sound was coming, Spence asked, "Dog?"

"Yes. He's about eighteen months old now."

"What's the breed?"

"Doberman pinscher."

At the sound of Eimear's voice, the audible indications of frustration grew louder.

Without raising her voice, she directed, "Razor, sit, quiet."

The sounds ended immediately.

"Your dog's name is 'Razor'?"

She smiled. "It suits him. He is rather sharp."

Spence thought, Wow. I was off by a mile on that one.

Wishing to leave his incorrect assessment and set the interview tone, Spence repeated, "Thank you again for your time."

Locking her deep, emerald-green eyes onto Spence, she countered, "As odd as it may sound, I've been looking forward to this visit. I've never been interrogated before, and I needed a break from work. So, tell me. What can I do for *you*?"

"First off, let me assure you this is *not* an interrogation. Interrogations are for those that are unwilling to be totally forthcoming. That's not you, I'm certain. You allowed for me to come and visit. I simply want to talk with you. I want to talk with you about an incident that occurred between your brother, Robert and Duke Kacmar a while back. But before we do, if you don't mind, would you tell me about yourself?"

"Me?" Pausing for a moment, "I'm originally from Chicago. Moved down here to get away from the cold, the wind, and the snow. I'm *way* into computers, coding, and related technology of all sorts. My work life involves consulting in IT security and program augmentation with various entities. Most of my work requires me to sign a nondisclosure agreement, so I can't say much about that. For relaxation, I like to play with code and develop apps. But here lately, even that hobby has turned into a significant revenue stream. And that's pretty much it."

"Pretty much?"

"Well, I like to spend time walking on the beach, and I like to read."

"I like to read as well. Do you have a favorite genre?"

She shifted slightly on the couch and laughed nervously. "I like to read the classics and, most especially, Poe. That's funny, isn't it?"

"Not at all. Do you know Poe in addition to being a writer and a poet was into cosmology and cryptography?"

Hopping up from the couch, she exclaimed, "I certainly do! Come over here and look at this."

Spence, following her and endeavoring the keep the conversation going asked, "What's your favorite poem by Poe?"

"Eldorado."

"What's it about?"

"It's a metaphor about the search for happiness, success, or whatever it is that's important to you. I think we're all searching for *that something*, don't you?"

"I do."

"I wonder what you're searching for?"

Spence offered no reply.

Leading him over to a wall-sized, antique bookcase, she opened the leaded glass door, then pointing to the top shelf, she told him, "These are all first editions." She repeated the words joyfully. "First editions. Can you believe it?" She ran the index finger of her left hand over several of the books.

Next, pointing to two lower shelves, she said, "These are biographies. I like to read biographies of Poe." She stared inquisitively into his face. "You probably think I'm strange."

"Not at all. Not at all," he repeated. "I read Poe as well, but I've got to tell you: I'm really into Dickens. I especially like to read Charles Dickens. And if you like the macabre, you should try reading some of his short stories. A great example is 'The Haunted Man and the Ghost's Bargain.' I'll give you this: Poe does an outstanding job of giving us insight into *his* disturbing world. Dickens, however, places the dreadful into the world in which *we* live. If you want, sometime I'll get you a list."

"That would be great. Thank you." Turning, they both returned to their respective places.

Picking up, where they had left off, she offered, "So, go ahead and ask away."

"First off, could you tell me about your brother?"

"Robert, my brother is a very good man. He handles all my business concerns so that I can direct my attention to services and products. He has a master's degree in business administration and a bachelor's degree in marketing. We are equal partners in our corporation. He has sacrificed a great deal to bring us to this point."

"What about your brother's temperament?"

"No better or worse than anyone else's. He's pretty easygoing up to a point. I'll admit he tends to be overprotective when it comes to me. Like all of us, if you push him too far, you'll get a rise out of him."

"On a scale of one to ten, with one being the least and ten being the highest, what would you say is the topmost temper-rise number he has ever reached in your presence?"

"I would say a seven."

"And what did that circumstance entail?"

"A robust debate with a client over a lack of payment."

"How would you describe a robust debate?"

"People arguing with raised voices, each trying to prove their point."

"Tell me about the times your brother would have been at the point of an acrimonious physical action?"

"I don't think my brother is capable of violence concerning a business-related circumstance."

"Business-related?"

"Well, if someone were attacking me physically, he would come to my defense. He played rugby in college and has kept himself in good shape since."

"If you would, please tell me about the incident involving your brother and Mr. Kacmar?"

"I had developed an app. The app was designed to assist in trouble shooting a security system for a specific computer operating system. He—Kacmar—had bought the patent for an app that was remotely similar for a completely different operational system. He filed a suit declaring patent infringement. My brother hired a lawyer to handle the case. And that was good enough for me. I told my brother to let it go at that—let the court decide. But Kacmar kept calling me repeatedly making all kind of threats and accusations, trying to force me into settling."

"Finally, my brother had enough and went over to his house trying to get Kacmar to stop. Kacmar took out a protective custody order against my brother and nothing happened after that. My brother stayed out of it from then on. Ultimately, the suit was resolved in our favor and that was it."

"Tell me: where were you Monday night?"

"I was here, working most of the night. I'm doing some work for a company located in Singapore, so due to the time difference, I was on the phone and in front of my computer for the better part of the night. They wanted to continue working right on, but when I heard the clock in the hall chime, six, I'd had enough and told them so. You can check my computer log or phone records if you need to."

"How about your brother?"

"You'll have to ask him. I don't know."

"Did your brother ever talk to you about the incident at Kacmar's house?"

"Yes. He said, that he went there to tell Kacmar to stop calling me. He said Kacmar wouldn't listen and told him to get off his property. At that point, it got into a shouting match. Finally, I think a neighbor called the police. The police arrived, ordered my brother to leave. He did and that was it."

"Did you have anything to do with Kacmar's death?"

"No."

"Who *could* have killed him?"

"A lot of people, I would think. He had bad-mouthed and screwed over a lot of people. Our attorney had a background conducted on him and his firm. There was a long, long trail of cases such as mine—most, a lot worse."

"Why do you think someone would kill Kacmar?"

"Because they had murder in their heart. Maybe due to anger or revenge."

"What do you think should happen to whoever killed him?"

"I think they should be punished to the fullest extent of the law. I'm not for the death penalty, but at the very least, I would say, they should go to prison for the rest of their life."

"Is there anything else about this case that you know that I should know?"

"No."

"Is there any question that I've neglected to ask you?"

"No."

Closing his notebook and returning his pen to his shirt pocket, Spence smiled. "How do you think Poe would have written this case?"

With the smile coming back to her face, she said, "I think the whole thing is Poe-like enough as it is. I mean him lying there next to the cannon with a screwdriver or something sticking out of his chest—that's straight Poe 101. My good friend Linda called me and told me all about it. She told me, and the media has confirmed that, apparently, he's not the only lawyer that bought it."

"Linda?"

"Yes, she's a waitress. A lot of law enforcement officers eat there where she works. She says that just listening there is better than having a scanner."

"Where does she work?"

"Cox Family Restaurant. Do you know it?" she asked as she refilled her tea glass.

"I'm familiar with it. What's her name?"

"Sorry, Mr. Detective Man, I'm not gonna drag my friend into something. You'll just have to put on your deerstalker hat and figure that one out for yourself."

"Fair enough. Listen, if I need to talk with you again, can I call you?"

"Sure, but there's a catch. Give me a piece of paper and your pen."

She wrote a number on the paper. "Here use this number. That other number is my business phone, and I don't check it half the time—busier than I want to be as it is. Now, here's the catch: give to me *your* phone number. And I don't want some wastebasket number."

Spence took out one of his cards and handed it to her.

"That number is directly to me. Okay then. Again, thank you, Eimear, for your time and your willingness to talk with me."

Spence stood up to leave. She stopped him up short.

"Listen—one *more* thing. You're right. I've sat here, answered all your questions, served you tea, and shown my books to you—things I rarely do for anyone. Now, I would say it's *my* turn. I think *you* should do something for *me*."

Spence sat back down. "What do you mean?"

"Well, I also like to write poems with riddles—maybe it's a Poe thing—I don't know. So, this riddle is entitled, 'What's Her Name?'" Smiling, she asked, "So, Mr. Detective Man, are you willing to step up to the plate?"

Returning the smile, Spence countered. "Take your best shot."

"All right, here goes,

'From the first have I been in place—
A plumb line for the human race.
Neither storm nor tempest force—
Shall move me from my hallowed course.
From age to age I am the same—
And those who seek me, know my name.'"

Eimear sat back on the couch, crossed her arms and demanded, "Okay. What's the name?"

"Hold on. Give me a second to think."

Smiling, she countered, "Hurry up, Mr. Detective Man. I don't have all day. I'm a busy woman, you know."

After a moment, Spence took a piece of paper from his notebook and methodically wrote something, folded, and handed it to Eimear. She unfolded the paper, read it, looked at Spence, and laughed heartedly.

"Well, I guess Mr. Detective Man is smarter than he looks."

"I'd almost have to be," he lamented. "But before I go, let me tell you this, Miss Smart App Maker, I have a riddle or two myself. So, should things clear up and we ever have more time, we'll just see how smart *you* are. Hear this, however: you had better bring your A game because there will be a wager attached to mine."

"Money?"

"No, not money. I'll come up with something."

Having said that, Spence got out of his chair for the second time, extended his right hand, and said, "Thank you again for your time. This has been, without a doubt, the most enjoyable interview I've ever had the pleasure to conduct."

The handshake stayed in place just a little bit longer than convention would have required.

Eimear walked him to the door. "I'm looking forward to solving the riddle."

"Don't get your hopes up. You know, some people just can't handle disappointment. For all I know, you might be one of those."

"I sure hope things clear up."

Looking her straight in the eye, Spence acknowledged, "I hope things clear up as well."

As Spence walked to the car, she continued to hold the door open, only closing it after he had driven out of sight.

Driving back to the sheriff's office, Spence was lost in thought. Out of the car and standing in the parking, he called Leigh.

"Hey, Leigh. How're you doing?"

Having listened to her personal update and offering a couple of affirming responses, he told her, "I need a deep-dive background on someone." After a short pause, he answered, "Eimear O'Neill. That's E-I-M-E-A-R and O'Neill with two Ls."

Leigh repeated the name and spelling back to him.

"That's it. Thank you. Talk to you later."

He then entered her name and number into his phone.

Walking back into the conference room, he found Rollins working through a mound of paperwork.

"How'd it go?" Rollins asked.

"If we need to, we can check her computer and phone logs, but I'm thinking she was not involved in any way."

"What's she like?"

"An attractive, intelligent, wealthy woman who knows how to find a good friend as well as how to be one. And who also has a razor."

"A razor?"

"I'll tell you later."

CHAPTER SIXTEEN

A Plea, a Bribe, and a Surprise for a Ride

I T WAS GETTING late in what had been a long day. Rollins continued to plow through the paperwork. Spence altered between completing a summary of his interview with Eimear O'Neill and returning email and text messages on his phone.

The door opened, and in walked Dixie Bell Lee. Sans the impeccable uniform, she was outfitted in a black pencil-skirt suit set with a white camisole. She had a badge holder hung around her neck with a silver-colored chain. She immediately walked over to the table, sat down and buried her head into her folded arms.

Spence fired the opening shot. "My, oh my, how the mighty have fallen." She ignored the volley and despaired. "Help me, Lord. I can't breathe."

That statement was enough to pull Rollins up from the paperwork, "What do you mean?"

With her head still buried in her arms, "I've been with a pack of media types posing as journalists all the live long day. I've breathed in so much hair spray fumes my lungs are burning. I've been asked so many inane questions that my mind is numb. One reporter—and I use the term loosely—wanted to know if any of these incidents could have been related to climate change."

Raising her head slightly and looking at Rollins, she offered, "I'll trade you."

"Nope," Rollins replied and returned to the paperwork.

"Then give me something—anything—just so I can throw it out there and they can chew on that for a while."

Spence took a copy from the public portion of the initial case report and slid it over to her.

"Have enough copies of this made and give it to them. That service ought to buy you a little time and some fresh air."

Just at that point, a text message flashed on Spence's phone. He read it, stood up, told the two, "I'll be back in a minute," and left the room. He walked out of the building entrance and waiting for him was the same vehicle that had appeared by the fence at the graveyard. He walked over to the partially opened passenger window, greeted the driver and passenger, and listened.

After a few minutes, he said, "Okay. Thanks. Let me know when you find out more." When he tapped twice on the top of vehicle, the window went up completely, and the driver quickly drove away. Spence stood there a moment, gathering his thoughts, then turned, and went back into the building.

Back in the conference room, Spence began to brief the two on some of what he had learned. Rollins and Dixie were both wise enough not to ask from where Spence had gotten his information.

"Reportedly, there have been twenty-seven incidences of fatal attacks on lawyers across the fruited plain."

Dixie looked at him, made a right-handed fist, and jabbed it up and down by way of a nonverbal question.

"Yes, all were killed with screwdrivers."

"Well, when this information gets out, I'm guessing the next airheaded media question I'll be asked is, 'Do you think screwdrivers should be banned?'"

He paused a moment before continuing. "Just about every federal agency from the CDC to Homeland Security has formed a task force, and I expect more will climb onto the bandwagon."

Looking directly at Rollins he added, "Soon—very soon—they are going to want for you to share whatever you have. But due to the fact that the other related North Carolina incident, involved a lawyer who was also a highly placed North Carolina state employee, located in Raleigh, I don't think you'll be inundated with offers to help. The same goes for the feds as they've got their own hands full."

"You think, at some point, any of these other entities are going to share what they have with us?" Dixie asked sardonically.

Spence advised her, "Don't hold your hair-sprayed breath. You know it's always a one-way street. There's going to be a secure, daily, virtual informational conferring system set up so that all the impacted investigative entities can share the information that they have."

Rollins chimed in, "Unless the sheriff or the chief tells me differently, I'm not sharing anything until someone shares something with me. And even then, it will be a quid pro quo with that one particular entity. I'll get someone assigned to attend the virtual sessions, but I know that's going to be a one-way-only informational street."

Continuing, while looking at Rollins, he said, "Understood. And here's the thing, I'm suggesting, we're going to have to be more divergent in developing our lines of inquiry. This situation is a nationally impacted undertaking. It has to involve some type of coordinated operation. While I don't think we should eliminate the idea that it could be a personal grievance type of an occurrence, the more salient possibility seems to me, that what's going on here is planned and orchestrated well beyond the local or state levels. But at the end of the day, you're the boss."

"I agree. And for the time being, I want the details about the details about the details to stay with the three of us, along with the sheriff and chief."

Dixie and Spence signaled their agreement with their silence.

As if on cue, ADA Russell, burst into the room opening the door with one hand while texting with the other. Helping himself to a seat and pushing back onto the rear legs of the chair, he said, "Well, as you speculated, the district attorney has tasked me with this case—should it come to trial. So, if you need me, I'm available. Where are we?"

Rollins began to fill in some of the blanks. "Spence interviewed Miss O'Neill and I interviewed her brother, Robert. I don't think he is in the loop in this case."

Looking at Spence, Russell asked, "What about her?"

"I have a high degree of certainty that she isn't involved."

Russell shifted his gaze to Rollins while raising his eyebrows as a form of inquiry.

"No, I'm telling you, same with him. I'm gonna check his alibi, but I feel certain that it will pan out."

Lastly, to Dixie, "And what has our media consultant contributed to the cause?"

"Bite me."

"Anything else?"

Sliding a picture over to Russell, Rollins added, "I've got a picture of the screwdriver from the medical examiner. Tomorrow, Spence and I are going to visit the hardware and big box stores to see who carries this type of screwdriver and, if so, what kind of information can they provide us regarding sales."

Russell glanced at the picture and slid it back. Not bothering to pick up his phone from the table, he read a text message that had appeared.

"That's the DA. Y'all be okay with me sharing what you've told me with him?"

Rollins affirmed, "No problem."

Dixie, with a glimmer of hope in her eyes, wondered, "Do you think the DA would be interested in holding a press conference? I've already gotten a thumbs down from the chief and sheriff with regard to speaking to the media at this point."

"I can ask him. I'm heading back over to the office in a few."

"I'll walk over with you. If he agrees, you can be my best friend for the day, and I'll buy you a drink."

"Just can't get enough of me, can you woman?"

"Listen. In this short time, since we were at the cemetery, I've learned something about myself."

The three men asked in unison, "What?"

"There's no level of degradation I'll not stoop to in order to get out of just one press briefing." Looking at Russell, she continued. "Even if it means being seen in public with you and then having to buy you a drink." She stood up. "Come on, let's go."

Smiling at both men, he said, "Know this, gentlemen: it isn't easy being God's gift to women."

"Take me now, Lord," Dixie prayed.

"Nothing like waiting for the next shoe to fall," he observed as he and Dixie walked out the door.

The two were gone. Spence repeated, Russell's question, "Where are we?" Only this time, the emphasis was on the *we*.

"Here's where we stand. I'm relatively certain that the O'Neills were not involved in lawyer Kacmar's death. I've got a picture of the murder weapon we can take around tomorrow. I'm waiting on the autopsy, phone, and computer analysis reports. I'm waiting on the field reports from the knock and talks being conducted in Kacmar's neighborhood and around the cemetery. I've asked the clerk of court's office to work me up a listing of Kacmar's filings over the last two years so we can eyeball the names. I know this murder is an element within a much larger undertaking."

"All right, good. Now, what about any extremist groups in the area?"

"The police department has a criminal intel officer. I'll call her and see if we can meet with her tomorrow as well. I'll be back in a minute."

While Rollins was out, Spence mentally walked his way back over the day. So much had happened and been said since Tuesday morning, that he knew he needed to separate the vital from the noise. The last thing he wanted was for Rollins and himself to fall into a confirmation bias mindset. He wanted to make sure he was cognizant of what was *there* as well as what was *not there*. He wanted to remind himself that everything he thought at this point just might be wrong. As he had often told his investigators and his students, "Don't be too ready to believe what you think."

Rollins's return terminated his reflection.

"She can meet with us tomorrow at two. That will give us time to take the picture around and see what we can learn."

Gathering up his unfinished paperwork, he said, "That's enough for today. I think I'm gonna go for a ride and clear the cobwebs out of my head."

"Well, keep the shiny side up."

"I intend to."

Spence left the building and headed to the parking lot. Picking his helmet up from the seat, he saddled up, started the engine, and moved out. It wasn't until twenty minutes later that he realized the bike had taken him out Dill's Point Road near to the intersection of Jade Street.

When he got to the Jade Street intersection, he slowed down momentarily, sped up, and continued to the very end of Dill's Point Road. There, he turned around and headed to the hotel.

CHAPTER SEVENTEEN

Searching, Seeking, and Sermonizing

S PENCE AND ROLLINS spent Thursday morning endeavoring to make the rounds of every store in the county that sold screwdrivers. First, they would look over the inventory displayed and then speak to someone on the floor. After showing a picture of the screwdriver recovered at the autopsy, they would inquire if the store had ever sold that brand and if they knew of some stores in the area that did. While nothing emerged from their inquiries, Spence took advantage of the moment and *planted* two or three call-me cards in the parking lot of each location.

Rollins lamented, "If there's another store around here that sells screwdrivers, I don't know about it."

Pointing to the picture, Spence observed, "Think about this. The screwdriver doesn't exactly look new. Maybe it was purchased at an antique store or maybe even a yard sale. What you could do is have patrol officers check out any antique stores in their zones, and if they find anything promising, they could give us a heads-up, and we can make a visit. Also, your contacts in the surrounding counties of Onslow, Jones, Craven, and Beaufort might take a look-see for you when they're out and about."

"Good idea. I'm not going to release copies of this picture, but I can let them all know what I'm looking for. It's like looking for a needle in a haystack."

"Exactly."

Taking an exaggerated look at his fifteen dollar, men's green, army, quartz watch, Spence observed, "Well, look at the time—lunch already. And since our meeting isn't until two, we can stretch it out, talk things out and see if anything else pops up."

"Where do you want to eat?"

"I'd like to go back to Cox Family Restaurant if that's okay with you."

"Works for me."

At the restaurant and before they got out of the car, Rollins said, "Give me a couple of your cards, and I'll put them out. I think I'm going to start doing that. It's not a bad idea, even if you did think of it."

"Then do me a favor. While I'm here, don't put them out at the same location. After I head back to the mountains, you can *seed* them anywhere and everywhere."

"Fair enough."

"Let me know how it works out for you. Just something else for which you owe me."

"I'm forever in your debt."

"Enough to buy my lunch?"

"Not quite. Just missed it by a hair."

Just as they had settled into their booth, their orders were quickly taken. Both men sipped their tea while lost in thought. A waitress walked by looking at her order pad.

Spence caught her attention. "Excuse me, ma'am, I'm not from around here. Someone told me this was the second-best place to eat in the county."

As she knew Rollins, she glanced quickly at him. He nodded his head slightly indicating everything was copasetic.

Showing a furrowed brow, she asked, "Did they happen to mention what the very best, place to eat happened to be?"

"If they did, I've forgotten it. Where would you think it might be?"

"You're sitting in it."

Returning her focus on Rollins, she asked daringly, "Isn't it true, Jesse, this *is* the best place to eat?"

"Why else would I be sitting here?"

Smiling and nodding her head, she said, "There you go." She turned back at Spence. "Who told you we were second best?"

"Someone I met in passing, but I do remember they said a good friend of theirs worked here."

"Who?"

"Linda something. I can't recall the last name."

"Linda Compton?"

"Is that the only Linda who works here?"

"Yes."

"Then that must be it. Is she working today?"

Looking at her watch, she said, "Her shift ends in a few."

"Would you please ask her to drop by for a second if she gets a chance?"

She pointed the eraser end of her pencil at Spence as she left. "Okay. This *is* the best place to eat."

Holding his glass of tea midway to his mouth, Rollins asked, "What was that all about?"

"Just practicing and trying to see what I can find out."

A few minutes later, Linda made her way to the table. "Hey, Jesse. What's going on?"

Standing up and extending his hand, Spence offered, "You must be Linda. I'm Tim Spence. It's nice to meet you."

She shook his hand. "Should I know you?"

"No. Not at all. I just crossed paths with someone recently who had good things to say about you."

"Who?"

"I can't remember." He looked at Rollins. "Working in this case, we've talked to so many people in the last couple of days, in my mind, it's like one big conversation. I've lost count of who's who and who said what."

"The murder in the Old Burying Ground?"

"That's it. The murder in the Old Burying Ground. It's a puzzler."

"For sure. I heard that a bunch of lawyers had been killed. This guy was just one of 'em. He got stabbed with something, and they found him in the graveyard."

"They found him in the graveyard."

"Yes. Deader 'n four o'clock."

"Wow. You know just as much as we do."

"People gonna eat, and people gonna talk. Think for a minute. Who told you about me?"

Spence paused. "I just can't seem to pull it up."

"Was it a man or a woman?"

He pausing. "I think it was a man. I can't be sure. I just wanted to meet you for myself. I hope I haven't held you up."

"Nope. I'm through here for the day."

"Well, Linda, I'm glad to meet you, and it has certainly been nice talking to you too."

She looked at Rollins. "Take care, Jesse." The she turned and walked away.

As Spence returned to his seat, the food arrived.

He shared with Rollins what Rollins already knew. "We're going to have to keep a tight lid on anything we discover." At that, the two casually made their way through the meal, talking about everything but the case.

On the way to the police department, Spence's phone rang. First glancing at the display, Spence then placed the phone to his right ear.

"Eimear. What a nice surprise. To what do I owe this pleasure?"

Rollins took his eyes off the road long enough to throw a quizzical glance at Spence.

"So, Mr. Detective Man, checking up on me, are you?"

"What makes you say that?"

"A little electronic bird just called me."

"What, a mockingbird?"

"No, a wise owl."

"Hm. I can't recall your name having come up in any conversations. You're going to have to be a little more specific, I'm afraid."

Laughing, she countered, "You want specifics? I'll give you specifics. From right here in my seat, I'll modify your computer so that the only thing it will be good for is a plant base. I'll torque your cell phone where it will only work as a door stop. Do you believe me?"

Spence echoed her laughter. "Without a doubt."

With her voice taking on a more serious tone, she continued. "I know you have to do what you have to do. But look, when you no longer consider me or my brother as suspects, call me. Okay?"

Immediately, he answered, "Count on it."

Spence ended that call. Without taking his eyes from the road, Rollins, who had only heard one side of the conversation, asked, "What was that all about?"

"Just taking out some antivirus protection for my computer and my phone."

Rollins pulled into the back of the police department to avoid the media. Spotting a uniformed officer with Atlas-sized muscles bulging out of his chest and the arms of his short-sleeved uniform shirt, he called, "Hey, Chicken Micky, would you please park my car so that we can go in the back and avoid the reporters? We'll be up in Lakisha's office."

"Sure, Jesse. I'll be glad to. I'll bring the keys to you."

"Thanks. I owe you."

Spence looked at Rollins and asked, "Chicken Mickey?"

"Oh—funny story. Mickey is the apple of his grandmother's eye—always has been. Each Sunday, they have dinner at her house. She's constantly asking him, 'Chicken, Mickey?' as she holds the platter of chicken out to him. After a while, the phrase became a name. That's what everyone calls him, 'Chicken Mickey.'"

Spence said, "That's probably why he spends so much time in the gym."

They made their way to an office door upon which, in big, bold letters, was the command, Knock. Having followed the posted command, there was a pause, a klaxon-like buzz, and a loud click as the lock released. Entering the room, they saw three large, darkened computer screens.

Rollins began to make the introductions. "Tim, this is Lakisha Summers, the criminal intelligence officer for the police department. Lakisha, this is—"

Lakisha cut him off and finished the introduction herself, "Tim Spence. One of the founding partners of the Academy of Investigative Resources."

She walked over to Spence and shook his hand. Answering a question that had yet to be asked, she advised, "I'm highly peculiar as to whom I let enter into my world. I like to know a *little something* about them before I buzz them in." Having said that, with a wave of her hand, she pointed out the entire scope of the office as her world.

"Duly noted," Spence acknowledged.

Lakisha walked over to a small wooden conference table in the corner of the room well away from her computer screens.

"Let's take a seat."

She opened. "Okay now. What can I do for you?"

Rollins picked up the inquiry. "We wanted to talk to you about extremist groups here in North Carolina."

Lakisha affirmed with a slight nod.

"And we were wondering, how many groups do we have here in North Carolina?"

"Depending on the wide variety of definitions as to what constitutes an extremist group, somewhere between twenty-five and forty."

From a folder previously placed on the table, she took out and unfolded a North Carolina map. "Here are the locations of the suspected and known groups across the state. The red square indicates the known, and the amber square indicates the suspected."

Again, pulling from the folder, she added, "Here is a listing, location, and summary of all of these groups, as my intel indicates, *today.* You can keep this and the map. Tomorrow might show something slightly different by way of location and status. The situation is very fluid." She continued. "I know the two of you're working the Kacmar case. I know the incident here is a part of a pattern shown to be of a much wider scope. What I don't know is how can I help you?"

Spence jumped into the conversation. "Do you think any of these known or suspected groups could be a player within this pattern?"

"No, I don't. But I'm not *in love* with my assessment. It could change. These groups range in sophistication from meeting in the basement of someone's home to the utilization of encrypted platforms. Their angst may be focused upon race, creed, color, or freedom as they define it—you name it. However, I've not seen anything to this point where lawyers have been the collective angst of a group or a web of groups. That being said, America, as a whole, has little esteem for the legal profession. Poll after poll shows only a small percentage of Americans that were surveyed believe lawyers make much in the way of a positive contribution. Think about it, Carl Sandburg—nice as he was—wrote a telling poem about them. Even Shakespeare had something to say. I'm not saying that America's perception is correct. I'm just saying that *it is what it is* and that people's perception *is* their reality."

Spence took a moment to process what Lakisha has shared and summarized. "So, it could be that whatever is behind the curtain of these murders is off the radar?"

"That's my take—at this moment. Believe me: there's no small amount of inquiry among intel officers—local, state, federal, private sector—such as myself about this very issue, but to this point, I've seen no actionable information. I do have one person on the edge of my consideration, but I want to do a bit more digging before I put a name out there. If something significant pops up, I'll let you know. If you don't hear from me, you'll know it didn't pan out."

Lakisha stood up. Rollins and Spence took the hint that the meeting was over and did the same. Walking over to Spence, she handed him her card.

"Know this: In two years, I'm gonna be knocking on your door. I want two more years in the chair—the last year, in which I'll be training my replacement. Then, I'll be good to go."

Spence took her card and gave her his. "I'll be waiting to hear from you. It's been nice meeting you and thank you for your time and information."

When Rollins opened the door to leave, he found his car keys taped just below the command. Apparently, Chicken Mickey was not eager to knock.

As they walked across the parking lot to the car, Rollins accused Spence. "You have no pride whatsoever, do you? You're like a thief in the night, stealing people from anywhere you can."

"You know my motto: them that takes has. Tell me something: Doesn't she ever smile?"

"I see her smile every Sunday in church," Rollins admonished delicately.

Back in the conference room, Rollins found the summary of the knock and talks. After, they had reviewed the summary—finding nothing in the way of actionable information—the two evaluated their inquiry-related activities from the gravesite to that point.

"I'm gonna run to my desk and see if I've received anything from the any of the untold number of taskforce entities," Rollins noted as he got up and left the room.

Spence thought, I can answer that one for you.

He took advantage of the break to check his texts and emails and make a quick phone call to Leigh, requesting an update on the inquiry by phone for the Bill Dockery inquiry and Eimear before he called it a night.

"Sometime before midnight, please."

Rollins returned with a piece of paper in hand, much to Spence's surprise.

"Don't get your hopes up. It's only a request for the information I've gained so far."

Having said that, he fed the paper into the shredder that had been placed in the room at the very start of the inquiry.

"Okay. Let's call it a day. All I want to do is brief the chief while we're here, call my sergeant, and let him run the information up the chain. Until we get the results of the forensic analysis of Kacmar's computer and phone as well as the autopsy report, we're at a standstill. Tomorrow's Friday. We'll meet here at nine and do some more divergent thinking. If anything pops up tonight, I'll call you. You do the same and call me."

"Works for me."

They left the room. Rollins went down the hall to round up the powers that be, and Spence made his way to the parking lot and waited for Rollins. Back on his bike, he went straight to the hotel. He spent the evening returning planted-card inquiries and learning all that he could from and about the individuals—taking the time to make a record of all. While eating the salad he had sent to the room, he fielded the update on the Dockery inquiry and the background on Eimear. He directed a couple of additional steps to be taken in the Dockery inquiry.

"That's all she wrote," he said out loud.

Later, crawling into bed, he found that this was not the usual routine of falling asleep as soon as his head hit the pillow. Something was working around in the back of his mind, and he just couldn't seem to bring it forward. After a while, fatigue won out, and his mind turned the whole problem over to the subconscious.

CHAPTER EIGHTEEN

Two Turns around a Graveyard— Drawing the Next Card

F RIDAY MORNING FOUND Rollins and Spence sitting at the conference room table, coffee in hand. For some time, the two were lost in thought staring at the sparce documentation laid out on the table. As the media, feeding frenzy on a story of national implication mounted, so did the pressure they put on themselves to come up with "something."

Spence broke the reverie. "How did your briefing with the chief go?"

"As well as to be expected. I laid everything we had out there and told him what we had accomplished to this point. I asked him for any lines of inquiry we might have missed and as to what other steps we could take."

"What did he say?"

"That it looked like we had the bases covered and to let him know when the electronic forensic and autopsy reports came in. After that, I called my sergeant and brought him up to date."

"Excellent."

Again, silence blanketed the room.

Finally, Spence took a deep breath and noted, "We're not going to solve anything sitting in this room. Let's go back to square one. What say we go back to the Old Burying Ground, look around, change perspective, and walk our way back through everything we have undertaken to this point?"

"That works for me."

Gathering the documents and placing them into a light, tan file folder, Rollins said, "Let's go."

Back at the Otway Burns site, Rollins pulled out one of the crime scene photos showing Kacmar propped up with the screwdriver still in place.

Pointing at the deceased's shoes, Rollins noted, "See the material on the bottom of his shoes. I'm thinking he walked in here under his own power."

"I think so too. You can see the crushed stone from the path, bits of leaves, and tiny pieces of wood on the soles."

Pointing at the fence behind them, Spence said, "If the gate was locked, they would have to have made it over the fence. But what would have motivated or caused Kacmar to walk here—assuming that he did—and climb over a formidable fence?"

"Someone could have been holding a gun on him."

"I'm thinking two possibilities. One, as you said, he could've had a gun or some other weapon held on him. Two, he was surreptitiously motivated to come here. What other possibility am I missing?"

"Maybe he wasn't fully in control of his mental faculties," Rollins added.

"That's a good point."

Continuing, Rollins observed, "You know, all this time I've been thinking that there was just the two of them—Kacmar and whoever—but there could have been more than one perp involved."

"For sure. What about this? Let's slowly walk the inside of the fence line. Maybe we can see what the most advantageous way would be to break into the graveyard. Your call."

"Good idea. Let's take it one step further. Let's walk it counterclockwise and then turn and walk the perimeter, clockwise. That way we'll have the opportunity to gain two perspectives."

Stepping up to the fence by Craven Street, the two slowly began to walk the perimeter, scrutinizing the ground and the fence. As, they walked, they continued to mind map what they knew, what they knew that they didn't know, and theorize as to what they didn't know that they didn't know. It helped that Rollins had taken and excelled in Spence's e-learning class, Divergent and Convergent Thinking. As they conversed, it struck Spence that the pupil was becoming as good as the teacher. For Spence, the only thing better was when the pupil became *better* than the teacher. He had no doubt that, with Rollins, that would, in time, prove to the case.

Eventually, they found themselves back at the cannon. After pausing for a few minutes, they reversed their course and repeated the trek. By this time, the tours had started. This turn was more contemplative than communicative. Both were processing, turning data over in their minds like a crystal, anticipating that examining information this way or that way would cause the bright light of revelation to bring forth a new line of thought.

At their journey's end, Rollins's phone musically indicated that he had received a text.

After reading the text, he shared with Spence. "The forensics on the electronics will be here on Monday."

Looking at his watch, Spence replied, "Great. Let's take a break and get some lunch."

"Where do you want to eat?"

"Your call. I picked last time."

"Let's go back to the Beaufort Grocery Company. I would like to have the opportunity to eat the Queen's Club in its entirety."

He had not forgotten that they last time they were there, Bo had appropriated half of his meal. As entertaining as the card trick had been, it was not worth a half of his sandwich as the price of admission.

On the way out, they dutifully stopped to pay their respects to the little girl buried in a keg of rum. As they stood, staring at the array of memorials laid upon her grave, Spence reflected upon the card he had discovered there.

"By itself, it may be nothing. But I don't believe in coincidences. Finding a card here and a similar card at Kacmar's house is *not* a coincidence. One card allowed for taking money from others. The other card allowed the holder to get out of jail. After we eat and get back to the office, we'll talk this over. It's hard for me to think on an empty stomach, and we need to think about those cards."

"I agree."

Having made their way to the gate, they paused to allow the next tour group to enter the graveyard as they waited for their tour guide.

After enjoying a lunch that allowed for the completion of the entire meal, they went back to the office, directly to the conference room.

Rollins laid out in front of them the clear, separate evidence bags containing the two cards recovered from the house and the gravesite. The bags were appropriately marked with the case number and other requisite documentation.

Spence opened the cognitive considerations. "What do you think?"

"We agree that finding a card at the grave and another in Kacmar's house is a bridge too far to be a coincidence. Somehow, whoever left the card *is* tied to the case. But how is the wording on the first card linked to Kacmar?"

Spence tapped his right index finger on the bag containing the card taken from the gravesite.

"The card authorizes the holder to take money from the others. Kacmar was a lawyer specializing in ersatz civil litigation, the purpose of which was to take money from individuals or corporations. His body was found by a cannon from a ship that was authorized to take whatever from others on the open sea. Could those facts all be connected?"

"That's a good fit, at least for the way things stand right now. That being the case, what's the purpose of the writing on this second card?"

"You know what? We have got to remind ourselves to be thinking *macro* as well as *micro*. Kacmar was just a part of a score of lawyers that bought the farm across the country—all in a similar manner. This case is not an isolated event, but rather part of a larger—for lack of a better term—operation. If the killer did leave the cards—and that's where my head is right now—then whoever this is, knew we would be searching Kacmar's house. They wanted for us to find the card. That being the case, I see three possibilities for this last card. One, it's just meant to throw us off by going down a dead end and has no connection at all. Whoever killed Kacmar may or may not still be around. Two, it's somehow linked to Kacmar, and we have yet to figure that out. Three, it's linked to something that has *yet* to occur or has already occurred, and we just haven't discovered it yet."

"I don't want to think about what's behind your door number three."

"Neither do I, but it is what it is. What do you want to do next?"

"I'm thinking I'll could go ahead and submit these cards into evidence. It would take a while, but I'd like to have them checked for fingerprints and DNA."

"Good idea. My gut tells me to keep knowledge of these cards to ourselves. Let me throw this out. You're right: it *will* take forever to get any results from the state lab. I know a certified, private lab here in North Carolina that can do the turnaround much quicker. I can make a call and get the fee knocked down so that it won't break the bank. It's your call. Do you want to run it up the flagpole?"

"Yeah. Give me a few and let me see if the sheriff salutes."

While Rollins was gone, Spence pulled his phone from his pocket and began to play catch-up. His first call was to Leigh to receive a brief update on the salient undertakings of the partnership. Most AIR operations were moving forward smoothly, but with two cases, he added additional steps that he wanted to be taken—the Dockery inquiry, in particular.

Next, he perused his emails. Some, he answered, but most, he forwarded onto the appropriate person for disposition. After that task was completed, he started in on his text messages. Except for one text, all required only short answers to clear the boards. Looking at his watch, he noted that forty-five minutes had passed in the blink of an eye. He was just starting to listen to the messages in his voice mail when Rollins returned.

"All right, the sheriff signed off on having the private lab do the analysis. I'm keeping the informal chain of evidence log up to date. We've got to be able to document a valid chain of evidence coming and going. I'll need to include the pertinent information regarding the lab."

Spence checked the contact listings on his phone. He found what he was looking for and used one of his hotel pens to write the name, address, and lab certification number on a page from his legal pad. As soon as he handed it over, Rollins was quickly out the door.

Spence touched the speed dial for a direct number into the lab. After two rings, there was a pickup, and a familiar voice answered, "Lab."

"Gary Barnes. How's the oldest lab rat in the history of forensics?"

"Hanging on by the tips of my fingers. How's the world's worse investigator that couldn't find a discarded hypodermic needle on a San Francisco sidewalk?"

"Better than I deserve. You still living in Cary?"

"Yes—Corralled Area for Relocated Yankees!"

"It does sadly sound to me like you've lost most of your Southern accent."

"All I need is about fifteen minutes on the golf course with you, and I'll be right as rain."

"Before you know it, you'll be eating bagels and cream cheese three times a day. Listen, I do need a favor."

"I knew that the minute I heard you speak. You never call. You never send me flowers or candy. What have you got, and what do you want?"

"There will be two cards coming your way from the Carteret County Sheriff's Office. We need them tested for fingerprints, DNA, and anything else you can tell us." Lowering his voice, Spence added, "This is important."

"I understand. I'm aware of what's going on. I'll take care of it."

"Thank you. Two last things, please. When you've completed the analysis, would you call me first with the results before we send someone to retrieve them? Secondly, would you not enter anything into your computer system regarding this until I give you the go-ahead?"

"You've got it."

"Thank you, Gary. I owe you."

"Just a token of appreciation for the solid you did for me."

"Ain't nothing but a thing."

With that summation, the call ended.

Ultimately, the lab results, other than the fact the ink was the same on both cards, were nil. A uniformed officer was sent to recover the cards and return them to Rollins.

While waiting for Rollins, Spence took advantage of the solitude to return phone calls.

"Two down. Seven to go."

Just as he started to make the third call, Rollins returned to the conference room.

Spence gave him an update. "I called the lab and they'll be standing by."

"Great. I've got a uniformed officer in a marked car heading that way, evidence in hand."

Gathering up the papers and returning them to the folder, Rollins noted, "I think we have done all the damage we can for the day. It's Friday. You want to come over for supper? We're calling in pizza."

"Let me take a rain check. I think I'll get in a ride out twenty-four back to Swansboro. See what I can get into. If anything comes up this weekend, will you call me?"

"For sure. By Monday, we should have the autopsy report along with the electronic forensics. Hopefully, we can use whatever is there to stir the pot and move forward. It has been a week, hasn't it?"

"One time. It'd be nice if we could wrap up our little piece of this national puzzle once and for all. Then I could return to my vacation."

As they left the office and went their separate ways, they had no way of knowing that their little piece of the puzzle was to become much bigger, much more complex, and much more deadly. Oh yes. There was, most assuredly, something behind door number three—something that would prove to be most challenging.

When Spence got to his room, there was a hotel envelope taped to his door. Inside the envelope was a handwritten note: "Am I still a suspect?" The note was signed simply with a capital *E*.

With that inquiry, Spence knew his phone log had just jumped from seven to eight.

"No ride this evening," he decided.

"I'll just have a sandwich, a small salad and a beer sent up to the room."

CHAPTER NINETEEN

A Better Ride, a Series of Reports, a Transcript Review

S ATURDAY AND SUNDAY had been good to Spence. For the most part, when he wasn't fishing, he was riding. He dedicated two hours each evening after supper for work. Saturday morning during breakfast, he checked in with Ann at the restaurant to get an update as to her transportation predicament. She told him that her new ride, a much later, preowned model with very little mileage and a lifetime powertrain guarantee, would be hers in just a matter of days.

"I can't thank you enough," she said as she poured his coffee. "You have no idea how much this means. I can make the payments and won't have to spend everything on repairs."

"I think I do have an idea, and you're more than welcome. Just, when the time comes and you're in a position to help someone, pay it forward. Now what do you have in mind for breakfast?"

Sunday morning, for his way of thinking, he slept in late—eight a.m. After a quick cup of coffee, he ran on the beach. An energy bar and a second cup of coffee sufficed for breakfast. Then he headed straight for the bike. Heading up Highway 70, he spent the day meandering around James City and New Bern. On the way back, he rewarded himself with an early supper consisting of a cheeseburger and fries from the Sea and Soul food truck.

Back at the hotel, he checked at the front desk to see if a package had arrived. The package was wrapped in brown paper with only his name and no mail-service indications. From there, he walked out the back of the hotel to Molly's Beachside Bar. After one beer and one business card exchange with a real estate developer with whom he created the opportunity to engage, he made straightaway to his room. He made one phone call to express thanks for the package and thoroughly reviewed the material within the package. After his review, he called Leigh's office phone and left a recorded message listing several steps he wanted to have taken as a result of his review. After that, it was lights out.

Having arrived early Monday morning, he waited patiently in the parking lot of the sheriff's office for Rollins to arrive. Soon, coffee in hand, they were ensconced in the war room.

Spence got the week started. "Anything come up over the weekend?"

"I got a notification late yesterday that the reports are all in. After I finish this coffee, I'll go sign them out from the evidence tech. How was your weekend?"

"I had an outstanding weekend—fishing, running, riding, browsing, and eating. How about you?"

"Saturday, we took the girls to the beach. Yesterday, after church we had potluck on the grounds." Rollins placed a special emphasis on the word *church* while raising his eyebrows and establishing direct eye contact with Spence. Spence understood the meta-message.

Rollins wasn't ready to let it go.

"I started to pray for you, but God said not to bother."

Not waiting for a response, he continued. "After that I took a Baptist-hour nap for most of the afternoon. Woke up long enough to eat some chili dogs, spent some time with the girls, and called it a day. Now, here I am."

Spence stated the obvious. "The media is having a feeding frenzy on the murders of all of these lawyers."

"Don't I know it? I've kept the sheriff, the chief, and all the other stake-holders in the loop. Thankfully, they understand the massive scope of this thing and that it isn't just a simple, 'get-back-at-a-lawyer' case. I'm sure D has more than got her hands full. I'm more than glad that she is doing what she is doing and we're doing what we are doing."

Placing the empty coffee cup on the table, he declared, "I'm gonna go get the reports, and we'll start there." He looked at Spence's package. "What's that?"

"We'll get to it after the reports."

"Ten four."

During Rollins's absence, Spence called Leigh. "Anything I need to take care of?"

"One thing. I'm gonna transfer you. Call me if you need me. Have a good day."

Spence listened. The briefing ended.

"Thank you. Please tell them good job. Talk to you later."

Rollins returned, reports in hand. Both transitioned into the silent mode as they reviewed the reports. In the fullness of time, Rollins took a deep breath, exhaled, and lamented, "Not much here."

"Nope. No defensive wounds on Kacmar, no foreign skin sampling from under his fingernails, and nothing but alcohol detected in his system. The screwdriver *was* the cause of death. His computer and cell phone had no indications of any acrimonious exchanges. His phone never left the house on the night he was murdered so tracking him by that's not in play. We did learn that the time of death was somewhere between four and five a.m. That's it."

"Let's just let this information, or lack thereof, percolate. Maybe something will come to us. In the meantime, I've got something else we can review. I just don't know if there's a great deal within this interview transcript that will help. I've read through it a couple of times. Maybe you'll find something that I've missed."

"Right now, I'll take anything I can get."

"Here is a transcript of an interview related to the murder of a lawyer during the same window of time as ours and all the others."

Rollins knew not to ask Spence where and how he came into possession of the transcript. The concept of need-to-know was hard and fast.

Spence added, "It isn't that long but I got us a couple of additional lines of inquiry for us from it."

"What are they?"

"It would take away all the fun if I told you. Besides, you might find something I missed. Listen, transcripts are an excellent source of information missed by too many investigators. Transcripts aren't just a record of an interview. If the reader of the transcript is linguistically knowledgeable, they provide guidance for question development for subsequent interviews and can help to solve a case."

Having said that, Spence pointed to the transcript and said, "Show me what you've got."

While you read it, I'm gonna go get another cup of coffee. Back in a bit."

Rollins placed the document on the table and began to read:

IR Auten: The time is 13:35. My name is Detective Auten, and this is my partner, Detective Edwards, and we're in an interview room at the Justice Center. And we're here with J. R. Harrington. Is that Jimmy Robert Harrington?

IE: James Robert Harrington.

IR Auten: And what's your birthdate, Mr. Harrington?

IE: June 15, 1978.

IR Auten: Okay. Prior to us talking to you, I want you to know you're not under arrest. This is what's known as a noncustodial interview. You do not have to talk with us, and you're free to leave at any time. Do you understand that?

IE: Yes.

IR Auten: That being the case, are you willing to sit here and talk with us?

IE: Yes. I just want to know what this is all about.

IR Auten: We'll get to that. Are there any questions about what I just shared with you?

TO JUSTIFY THE WICKED

IE: (unintelligible)

IR Auten: Okay, you've got to speak up louder than that.

IE: Okay, no.

IR Auten: Okay. All right, what we're gonna do is—we want to—we're investigating, obviously, the death of lawyer Ray Greenwood.

IR Edwards: Someone told us that.

IR Auten: Yeah, and we're going to need to talk to you about that.

IE: All I know is what I've seen on the news.

IR Auten: How long have you known Greenwood?

IE: Officially? Probably close to three years. Three years with the civil suit.

IR Auten: Have you had any contact with him since then?

IE: Off and on.

IR Auten: What's your opinion of Greenwood? What was the—

IR Edwards: How did you know him?

IE: Well, I had filed a suit against a guy that had rear-ended me. Broke my back and knocked out my front teeth. I was out of work. Lost a lot of money. Greenwood was the attorney for the guy that hit me. What he did was—

IR Auten: Recently have you contacted him?

IE: No.

IR Auten: Not since the civil suit?

IE: Not really.

IR Auten: Do you think you were fairly compensated as a result of your suit?

IE: No.

IR Edwards: Why not?

IE: He turned everything around. Made it look like part of the fault was mine. I was just stopped at an intersection.

IR Edwards: Is that what was determined?

IE: We went through the court and everything. Everything is done. And then he did something, and all of a sudden, the amount they gave me was more than cut in half.

IR Auten: How was your attorney? What that a...?

IE: The first attorney?

IR Auten: Yeah, was there problems with him too?

IE: Absolutely. He didn't do what he was supposed to do representing me.

IR Auten: Uh-huh. I understand Greenwood had made a couple of crime... crime reports or something?

IE: Ah, we have a big fight about a year and a half ago, you know. He made a report. I didn't make a report. And then we had an altercation about six months ago maybe. It wasn't a physical argument. I kicked his door or something.

IR Auten: And he made a police report on those two occasions?

IE: Mm-hmm. And I stayed right there until the police came, talked to them.

IR Edwards: Were you arrested at one time for something?

IE: No. I mean, we had an altercation. I don't know. I know I ended up doing community service.

IR Auten: So you weren't arrested?

IE: No, I was never really arrested.

IR Edwards: They never booked you or...

IE: No.

IR Auten: Can I ask you when's the last time you've slept?

IE: I got a couple of hours sleep last night. I mean, you know, I was asleep a few hours when the phone call came that y'all wanted to talk to me.

IR Edwards: Did Greenwood have a housemaid that lived there?

IE: I believe so, yes.

IR Edwards: Do you know her name at all?

IE: Anna, Anna, something like that. Her name was on the police report.

IR Auten: We didn't see her there. Did she have the day off perhaps?

IE: I don't know. How would I know what schedule she's on?

IR Edwards: J. R., what do you think? We can maybe just recount last night…

IR Auten: Yeah. When was the last time you saw Greenwood?

IE: I was leaving a classical musical concert. He was there too. He took off, and I was talking to one of my business partners.

IR Auten: Where was the concert?

IE: Raven Center.

IR Auten: And was that for one of your children?

IE: Yeah, for my daughter, Jill.

IR Auten: And what time was that yesterday?

IE: It ended about nine thirty, quarter to ten, something like that, you know, in the ballpark, right in that area. And they took off.

IR Auten: They?

IE: Him and whoever he was with.

IR Auten: And then you went your own separate way?

IE: Yeah.

IR Auten: Was Greenwood driving?

IE: I don't know.

IR Auten: What kind of car were they in?

IE: A black car.

IR Auten: What were you driving?

IE: My Cadillac.

IR Auten: Do you own that Ford F150 that sits outside your house?

IE: My company owns it.

IR Auten: So that's your vehicle, the one that was parked there on the street?

IE: Mm-hmm.

IR Auten: And it's actually owned by your company?

IE: My company, yeah.

IR Auten: Who's the primary driver on that? You?

IE: I drive it. My ex-wife drives it. You know, it's kind of a…she's part owner of the company.

IR Auten: All-purpose type vehicle?

IE: All-purpose, yeah. It's the only one that my company insurance will allow me to let anyone else drive.

IR Auten: Okay.

IR Edwards: When you drive it, where do you park it at home? Where it is now? It was in the street or something?

IE: I always park it on the street.

IR Edwards: You never take it in the...

IE: Oh, rarely. I mean, I'll bring it in and switch the stuff, you know, and stuff like that. I did that yesterday, you know.

IR Edwards: When did you last drive it?

IE: Yesterday.

IR Auten: What time yesterday?

IE: In the morning, in the afternoon.

IR Auten: Okay, you left there, you're saying, about nine thirty or quarter to ten, or you left the concert?

IE: Yeah.

IR Auten: And you spoke with some of your business partners?

IE: Yeah, we were just standing there talking.

IR Auten: Okay, what time did you leave the concert?

IE: Right about that same time. We were all leaving. We were all leaving then. One of the partners said something to me about me joining them for a late dinner, and I said no thanks.

IR Edwards: Listen, we wanted to interview one of your business partners, and he declined to talk to us. Why do you think...

IR Auten: Where did you go from there, J. R.?

IE: Ah, home, home for a while, got my car for a while, tried to find my girlfriend for a while, came back to the house.

IR Auten: Who was home when you got home?

IE: Jill.

IR Auten: Jill? Anybody else? Was your ex-wife, Scarlett, there?

IE: No.

IR Auten: Isn't that her name, Scarlett?

IE: Scarlett, yeah. Franklin. She changed her name back after we got divorced. We're good, though.

IR Auten: So, what time do you think you got back home, actually physically got home?

IE: Ten something.

IR Auten: Ten something? And then you left, and…

IE: Yeah, I'm trying to think, did I leave? You know, I'm always…I had to run and get my daughter some flowers. I was actually doing the concert, so I rushed and got her some flowers, and I came home, and then I called Sandra on her landline as I was going to her house, and Sandra wasn't home.

IR Auten: Sandra is your girlfriend?

IE: Girlfriend, yeah.

IR Auten: Sandra who?

IE: Avendano.

IR Auten: Could you spell that for me?

IE: A-V-E-N-D-A-N-O.

IR Auten: Do you know an address on her?

IE: No, she lives on Sprague Street, but I think she's out of town.

IR Auten: You got a phone number?

IE: Yeah (number deleted).

IR Auten: So, you didn't see her last night?

IE: No, we'd been to a big affair the night before, and then I came back home. I was basically at home. I mean, anytime I was…whatever time it took me to get to the concert and back, to get to the flower shop and back, I mean, that's the time I was out of the house.

IR Auten: Were you scheduled to play golf this morning someplace?

IE: At the country club.

IR Auten: What kind of tournament was it?

IE: Ah, it was business grouping, with special clients.

IR Auten: Oh, okay. What time did you leave last night, leave the house?

IE: To go to the airport?

IR Auten: Mm-hmm.

IE: About…the Uber was supposed to be there at eleven thirty. Normally, they get there a little earlier. I was rushing around—somewhere between there and twelve.

IR Auten: So approximately eleven thirty to twelve?

IE: Eleven thirty, twelve, yeah, somewhere in that area.

IR Auten: And you went by Uber?

IE: Yeah.

IR Auten: Who's the Uber driver?

IE: Ah, you have to ask my administrative assistant.

IR Edwards: Did you converse with the driver at all? Did you talk to him?

IE: No, had never picked me up before. Most of the time, I have a regular driver I drive with and converse. No, just about rushing to the airport, about how I live my life on airplanes, and hotels, that type of thing.

IR Edwards: What time did the plane leave?

IE: Ah, twelve forty-five, the flight took off.

IR Auten: What airline was it?

IE: A charter airline. Private company.

IR Auten: Private company? And it took off at twelve forty-five to New Orleans?

IE: New Orleans.

IR Edwards: So yesterday you did drive the F-150?

IE: Mm-hmm.

IR Edwards: And where did you park it when you brought it home?

IE: Ah, the first time probably by the rose bushes. I'm trying to think, or did I bring it in the driveway? Normally, I'll park it by the rose bushes, sometimes…

IR Edwards: On Davis or Davison?

IE: On Davis, yeah.

IR Edwards: Where did you park yesterday for the last time, do you remember?

IE: Right where it is.

IR Edwards: Where it is now?

IE: Yeah.

IR Edwards: Where, on…?

IE: Right on the street there by the rose bushes.

IR Edwards: On Davis?

IE: No, on Randolph.

IR Edwards: You parked it there?

IE: Yes.

IR Edwards: About what time was that?

IE: Five something…six o'clock, I don't know, right in that area.

IR Edwards: Did you take it to the concert?

IE: No.

IR Edwards: What time was the concert?

IE: Over at about nine thirty. Like I said, I came home, I got my…I was going to see my girlfriend. I was calling her, and she wasn't around.

IR Edwards: So you drove the…you came home in the Cadillac, and then you got in the F-150…

IE: In the F-150, 'cause my phone was in the F-150. And because it's a F-150. It's a F-150, it's what I drive, you know. I'd rather drive it than any other car. And, you know, as I was going over there, I called her a couple of times, and she wasn't there, and I left a message, and then I checked my messages, and there were no new messages. She wasn't there, and she may have to leave town. Then I came back and ended up sitting with Jill.

IR Edwards: Okay, what time was this again that you parked the F-150?

IE: Five something, maybe. We had…went and got a burger, and I'd come home and kind of leisurely got ready to go. I mean, we'd done a few things…

IR Edwards: You weren't in a hurry when you came back with the F-150?

IE: No.

IR Edwards: The reason I asked you, the vehicles were parked kind of at a funny angle, stuck out in the street.

IE: Well, it's parked because…I don't know if it's a funny angle or what. It's parked because when I was hustling at the end of the day to get all my stuff, and I was getting my phone and everything off it, when I just pulled it out of the gate there, it's like it's a tight turn.

IR Edwards: So, you had it inside the compound, then?

IE: Yeah.

IR Edwards: Oh, okay.

IE: I brought it inside the compound to get my stuff out of it, and then I put it out, and I'd run back inside the gate before the gate closes.

IR Auten: What's your office phone number?

IE: (number deleted)

IR Auten: And is that the local area code 214?

IE: Yes.

IR Auten: How did you get the injury on your hand?

IE: I don't know. The first time, when I was in New Orleans and all, but at the house, I was just running around.

IR Auten: How did you do it in New Orleans?

IE: I broke a glass. One of you guys had just called me saying you wanted to talk to me, and I was in the bathroom, and I just kind of zoned out for a little bit.

IR Edwards: Is that how you cut it?

IE: Mmm, it was cut before, but I think I just opened it again. I'm not sure.

IR Edwards: Do you recall bleeding at all in your truck, in the F-150?

IE: I recall bleeding at my house. and then I went to the F-150. The last thing I did before I left, when I was rushing, was went and got my phone out of the F-150.

IR Edwards: Mm-hmm. Where's the phone now?

IE: In my bag.

IR Edwards: You have it?

IE: In that black bag.

IR Edwards: You brought a bag with you here?

IE: Yeah, it's…

IR Edwards: So, do you recall bleeding at all?

IE: Yeah, I mean, I knew I was bleeding, but it was no big deal. I bleed all the time. I play golf and stuff, so there's always something, nicks and stuff here and there.

IR Edwards: So, did you do anything? When did you put the Band-Aid on it?

IE: Actually, I asked the girl this morning for it.

IR Edwards: And she got it?

IE: Yeah, 'cause last night with Jill, when I was leaving, she was saying something to me, and I was rushing to get my phone, and I put a little thing on it, and it stopped.

IR Auten: Do you have the keys to that F-150?

IE: Yeah.

IR Auten: Okay. We've impounded the F-150. I don't know if you know that or not.

IE: No.

IR Auten: Take a look at it. Other than you, who's the last person to drive it?

IE: Probably Scarlett. When I'm out of town, I don't know who drives the truck, maybe my ex, maybe my daughter.

IR Auten: The keys are available?

IE: I leave the keys there, you know, when Scarlett is there because, sometimes, she needs it, or Jill was gone and wasn't coming back until today, and I was coming back tonight.

IR Auten: So, you don't mind if your ex-wife uses it, or...

IE: This is the only one I can let her use. When she doesn't have her car, 'cause sometimes her husband takes her car, I let her use the truck.

IR Edwards: When was the last time you were at Greenwoods' house?

IE: I didn't go in. I would never go in his house. I haven't ever been in his house. The last time I was at his house you know, six months. We had that altercation.

IR Auten: How did that happen? Did you just park and go up to the house?

IE: Up to the house.

IR Auten: Is there a kind of walkway out front from the driveway?

IE: Yeah.

IR Auten: But you never went inside the house?

IE: I haven't been in the house.

IR Auten: Has he been trying to contact you?

IE: Not that I know of.

IR Auten: Nothing's going on, huh?

IR Edwards: Do you know where Greenwood went, the others with him, for dinner last night?

IE: No. Well, no, I didn't ask.

IR Edwards: I just thought maybe there's a regular place that they go.

IE: I wouldn't know.

IR Auten: You haven't had any problems with him lately, have you, J. R.?

IE: I always have problems with him, in my mind, you know? Every time my back starts to hurt or every time I look in the mirror and see my dental implants, I have a problem with him.

IR Auten: Did Greenwood have words with you last night?

IE: Pardon me?

IR Auten: Did Greenwood have words with you last night?

IE: No, no, no.

IR Auten: Did you talk to him last night?

IE: No.

IR Auten: But you didn't have a conversation with him?

IE: No, no.

IR Auten: What were you wearing last night, J. R.?

IE: What did I wear on the golf course yesterday? Some of these kind of pants, some of these kind of pants—I mean I changed different for whatever it was. I just had on some…

IR Auten: Just these black pants.

IE: Just these…they're called…something I don't remember.

IR Auten: These aren't the pants?

IE: No.

IR AUTEN: Where are the pants that you wore?

IE: They're hanging in my closet.

IR Auten: These are washable, right? You just throw them in the laundry?

IE: Yeah, I got several pair.

IR Auten: Do you recall coming home and hanging them up, or…?

IE: I always hang up my clothes. I mean, it's rare that I don't hang up my clothes unless I'm laying them in my bathroom to wait to do something with them, but those are the only things I don't hang up. But when you play golf, you don't necessarily get dirty pants.

IR Edwards: What kind of shoes were you wearing?

IE: Tennis shoes.

IR Edwards: Tennis shoes? Do you know what kind?

IE: I don't know. I'd have to check.

IR Edwards: Are they at home, too?

IE: Yeah.

IR Edwards: Was this supposed to be a short trip to New Orleans so you didn't take a whole lot?

IE: Yeah, I was coming back today.

IR Edwards: Just overnight?

IE: Yeah.

IR Auten: That's a hectic schedule, fly there to play golf and come back.

IE: Yeah, but I do it all the time.

IR Auten: Do you?

IE: Yeah. That's what I was complaining with the driver about, you know, about my whole life is on and off airplanes.

IR Auten: J. R., we've got sort of a problem.

IE: Mm-hmm.

IR Auten: We've got some blood on and in your F-150. We've got some blood at your house, and sort of a problem.

IE: Well, take my blood test.

IR Edwards: Well, we'd like to do that. We've got, of course, the cut on your finger that you aren't real clear on. Do you recall having that cut on your finger the last time you were at Greenwood's house?

IE: Greenwood's house?

IR Edwards: Yeah.

IE: No. It was last night.

IR Edwards: Okay, so last night you cut it—

IR Auten: Somewhere after the concert?

IE: Somewhere when I was rushing to get out of my house.

IR Auten: Okay, after the concert.

IE: Yeah.

IR Auten: What do you think happened? Do you have any idea?

IE: I have no idea, man. You guys haven't told me anything. I have no idea. When you said to my daughter, who said something to me today, that somebody else might have been involved, I have absolutely no idea what happened. I don't know how, why, or what. But you guys haven't told me anything. Every time I ask you guys, you say you're going to tell me in a bit.

IR Auten: Well, we don't know a lot of answers to these questions yet ourselves, J. R., okay?

IE: I've got a bunch of guns, guns all over the place. You can take them. They're all there. I mean, you can see them. I keep them in my car and F-150 for an incident that happened a month ago that my former in-laws, my ex-wife, and everybody knows about that.

IR Auten: What was that?

IE: Going down to…and cops down there know about it because I've told two marshals about it. At a mall, I was going down for some social event, and I had just left—and it was like three thirty in the morning, and I'm in a lane, and also the car in front of me is going real slow, and I'm slowing down 'cause I figure he sees a cop, 'cause we were all going pretty fast. And I'm going to change lanes, but there's a car next to me, and I can't change lanes. Then that goes for a while, and I'm going to slow down and go around him but the car butts up to me, and I'm like caught between three cars. They were a bunch of guys in those cars, and they were not letting me go anywhere. And finally, I went on the shoulder, and I sped up, and then I held my phone up so they could see the light part of it, you know, 'cause I have tinted windows, and they kind of scattered, and I chased one of them for a while to make him think I was chasing him before I took off.

IR Edwards: Were you in the F-150?

IE: No.

IR Edwards: What were you driving?

IE: My Cadillac. It has tinted windows and all, so I figured they thought they had a nice little touch…

IR Edwards: Did you think they were trying to rip you off?

IE: Definitely, they were. And then the next thing, you know, I went home. At four in the morning, I got there, and when Jill woke up, I told her about it, and told her mother about it, told everybody about it, you know? And when I saw two marshals at a mall, I walked up and told them about it.

IR Auten: What did they do, make a report on it?

IE: They didn't know nothing. I mean, they should have some kind of a report and remember I told them.

IR Auten: Did Jill mention that she'd been getting any threats lately to you? Anything she was concerned about or threats to her safety?

IE: To her?

IR Auten: Yes.

IE: From?

IR Auten: From anybody.

IE: No, not at all.

IR Auten: Is she very security conscious? Does she keep that house locked up?

IE: Very.

IR Auten: No one has come to the house making threats or anything to you or her, right?

IE: Not that I know of. I'm sure she would have said something.

IR Auten: Oh, okay. Does the electronic buzzer work?

IE: The electronic buzzer works to let people in.

IR Auten: As far as we can tell, you're the only one who had a strong enough beef with Greenwood to want him dead.

IE: You think I killed him?

IR Auten: We're just saying you got motive, you got means.

IE: Him being dead doesn't benefit me.

IR Auten: It is if you think of revenge as a payback benefit.

IR Edwards: Where did you get the screwdriver?

IE: Screwdriver? What screwdriver? I'm starting to think I need my lawyer in here.

IR Auten: That's up to you. We're just trying to get your side of the story.

IE: My side of the story is this: I didn't kill him.

IR Auten: If it was something like self-defense…

IE: I didn't do it.

IR Auten: I can understand this.

IR Edwards: Things like this happen all the time, you know?

IE: There's only one thing to understand. I didn't do it.

IR Auten: Think about it. Who else would have a motive to kill him?

IE: I don't know, but I'm sure I'm not the only person he's shafted.

IR Auten: You mean screwed over?

IE: I guess. I was just stopped at the intersection.

IR Auten: Was this something you planned or was it on the spur of the moment?

IE: There's no plan. There was no plan. I didn't kill him.

IR Auten: You know the jury is going to hear this recording.

IE: Fine. They'll hear me telling you, hard as I can, I didn't do it. They'll hear me telling the truth.

IR Auten: My partner here, Detective Edwards, doesn't believe you either.

IE: Well, then you're both dead wrong. I didn't do it.

IR Auten: You know, between us, we have over forty years of experience doing this. You don't think we can spot a lie when we hear one?

IE: I think I need my lawyer.

IR Auten: That's entirely up to you.

IR Edwards: Did Mr. Pack, your attorney, talk to you anything about this polygraph we brought up before? What are your thoughts on that?

IE: I had told him that I was willing to take it, but now after listening to the two of you, I've changed my mind.

IR Edwards: Well, you're not compelled at all to take this thing, number one, and number two—I don't know if Mr. Pack explained it to you—this goes to the exclusion of someone as much as the inclusion so we can eliminate people. And just to get things straight.

IE: But why would you try to eliminate me if you've already made up your minds that I did it?

IR Edwards: Oh yes. We use it for elimination more than anything.

IE: Well, I'll talk to him about it. Maybe, but definitely not right now.

IR Edwards: Understand, the reason we're talking to you is because of the problems you've had with him in the past.

IE: I know now, apparently, I'm the number one target—apparently your only target—and now you tell me I've got blood all over the place.

IR Edwards: Well, there's blood at your house in the driveway, and we've got a search warrant, and we're going to go get the blood. We found some in your house. Is that your blood that's there?

IE: If it's dripped, it's what I dripped running around trying to leave.

IR Edwards: Last night?

IE: Yeah, and I wasn't aware that it was…I was aware that I…you know, I was trying to get out of the house. I didn't even pay any attention to it, I saw it when I was in the kitchen, and I grabbed a napkin or something, and that was it. I didn't think about it after that.

IR Auten: That was last night after you got home from the concert, when you were rushing?

IE: That was last night when I was…I don't know what I was…I was in the truck, getting my junk out of the truck. I was in the house, throwing hangers and stuff in my suitcase. I was doing my little crazy what I do…I mean, I do it everywhere. Anybody who has ever picked me up says that J. R.'s a whirlwind, he's running, he's grabbing things, and that's what I was doing.

IR Auten: Well, I'm going to step out, and I'm going to get a photographer to come down and photograph your hand there. And then here pretty soon, we're going to take you downstairs and get some blood from you. Okay? I'll be right back.

IR Edwards: While we're waiting, let me get this straight. You've never physically been inside Greenwood's house?

IE: No.

IR Edwards: (To Auten) Got a photographer coming?

IR Auten: No, we're going to take him up there.

IR Edwards: We're ready to terminate this at 14:07.

Spence took his time getting back. Allowing time for Rollins to process the interview transcript, he stopped off and talked with other agency members with whom he had worked patrol or collaborated with in the past. His tour required two cups of coffee to complete his rounds. By the time he returned, Rollins had thoroughly reviewed the interview. They spent the rest of the morning until time for lunch dissecting the conduct of the interview in an effort to glean any, additional actionable information.

Before leaving, Spence fed the transcript pages into the shredder.

As Rollins closed the door behind them as they left, Spence caught his eye and wondered aloud, "What transcript?"

CHAPTER TWENTY

A Report, a Reveal, and a Ride

S PENCE AND ROLLINS decided that the Dock House Restaurant would *the* place for an early lunch. Russell had left a text message for Rollins that he would be needed in court at two p.m. Both decided to make it a light meal. Spence went for the chef salad, and Rollins opted for the garden salad with mahi. Both had iced tea.

They sat at an outside table covered with a bright-red umbrella covering. Normal conversation was replaced with looking at the endless yachts, the blue water, and the boats making their way up and down the water by Carrot Island.

Rollins broke the reverie. "I just never get tired of looking at this. It's always different somehow. One of these days, I'm gonna get myself a boat. I don't need a real big boat—just one we can cruise around in. Get out there on the water."

"I think that would be great—good family time and way to relax. Let me ask you this: What have you decided regarding the O'Neills?"

"I've taken them off the board. This case is not about somebody's angst about one particular lawyer. Here with our case, we're dealing with one-twentieth-something of a national case involving a score of other dead lawyers. Somebody or something has gone after lawyers as a group. I think someone is endeavoring to send a message. And whoever is doing it seems to have covered their tracks extremely well. Normally, I could say, 'This is not my first rodeo,' but the more we work this inquiry, the more I'm thinking this *is* my first case—at least of this type."

"This is a first case for all of us, not just you."

Seizing the moment, Spence told Rollins, "I need you to do something for me."

"Sure, what it is?"

Spence has laid out his request. Rollins responded. "I'll take care of it."

Just then, Spence received a text message. After having read the text, he said, "Excuse me for a moment." He walked out the adjoining parking lot to the black vehicle parked in the middle of the parking lot with the motor running. This time he crawled up and into the back seat, closing the door behind him. After five minutes he got out of the SUV and returned to the table where Rollins was finishing his salad. Rollins asked the obvious question, not with words but by establishing direct eye contact.

"Okay. All the murders followed a very similar pattern. As we know, a screwdriver was used in each case. No deceased cell phone or computer data has been of any use as actionable information. In each of the twenty-some cases, no one has been identified as a primary suspect resulting from a past adverse relationship with the deceased. The agreements from the suits are that this situation is a coordinated undertaking by an as-yet-unknown group or a collaboration of groups. In any case, it—they—whatever—are operating below everybody's radar. Whatever sources—if any—these multitude of task forces have reached out to have produced nothing. The only thing going on right now is the wannabes ranging from college professors to retired feds making the cable news rounds and repeating the same drivel from channel to channel."

"So apparently, no one is any further down the road than us."

"That seems to be the case."

Standing up from the table, Rollins placed his napkin on his plate and smiled at Spence. "Hey, will you take care of my bill? I've got to rush to make it to court in my never-ending quest to fight crime and just make the world a safer place for all of us."

"If you were as good at fighting crime as you're getting out of paying the bill, we could all sleep with our doors unlocked at night. Go on. I've got it."

Realizing that he now had some free time on his hands and that no one was waiting to eat and needing his table, he added to the pleasure of the moment by asking for a refill of tea. He reached for his phone, pushed speed dial, and waited. When his called was answered, he asked, "Guess who is no longer a suspect?"

"D. B. Cooper," was the instantaneous reply.

"Close, but Cooper is still on the board. No, surprisingly enough, it's the happy O'Neill family—Robert and Eimear."

"So that means you're going to take my picture down from the post office wall?"

"At least in this case."

"Well, I can't wait to begin my assimilation back into society."

"Just remember: one step at a time."

"I'll do that. Now that I'm off the hook, when you can, come by. There's something I want to show you."

"You get your hands on another first edition?"

"No. I wish. This has to do with your case."

There was a long pause, while Spence processed that piece of information.

"Well, you've got my interest now. Is there a time that works better for you?"

"Let's see. It's one fifteen now. Why don't you come over about five? We'll have an early dinner, and I'll walk you through what I have. Maybe there's something in this that can be of some value."

"All right, I'll see you at five."

Spence invested a few more minutes to turn over in his mind what Eimear had said. He sent a text to Leigh, "I'm heading back to the sheriff's office. I'll call you at two p.m. I would like to have the results of the status update on the Dockery inquiry."

Leigh immediately, returned the text. "I'll have the investigator standing by when you call."

When heading back, Spence decided to put everything aside and enjoy the walk. The sights, sounds and the walk itself served as a fifteen-minute, microvacation. Back at the sheriff's office, he was ready to go.

Back in the command center, Spence utilized his phone to review head-lines until exactly two o'clock. Shortly after hitting speed dial, Leigh answered simply, "I'm transferring you for the Dockery briefing."

"Thank you."

Immediately, the transfer was answered by a deep, rich voice. "Hey, boss. Here's what I've got."

Spence listened as the information was presented. At the conclusion he replied, "Thank you. Good job. I appreciate your depth of research and how quickly you resolved the issue. I'll not forget it. Now, if you would, please switch me back to Leigh."

Leigh answered, "What else can I do for you?"

"If you would, please have an invoice sent to Dockery and sign my name to the bottom. Thank you for keeping the ship from running aground."

"That's what I'm here for. You coming this way anytime soon?"

"I'm right in the middle of something."

"That's what I figured. I see the news. Stay safe."

Next, Spence pulled a business card from his billfold and dialed Dockery's number. In a brief moment, there was an answer.

"Bill Dockery."

"Mr. Dockery, Tim Spence, how are you sir?"

"I'm doing good, but I hope I'll be doing better as a result of your call."

"I have nothing but good news for you, sir. The issue has been resolved."

"Resolved? Just what does that mean?"

"You remember the concerns you shared with me that evening at the meet and greet?"

"Yes."

"Well, the circumstance with the related issues is no longer in play."

"But how….?"

"*How* is not the purpose of my call. What I'm delivering to you is the end result. The bottom line is you no longer have that problem. That's all I'm prepared to tell you."

A heavy silence followed. Spence waited patiently.

"I guess you've held up your end of the bargain."

"If we hadn't, I wouldn't accept your payment. You'll receive an invoice shortly."

"All right then. I'm grateful for all that you've done."

"I'll pass on your thanks to the person that made it happen. There's one more thing before I let you go."

"What's that?"

"If you don't mind, I'm going to keep your card. I can envision a number of circumstances wherein your shop and our operation would have the occasion to collaborate. It that something in which you would be interested?"

Dockery's voice brightened considerably.

"Most certainly. I would welcome the opportunity."

"Excellent. I'll stay in touch. And thank you for the confidence that you afforded to us by allowing us to resolve this matter. All the best."

With that summary, Spence ended the conversation.

Looking at his watch, he saw that it was well after three.

"Let's see. I need to be at the house by five. I have time for a short ride, get back to the hotel, change clothes and be there on time."

He left a note for Rollins that said, "Call me if you need me. If not, I'll see you in the morning. Spence."

He rode into Eimear's driveway with five minutes to spare. The door opened just as he walked up onto the porch. There stood Eimear and there sat, right beside her, none other than Razor. As soon as Spence stepped toward the door, Razor stood on all fours, eyes locked and in the ready position.

With her right hand, Eimear patted Spence on his left shoulder and decreed, "Friend."

Razor immediately stepped forward, sniffed the back of Spence's right hand, locked the sensory identification into his brain, turned, and walked into the house.

Spence breathed a sigh of relief.

Eimear was outfitted with bright white jeans. She had on a green twill shirt that perfectly matched her eyes. The sleeves were rolled up to just below her elbows. She was barefooted.

Spence on the other hand had on faded blue jeans a black, short-sleeved T-shirt and motorcycle boots.

"Well, well, well, if it isn't Mr. Detective," she declared with a smile.

Spence came back. "And if it isn't the formerly—if not currently—highly suspicious Miss Smart App Maker."

They both laughed at their new noms de guerre. At that moment, neither realized that in the fullness of time, those appellations would take on a much more meaningful depth of connection.

"Well, don't just stand there, come on in. Make yourself at home."

Spence looked around, continuing to admire the style and décor.

"How's your brother doing?"

"He's good—happy, as I'm to be off the hook."

"I understand."

"Do you?" she asked with a hint of doubt in her voice.

"Listen, you're not the only one upon whom the bright light of suspicion has shone. I know it's a hassle. And I know that sometimes it takes a while for that light to dim and go out. And I know how good it feels when it does. I also know how tenuous a security clearance such as yours can be, so I've arranged for the shredding of the summary of my interview with you and the removal of your name from any documentation. However, I couldn't do the same for your brother."

"Thank you so much. My brother doesn't have any level of security clearance with which to be concerned. But couldn't shredding those documents prove to be problematic for you?"

Laughingly, Spence replied, "Oh, sometimes the light of suspicion will blink back on for a little bit, but not for long. Besides—what documents? Anyway, what is it you wanted to show me?"

"We'll get to that, but first, let's eat. I'm starving."

As Eimear had stopped to put on a pair of leather boots, Spence had an idea they would be eating outside.

With that they walked through the house, out the back door and onto the patio. On the grill, were three large hamburger patties waiting to be cooked. A side table held all that one could ever imagine adding to a hamburger. Between two, beige, cushioned, outdoor lounge chairs rested a midsized, galvanized metal tub, full of ice and bottled beer. Ringlets of water ran down the long, brown necks of each bottle.

Spence asked, "Anything you want for me to do?"

"Nope. I've got it."

Hearing that Spence took a seat, stretched out and grabbed a beer. It wasn't long before she asked, "What do you want on your hamburgers?"

"Fix them like you fix yours."

"I put everything on mine."

"There you go."

Soon, before him was a platter with two big hamburgers, a long slice of pickle, and a mountain of French fries.

"Who could ask for anything more?" Spence wondered aloud.

"There you go," Eimear echoed as she claimed the other chair with hamburger and beer in hand.

Midway between the two, Razor happily played with a chew toy.

During the meal, their conversation served as a conduit to allow for the laying of a foundation for building a relationship. There's nothing *small* about small talk—phatic communication. The setting allowed for each to tentatively reveal something about themselves and learn something about the other. Like succeeding cable strands strung across a river to aid in the construction of a bridge, the rapport began to take shape and strengthen. Relationships are tenuous in the beginning. Time and circumstances serve to either abate or strengthen the connection. In this case, the linking was strengthening exponentially.

Eventually, Eimear facilitated the transition from the meal. "You ready to see something?"

"More than ready."

They quickly cleaned the patio and closed the chrome cover on the grill. Before going back into the house, they each grabbed a beer. Razor dutifully tagged along. Back inside, Eimear turned and locked the door.

Making their way deeper into the house, they came to a steel door painted the same color as the other interior doors. Eimear pressed a series of buttons on an electronic keypad and with a deep, audible click the door unlocked. Turning the doorknob and leaning heavily onto the door, she made way for Spence to enter the unexpected.

"Welcome to my world," she said as Spence endeavored to take it all in. The room was not unlike an inner chamber at NSA. There were no windows. Computers with small screens and computers with large computer screens were everywhere.

Immediately, Spence was surprised at how comfortable the room was despite all of the electronic equipment.

As if reading his mind, Eimear said, "There's a special HVAC unit installed just for this room. Neither computers nor I work well in excessive heat. Additionally, there's a separate electrical hookup to a natural gas generator in the event of a power failure."

"How are you connected...?"

Again, as if reading his mind, she said, "I have a number of redundant connecting systems. I'm not dependent on the efficacy of the local cable system to operate. Additionally, a complex encryption system is in place—again with redundancy woven into the setup."

"Encryption systems that you designed?"

"Just saying."

Continuing to gaze around in amazement, he said, "Well, I'm most assuredly impressed. Thank you for showing this to me."

"Oh. This is not what I wanted to show you."

"It isn't?"

"Nope. Step over here,"

Eimear reached down and typed into a keyboard. Immediately, the large computer screen came to life.

"What am I looking at?"

"That's the compilation of all the data related to the murders of the lawyers within the window of time that parallels your investigation."

"Where did all of this data come from?"

"Can't tell you that. But I *can* tell you that I've run this through my... an AI program and you can sit here and process the information. Nothing can leave the room other than what's in your head. And you can't tell anyone about this room or the source of your information—not even someone working with you on this inquiry. We good on that?"

"We're good."

Spence automatically, pulled up a chair preparing himself to process the information. Pointing to the screen he noted, "There's one piece of information in which I'm particularly interested in right off the bat."

Eimear immediately attacked the keyboard, and the screen went blank.

Spence stared at her with a look of questioning amazement on his face.

"Nope, not tonight. There's something that *I* want. You can't just be taking without giving something in return."

"And what's that?"

"I want a bike ride."

"You have to wear a helmet here in North Carolina."

"I had a full-faced helmet delivered today."

"Okay then, but one other thing—you can't get on the back of my motorcycle in white jeans. You'd look like surfer girl on the back of Moon Boy's scooter. It just can't happen. Your boots are fine. Just not the jeans."

"Got it. Wait for me in the den, and I'll go change."

As they left the room the door lock bid them goodbye with the same deep, audible "click." Razor chose to stay and keep Spence company.

Before Spence had time to settle into a comfortable leather chair with a book in hand, Eimear was back—decked out in standard-issue blue jeans and helmet in hand.

"Let's ride," she decreed.

"Keep in mind two things. When I lean, you lean with me in the same direction and hold on tight."

It took a while for her to become comfortable with leaning. But holding on tight didn't appear to necessitate any form of learning curve at all.

CHAPTER TWENTY-ONE

The Last Run

W HILE IN LAW school, the most salient directive drummed into Greg Garrett's head, class after class, was "win at any cost." That motto was etched on a brass plate in his office, positioned so that only he could see it as he sat behind his desk. Even more permanently, the motto was branded onto his brain. It comprised the main part of his professional DNA.

As a criminal defense lawyer, no machinations were, to him, beyond the pale. He viewed the fabrication or destruction of evidence as a valid means to an end. Finding "experts" whose only question to him was, "What do you want me to say?" was routine. Intimidating or bribing victims, witnesses or other stakeholders in a case were, to him, necessitated operational procedures. But always—*always*—there were, at a minimum, three degrees of separation between him and a nefarious act. Sure, he had been sanctioned numerous times by the bar in his home state and in various states for questionable practices, but he never violated either of the two, unpardonable, legal sins: intimacy with a client or appropriating monies from an escrow account.

He put in a great deal of effort to look the part via a lanky, six-foot, three-inch tall frame and a head full of dark-brown shoulder-length hair. His tailored suits were impeccable. The sleeve lengths of his shirt and coat were precisely to the point to allow his highly expensive watch to be seen. He wore a crested gold ring on the little finger of his left hand.

Make no mistake: his pretrial preparations were exemplary. As a result, his trial maneuverings were most effective. On direct examination, he was skillful at bringing forth and amplifying relevant information. But it was on cross-examination wherein he was at the top of his game. Using the testimony and exact words that the individual had stated during direct examination, he was adroit at picking apart, minimizing, and raising the fog of uncertainty on point after point. If the person testifying wasn't hostile at the beginning of cross-examination, they *would be* well before they were finished. Having the judge declare the individual hostile, the continued use of leading questions and questionable psychological practices were employed to endeavor to impeach the witness, at a minimum in the mind of one or more of those sitting in the jury box. He had a most subtle, nonverbal way of catching the eye of a juror as he asked a question as if to signal, "We know exactly what's going on here, don't we? Aren't *you* the clever one to see it too?"

He was especially keen to impugn the credibility, character or capability of those tasked with conducting the investigation involving his client. Even for the most stoic of investigative personnel, it was difficult to maintain composure when testifying.

It should come as no surprise, that due to his maneuverings—legal and otherwise—Garrett was highly sought after and subsequently, made a great deal of money. He was quick—as he deemed it—to reinvest into his operation. He hired the top-of-the-line private investigation professions to conduct his parallel inquiries. He traveled via chartered private jet. He stayed at the best hotels. Whenever he could, he would take on cases in locations wherein prosecutors, with political, personal agendas, were known to be soft on crime. Clients were wined and dined as royalty. He well understood, their positive word of mouth to their *associates* was far more effectual than any garish, television commercial. A successful representation would always lead to one or more additional engagements—a revenue stream that grew upon itself. He was a man with a plan and the plan was to always, at any cost, win. To him, victory in a case was almost as satisfying as his Scrooge-like affection for money.

To his credit, Garrett was a health fanatic. He neither smoked, drank, or *candied up* his nose. He was an avid runner. His light-boned frame didn't lend itself to weightlifting, but genetically, he was born to run—and run, he did. After an extended period of running, he would *zone in*. At that point, the clarity of thought would allow him to weave through an upcoming trial and analyze the unfolding of the procedure point by point. In the zone, he would *see* the thrusts of the prosecution. Consequently, he could prepare a variety of options for his own counterthrusts and parries.

At three in the morning, one would be hard pressed to label his run as late night or early morning, but labeled or not, it was the perfect time for him—he had the world to himself. Over time, he had developed a route so ingrained in his internal GPS that his *run* required no related thinking at all.

He would start at the Beaufort Yacht Station and run Pine Street to Live Oak Street. From there he would hang a right and run to Front Street. From Front Street, he would make a right on Pollock Street back to Pine. Following that pattern he would run the twelve block, grid that comprised the Beaufort Historical District. Finding himself at the intersection of Moore Street and Cedar Street, he would turn and run the grid in the opposite direction.

He was not far from turning off Pine Street to make his second passage down Turner Street when another runner emerged on his right and immediately fell into step with him. The presence of the other runner pulled him from the zone and brought him back into an unwanted state of awareness.

Slowing the pace and with no welcome in his voice, Garrett asked, "What are *you* doing out here this time of the morning?"

Operative countered. "I could ask you the same question. But I know the answer—this is the best time in the world to run. I'm surprised I haven't seen you out here before."

"I only get the chance to be here when I'm between trials. Right now, I'm preparing for a case that's scheduled to start later this month in Boston."

"I see."

By this time, the two were approaching the Beaufort Historical Site located at the one hundred block of Turner Street. The two-acre site consisted of a collection of eighteenth and nineteenth-century coastal, Carolina buildings. Among the curated buildings was the old jail built in 1829. The stark white, two-story building had a heavy, black metal door and walls that were twenty-eight inches thick. It housed not only the prisoners, but the jailer and his family. It remained in use until 1954.

Garrett's effort to reenter the zone was in vain. Operative demolished Garrett's initial cognitive, transitional pattern. "Hey, would you do me a favor and stand guard while I step behind the old jail and answer the call?"

The exasperation in Garrett's response was palpable.

"Stand guard?"

"Yes. I can't afford to be caught with my running shorts down. Come on, it will only take a moment."

Garrett accepted the fact that his run was about to be ruined.

"All right."

They both turned into the compound and slowed to a walk making their way past the wooden stocks to the back corner of the old jail.

Operative went around the corner of the building while Garrett walked rapidly back and forth in an effort to keep his heartrate up in order to quickly continue on his way.

After a few moments, Garrett advised, "I'm going to head on out before I cool down."

"Wait a second. Step around here and help me up. I sat down to retie my shoes, and now I can't get up. It's a cramp or something."

With a string of mental expletives, he walked around the corner over to where Operative was sitting on the ground with the right arm extended up in anticipation of an assist. Garrett leaned over and automatically extended his right hand. In one swift move, Operative used Garrett's right arm to pull him downward and, with the left hand, introduced the business end of a long screwdriver into Garrett's heart, which had been attempting to return to a normal heartrate. Garrett fell immediately to the ground. Now, upright, using a stick, Operative removed any shoeprints that may have been made.

Operative dragged Garrett's body around the corner of the building over to the steps in front of the black metal door of the jail. Again, the stick was used to remove the drag marks and footprints. After propping him up against the door and placing a card at the wooden base of the stocks, Operative turned and ran past the garden located behind the 1859 apothecary and doctor's office building, toward the broken, faded, paint-chipped, wooden, picket fence. Easily clearing the fence, Operative made straightway to Craven Street. At Craven Street, Operative turned left and ran into the night all the while removing the blue plastic gloves and securing them in a pocket for later disposal along with the old pair of running shoes. In less than four minutes from the time Garrett had rounded the corner of the building to when Operative turned left on Craven Street, the maneuver had been accomplished. Had it not adversely involved him personally, Garrett would have appreciated the depth of planning that had taken place to successfully accomplish the objective.

CHAPTER TWENTY-TWO

A Sojourner's Surprise, a Series of Discoveries, a Transitioning

JACKIE HOLLINGSWORTH HAD decided to live her life in reverse. She would travel—see the world—while she was young. At middle age, which she viewed as beginning at the age of thirty-three, she would settle into her family's food distribution business and ride it out from there on. Her parents had played no small role in her decision-making process. They provided her with a work ethic extraordinaire. As an only child, she had been *raised* in the family operation. Starting with sweeping the warehouse floors, when she could barely hold the push broom, she cleaned restrooms, washed trucks, learned to drive a forklift well before moving onto office operations. She graduated with a double major: accounting and supply chain management. All her high school and college classes were via e-learning platforms. This arrangement allowed for her to continue with her hands-on business operation experiences and gain her education concurrently. Through electronics, she was able to continue to partici-pate operationally in the business—thus drawing a salary—and feeding her wanderlust. Her parents' home in Salt Lake City served as basecamp between her travels.

On her travel list was the Outer Banks of North Carolina. That being the case, she now found herself on an early-morning stroll, twenty-three hundred miles from home, through the historical district of Beaufort. She was aware that the Robert W. and Elva Faison Safrit Historical Center didn't open until ten a.m. She wanted to just walk among the historical buildings in the quiet of the morning before everything started. Later, in the day, she planned to take a walking tour and then enjoy a boat, island tour sometime after lunch. She particularly wanted to see the wild horses on Shackleford Banks Island.

As she made her way from building to building, the old jail caught her eye. Next, she saw the wooden stocks, and finally, her eyes focused upon a figure resting on the steps of the jail. Her immediate thought was that it was an employee of the historical center who had responsibilities well before the ten o'clock opening. Having made that conclusion, she headed in that direction with the hopes of gaining some firsthand information on the best tours to take and best places to eat. She walked over to the reclining figure. Just as she spoke, "Excuse me," her eyes fell upon the implement protruding from the recumbent individual's chest. She elected to finish her sentence with a scream. Screams have a way of getting things started well before the appointed time. Jackie's goal to see the world had just afforded her the opportunity to see more of it than she had ever imagined.

Withing fifteen minutes after "the scream," a uniformed Beaufort police officer had cordoned off the area with yellow crime scene tape. Ten minutes after that, Rollins and the crime scene tech personnel were on site and operational. Twenty-five minutes later, Spence was side by side with Rollins. Finally, sixty minutes after Jackie's audible signal that something was amiss, Russell had made his way past the crime scene recorder dutifully keeping a record of who came onto and who left the site along with the respective times.

Holding his phone out to Spence and Russell, Rollins showed them a picture of the deceased.

"Anybody know this guy?" he asked.

After a moment, Russell answered, "His name is something Garrett. He's an expensive, high-profile criminal lawyer."

"Have you ever tried a case against him?"

"No. Listen, this guy is too big to fish in our little pond. His retainer from one client is probably as much as I make in a year. I've seen him at some local social functions put on by the county bar. He gave a short talk at one dinner on the cross-examination of a hostile witness."

Rollins asked, "Have you ever talked with him?"

"Not really. If the legal system were baseball, I would be low-A, and he is—was—major league. I'm certain he has—had—paralegals functioning with much more capability than me doing his legal research for him and making significantly more money than I do."

Russell took his phone from his right pants pocket. "Hang on. I can access the names, physical and email addresses of the regional attorneys."

After a few minutes for the search, he showed his phone to Rollins. "There he is."

Russell forwarded the information from his phone to Rollins's phone. Rollins then called for an officer to set up at Garrett's address and for someone to canvas his neighborhood.

For a few moments, Rollins and Russell silently continued to survey the scene visually and mentally. Spence had quietly taken a few steps back and had moved off to the side.

A crime scene tech dressed in a white, cotton polo shirt with Crime Scene written in bold, black letters on the back walked up to the pair. On the left collar, also in black, was embroidered "CCSO" for Carteret County Sheriff's Office. She wore black tactical pants.

Addressing Rollins specifically, the tech said, "So far, other than the screwdriver, we see driven into his chest, we've found nothing. We're taking pictures and making diagrams. If we find anything, I'll let you know."

"Thank you."

Spence had just as inconspicuously rejoined the two. Turning to Russell, Spence inquired, "By the way, are you carrying?"

"Not right now. Sometimes I forget," he replied, shrugging his shoulders.

Having overheard the conversation as she walked toward the group, Dixie added her two cents. "Listen, you need to take this situation seriously. They're killing lawyers. Apparently, it's open season on lawyers. You're a lawyer! I can see ole Bo's head mounted on the wall in somebody's den with a real long screwdriver below it on a little wooden tray. I can hear someone saying, 'Yeah, I bagged this one, but he was so dumb it wasn't much of a challenge. I think if I had asked him, he would have stuck himself with the screwdriver just to save me the trouble.'"

At this point, Russell knew enough to not fire a comeback. "Okay, so what do we have now?"

Rollins began to fill in the blanks. "Last name Garrett—a high-profile criminal attorney."

"Same MO?"

"Yep."

Giving full rein to her now highly activated sarcasm gene, Dixie observed, "Well, by now, I'm sure there's a group being formed with the purpose of banning screwdrivers. I just want to go on record right now: 'Screwdrivers do not kill people—people kill people.'"

Looking over her shoulder, she saw the media beginning to gather like vultures over a roadkill. Even though they were a good distance away, the four could hear muffled sounds of their increasingly louder, repetitive questions. Each endeavoring to talk over the others while holding outstretched microphones giving the appearance not unlike Lady Liberty.

"They look and sound like crowd of three-year-olds in the toy section at the Walmart," she noted as much to herself as to the three others. "Just wait. 'Mama' will be there in a little while."

Then looking at the others, she asked, "Did I say that out loud?"

Rollins got the quartet back on track. "If EMS has managed to calm down the woman that found him, I'm going to interview her. Also, we're going to need a warrant to search his house." He turned to Russell. "Can you help me with that?"

"For sure. I'll go get started. Come by my office when you get a chance. We'll work it up and get a judge to sign it." Having said that, he left and checked out appropriately with the record keeper.

Dixie reluctantly left as well, heading over to the media with a feeling in her heart not unlike that of the condemned walking up the thirteen steps to the hangman's noose.

With his gloved hand, Spence showed Rollins a card he had recovered from the base of the wooden stocks. Written on the card was the question "Who does the bridegroom pay?"

"I took several pictures, before I recovered it. We'll put this in a plastic bag and keep them along with the other two. I know there could be some chain-of-custody issues, but I don't think this case is going hinge on these cards. We *are* walking a fine line here—maybe too fine—but we need to contain some information of which only you and I are aware."

"Works for me. What do you think?"

"I'm certain it's a clue but I also think it's a teaser. We'll flesh it out later, but look, the first card allowed the participant to take money from others and we ended up with a dead patent shark. The second card provided a way out of jail. Now, here's a deceased high-profile criminal lawyer. This, third card—I'll have to think about for a bit. So far, we haven't received any notification that cards were playing a part in the other homicides. Not just here but across the country, it's lawyers that have been targeted. It will be interesting to find out if we're experiencing another round of attorney homicides or if this is an isolated case."

Spence's phone sounded an incoming text message. Taking out his phone he read, "Two things: 1] I didn't do it! 2] When you get a chance, come by, and we'll follow up on that piece of information you wanted. E."

Having read the message, Spence queried Rollins, "Is there anything you would like for me to do right now?"

"Nothing that I can think of right now. All the wheels are in motion. We'll wait to see what the autopsy report tells us, but I don't anticipate any surprises there."

"Then I'm going to check on something. I'll see you back at 'the room' later this afternoon."

Spence went to his bike, put on his helmet, and started on what had rapidly become a familiar route.

When he arrived, she was at the opened door. Her smile and eyes offered the greeting.

"Have you had breakfast?"

"No. There wasn't time. I got an early call from Rollins, showered up, and headed out."

"I saw the report on the station out of Washington, North Carolina. Someone had made a video of the scene with their phone and sent it directly to WITN. They must have recorded it before the officers arrived because it was close in. They have been playing it over and over. I'm sure by now their affiliates have a copy as well. How about some coffee and a scrambled egg sandwich with bacon and tomato? Everything is ready. All I have to do is make the toast."

"Thanks. I'm starving."

In the kitchen, Spence made himself at home. He took the cup beside the coffee maker and started to pour.

"Hey! I just drank out of that cup."

Continuing to pour, he asked, "Are you contagious?"

"I hope so, in some respects."

After taking a deep pull from the cup, he replied, "I'll chance it."

Soon, the fixings of the sandwich had been combined. She put the sandwich on a plate and set the plate on the polished, black granite of the ten-foot-long kitchen island. With his used and refilled coffee cup in hand, Spence walked around, pulled out a Randle tractor stool, sat down, and took a healthy bite out of the sandwich.

After another swallow of coffee, he looked at Eimear and asked, "I wonder if there were concurrent others or if this was just an isolated event?"

"I should know as soon as I fire up the system."

As Spence was now on the good side of famished, and not wanting to make a pig of himself, he slowed down his eating to make room for conversation in another direction.

"I really enjoyed our ride last night."

"I did too. But it was a little scary going over the bridge to Morehead City."

"You'll get used to it."

"How long have you been riding double on a motorcycle?"

"It's called 'riding two up,' and yesterday was my first day," he replied with a fake serious look on his face.

Immediately, coming back with an apt retort, she answered, "That's what I thought—a couple of times there, my life flashed before my eyes."

"I'll be more careful next time," he promised.

Having inhaled his sandwich, Spence refilled his coffee cup and turned to Eimear. "Okay, let's see what you've got."

Inside the computer room, Eimear logged on, and instantly, the multitude of computer screens throughout the room came to life. The dramatic transition from darkness to light reminded Spence of the Hendersonville, North Carolina, lighting of the Christmas tree on Friday evening, the day after Thanksgiving. Both events seemed to him to be rife with possibilities.

"Anything up there to indicate more cases along with ours?"

After scanning the appropriate screens, Eimear replied, "Nothing so far." Pointing to a specific screen, she noted, "Here's the compilation of Rollins and your Kacmar case."

That revelation caught Spence on his back foot. "Let me see."

Looking at the screen he saw that indeed the initial case report as well as the supplementals were displayed. He looked at Eimear. "I can't believe that. Let me text Rollins right quick."

Pulling out his phone, he quickly entered a text. "Have you forwarded any of the Kacmar case materials from out of the agency?"

After about three minutes the reply came. "Only the initial case report summary. The same information that was initially released to the media and the public. Nothing since. Why?"

Spence texted back. "I'll tell you later. In the meantime, I suggest you use only a stand-alone laptop for your supplementals and back it up on a couple of external hard drives."

Eimear asked, "What's the deal?"

"The only thing Rollins had sent forward was the initial case report, but everything is there on the screen. Let me make sure that Rollins washed you out before the information was *taken*."

They both went into the silent mode as they closely reviewed the documentation.

"Nope. You're not in there anywhere. That's at least one good thing. I'll brief Rollins when I see him face-to-face and see what he wants to do. In the meantime, there was one item yesterday that caught my attention. The summary from the Tennessee case showed that there was one individual that declined to be interviewed. Can you bring that up?"

After a series of audible clicks, the information appeared on the screen. Rather than entering the name on the notes app on his phone, he committed the name to memory.

"Anything else there?"

"No, that's it."

"I've got something that I need to do. Have you got the time to go with me?"

"Absolutely. Let me turn these off and get my helmet and I'm ready to go."

Shortly, they were on their way to the Dollar General Store on Live Oak Street. Spence purchased seven burner phones, along with ample plans, SIM cards, and accessories. He paid cash for the entirety of the purchase. They returned to Eimear's home where she helped him to set up the operation for each phone. Spence wrote the numbers down on a sheet of paper with an accompanying name to the side. "Me, Rollins, Eimear, Russell, Lee." Two numbers were listed with no accompanying names. That name was yet to be determined.

The phones were set up. Spence advised, "It's going to take a couple of hours for these phones to charge. I don't want to hold you up. I'm going for a ride to try and think some things through. I would certainly appreciate the company if you have the time."

"Oh, I've got the time. Where are we going?"

"We'll know when we get there."

"Works for me." She picked up her helmet.

The bike had chosen to make its way to Harkers Island. On the island, the two visited some shops and walked out to the boat ramp and watched the diamonds reflected on the water under a canopy of clear blue sky. The two talked about anything but the case.

He looked at his watch. "I'm ready to eat something—how about you?"

"I guess I could eat a little something."

It wasn't long before they were parked outside of the Fish Hook Grill on Island Road.

Eimear scoffed down a big double dog with chili, ketchup, mustard, relish, onion, and cheddar. She added a side order of fries for good measure. Spence had a more healthful serving of Hatteras clam chowder and a side salad with ranch dressing. Of course, they both had iced tea.

"You know there's a special place in hell for people that can eat like that and not gain weight."

"Not my fault that I have a high metabolism" she noted as she popped the last of the fries into her mouth. Seeing that Spence had one remaining golf ball-sized hush puppy remaining on his plate, she reached over, took it, and polished that off as well.

Both wished that the ride back to her house had taken longer. Back in her house, Spence gave to her the phone with her assigned number along with the number of the burner phone he would keep for himself.

"Anything to do directly with the case, please text or call with this phone. Otherwise, just get me on my regular phone. Look, I don't want to assume anything here and take up too much of your time, but if you want, I'd like to have dinner with you."

"You're not taking up too much of my time—on the contrary. Look, there's always a good chance of rain in the evening this time of year, so why don't I pick you up, say, around six?"

"Excellent."

Spence gathered up the remaining phones and walked to the front door. After she had opened the door, she moved in close and kissed him on the cheek. The kiss remained in place for a thousand one, thousand two, and thousand three. Breaking away, their direct eye contact remained even longer. It was not necessary for something to be said for something to be communicated.

Outside, Spence placed the remaining phones into the left saddle bag, started up the bike and headed out. On the ride to the sheriff's office, Spence realized that his life was undergoing a shifting paradigm. As he thought about it, he knew, for a certainty, that he had no problem with that reality at all.

CHAPTER TWENTY-THREE

A Caution, a Cognitive Exercise, a Coalescence

S PENCE ARRIVED AT the sheriff's office parking lot. He used the prepaid phone he had allocated to himself and called the firm's number. Leigh answered immediately after the first ring.

"Academy of Investigative Resources."

"Leigh, I need for you to do something for me."

"You've got it."

"Grab your personal phone, go outside, and I'll call you in five minutes."

With her phone in hand, she went outside and waited for the call.

When Spence called, she answered, "What have you got?"

"Until I tell you differently, please call me on this number. Give the number to each of the senior partners. Tell everyone else that if they need to talk with me, let you know—you'll relay the request, and I'll call them back ASAP on their personal phones. Have the tech spooks run security assessments on the phone system, the computer system, and sweep the entire compound for any video or listening devices. This is a priority one! Have them check the computer system *first* and request that everyone stay off their computer until the system has been cleared. After that check is completed, I would appreciate it if you would call me back and give me a status report."

"I'll take care of it—anything else?"

"There is."

Spence gave her the memorized name and the scant bit of information regarding the individual who had refused to be interviewed.

"At the point when the computer system has been cleared, assign someone to conduct a thorough background on this individual. Please let me know the findings as soon as it has been completed."

"I'll call you back when I have something."

"Thank you, Leigh. I appreciate you."

"As well you should," she replied laughingly.

Spence made his way into the room. He found Rollins and Russell digesting the latest information.

Preferring to stand and stretch after having spent time on the motorcycle, he asked both, "So what do we know?"

Rollins took the floor. "We just got word that there have been five more—including ours—reported attorney homicides in the last twenty-four hours. The other four occurred in states that were not part of the first round of homicides. So, counting Raleigh, that gives North Carolina a three count on attorney homicides, with only one being a resident of the state. The young woman who discovered the body had nothing of value to add. The area canvas has produced nothing. We did find out that the deceased's first name is Greg, and we located his house."

Russell, added, "We're waiting now for a search warrant to search his house."

"Is that it?"

Rollins lamented, "This case is like trying to pick up gelatin with your fingers—there's just nothing there."

Spence took a seat and handed the assigned prepaid phones to the pair.

Spence then briefed them on the fact that all their investigative documentation had found its way to the federal entity that was curating and supposedly disseminating portions of the information to authorized entities. Additionally, he requested that all case related communication between them take place using the burner phones. For the time being, he kept to himself everything regarding the individual that refused to be interviewed and his implementation of the background check.

Russell, who had not yet successfully developed Rollins's awareness for knowing when *not* to ask, queried, "How did you find all that out?"

Spence answered with silence and a friendly smile.

Before Russell could retort, a harried Dixie Bell Lee slammed open the door, burst into the room, pointed her right index finger at Russell, and commanded, "You!"

Gobsmacked, Russell could only mutter, "Me—what?"

"You, my unprincipled pettifogger are going to conduct the next media briefing along with questions and answers. Everyone has taken their turn in the barrel including your boss. And *he* has directed for *me* to tell *you* that you're next."

Having regained his composure and the color to his face, Russell replied, "Not a problem." He then raised his right arm and a thin, black magician's wand appeared in hand.

"In no time at all, I'll have them eating out of my hand. People will be saying, 'Not since Shakespeare took to the stage has there been such a performance.'" Having said that, he displayed the empty palm of his left hand, closed it, and when he reopened it, there was a wrapped piece of peppermint candy.

"I'm telling you, by the time I finish, they will all be weeping tears of joy, calling out my name and clapping. When is the next scheduled briefing?"

"Nine o'clock in the morning on the courthouse steps. By the way, here's your warrant."

Rollins grabbed the warrant.

"I'm going to notify the crime scene techs to meet me there and search the house. Then I'm going to see if I can get to the bottom as to how—or maybe why—the investigation documentation was sent out."

Spence advised, "Unless you specifically want me along, I'm going to stay here and see if I can develop any additional investigative steps we can take based upon what we know and what we know that we don't know."

Spence caught Rollins's eye contact and, within a millisecond, glanced at Russell and then at the door. Rollins understood the message, looked at Russell, and asked, "Would you like to come along?"

"Would I ever!" He rapidly jumped to his feet.

"Can I wear those little blue booties and plastic gloves?"

"Sure. Why not?"

"Great. You might want to take a picture of me looking around. That will come in handy someday when I run for district attorney."

Dixie caught the tail end of that conversation and added, "Should that day ever come, I plan to enter a nunnery."

Russell asked her, "Don't you think a coven would be more appropriate?"

Spence interrupted the bout in the middle of the round by asking Rollins and Russell, "By the way, you two, how did your court case end up?"

"Plead out," both answered in unison. The pair, along with D, began to make their way for the door.

While tossing the phone he had assigned to Dixie over to Rollins, Spence advised, "Here's Dixie's phone. Bring her up to code."

Closing the door behind them, the trio was gone. Spence could hear their fading banter as they walked down the hall.

Spence now had the room and the solitude to himself. His intent was to undertake a series of methodologies to structure his analysis of the available and unavailable information. Because the utilization of structured analysis operated contrary to the cognitive process the mind was wired to employ, he hoped the discipline required would result in additional actionable information and perspectives. He took his time to thoroughly work his way through each of the three structured platforms—*the possibility tree, the matrix, and the causal flow diagramming*. He had one more operation—*devil's advocacy*—that he wanted to undertake at a later point which would require the inclusion of one or more participants.

After four uninterrupted hours, he knew that the time and effort spent were more than worth it. He had gained a new perspective as well as what would prove to be a most productive action step. The concept was so simple that he had to laugh at the fact that the idea had not immediately been apparent to him after five minutes at the historical site. As satisfied as he was with the results of his cognitive undertakings, in the back of his mind, he knew that there was something else there that he just had not managed to bring forth.

He looked at his watch and saw that he was cutting it close to be ready for the six o'clock pickup. On the way back to the hotel, he resisted the temptation to *push the throttle*. He didn't want to put an Atlantic Beach police officer into the awkward position of having to give him a speeding ticket or himself in the embarrassing position of having to pay the ticket. He did, however, keep the bike's speedometer needle glued to the indicator of the posted speed.

Dressed and showered, he walked out of the lobby. He waited for a moment, watching vehicles loading and unloading under the gleaming white, hotel canopy. Then his eye caught a glimpse of a mobile work of art parked about fifty feet off to the side—a candy-apple-red 1954 Chevrolet, five-window pickup truck. He looked more closely and saw Eimear waiting patiently in the driver's seat. He quickly walked toward the truck like a kid headed for the lighted tree on Christmas morning.

Caressing the top of the hood with his left hand, he asked, "Is this yours?"

"Mine all mine."

"Tell me about it."

"It has a LS1 Corvette engine and the Corvette's front suspension."

Spence slowly walked around the truck. He looked at the big chrome grill, he saw the visor over the windshield and the brilliantly white, sidewall tires. Next, he took in the oak planks, laid out lengthwise in the truck's bed, each separated by a stainless steel slat. He opened the passenger door and saw the tan leather upholstery on the seats and side panels. There was just too much to see and absorb. Crawling into the cab, his left knee brushed against the gearshift flowering from the floor with a matching brown knob on the top.

"I could be buried in this truck and die a happy man."

Feeling the rush of cool air, he looked at Eimear who answered, "Well, at least you would be nice and cool in the grave. I had an air conditioning unit placed under the dashboard."

All Spence could declare as he fastened his seatbelt was, "*This* is a *truck!*"

"I know, right?"

As he continued to take it all in, he asked, "Where would you like to eat?"

"Sit back, relax, and enjoy the ride. We're going to another one of my favorite places to eat." With that she, engaged the clutch, put the truck in gear, eased off the clutch as she gently pressed the accelerator, turned right out of the parking lot and headed for Morehead City. Shortly, they were entering the parking lot at Smithfield's Chicken 'N Bar-B-Q on Arendell Street.

As she parked the truck, she asked, "Have you ever eaten at a Smithfield's before?"

"Many times. I'm just waiting for them to move further west in the state. Contrary to popular Raleigh belief, the state doesn't end at an imaginary vertical line drawn between Winston-Salem and Charlotte."

When they walked into the restaurant, the staff members who could see her greeted, "E!"

She happily acknowledged the salutation. "Here I am, again." It was obvious to all that she was a regular and welcomed guest. As they waited in line for their turn, Spence could smell the combination of pork, chicken, hush puppies and Brunswick stew. They both ordered the Bar-B-Q value pack, banana pudding and iced tea. Spence handed his credit card to the cashier. Having made the transaction, she returned the card, the receipt, and their respective drinks. The pair picked out a table in the far corner and made their way. Seated, they each took an obligatory drink of tea and settled in.

Eimear opened the dialogue. "Without revealing anything that you shouldn't, how is the case going?"

"You know as much as I do. Our two homicides are a microcosm of a nationwide conundrum—lawyers being murdered from one end of the country to the other. Rollins is following homicide investigative protocols to the T. Nevertheless, the old *tried-and-true* motives—such as to hide something, greed, revenge, jealousy, and the like—just don't seem to apply. We know there has got to be an impetus behind these homicides—nothing happens in a vacuum. I'm just not so sure that searching for a specific motive will be the gateway to getting to the bottom of this conundrum.

"Additionally, electronic *bread crumbs*, be they computers, phone forensics, internet searches, or social media, just aren't there. This lack of electronic evidence has made me realize that we have become too dependent, too comfortable with the utilization of electronics to solve cases. In this situation, it seems to me that what we have is a battle of wits in which our addiction to electronic-based solutions has put us at a disadvantage and is not going to carry the flag.

Whoever or whatever is doing this is, in my opinion, far beyond just wanting to send some kind of message. My perspective is that the homicides are the *means* to an end, not the end, itself.

Becoming more demonstrative in his narrative, while Eimear continued to listen attentively, Spence added, "And I'll have to say, they have played their hand well. What had become our investigative crutch—electronics—has been removed from the board. It's as if we've been, investigatively speaking, thrown back in time—no computers, no social media, no text messages, no cell phone towers. We're going to have to use something that, collectively, we have allowed to atrophy—our minds. And if there's one thing we, as a species, don't like to have to do, it's think deeply or for any protracted period of time."

Spence immediately realized that having the opportunity to speak this situation out loud had made him acutely aware of his own cognitions. He needed to hear himself articulate it to someone else to fully realize where his thoughts were. This thought process is a part of what had been in the back of his mind.

"I'm sorry. I got caught up. It was like the dam in my mind just broke."

"I'm the one that asked the question. But think about this—maybe it's not so much about a motive as it is about a cause."

"I wish I knew."

They looked down and realized their food had been set upon the table.

"Let's just eat and talk about something else."

Eimear could only nod her head in agreement as her mouth was already filled from a healthy portion of her barbecue sandwich. In her left hand were a pair of crispy French fries, each with ketchup on the tips, patiently waiting for their turn.

The turn taking and content of their conversation reflected their implicit need to learn more about the other and tactfully reveal more about themselves. Neither fully realized what was taking place.

After they had polished off the banana pudding, Eimear asked, "What would you like to do?"

"Your truck, you're driving. You call the shots."

"Okay then. What say we get back on the island and take a leisure drive down to the Bogue Inlet Fishing Pier at Emerald Isle?"

"Sounds good to me."

"Do you want to get a refill to take with you?"

"I'm not taking anything to drink inside that truck."

"It's just a truck."

"No, it isn't. It's *the* truck."

The thirty-minute ride from Atlantic Beach to Emerald Isle included an uninterrupted, oldies concert performed by the subscription service Eimear had wired into the truck. Spence was in his element. To him, although it was well before his time, the music of the sixties and the beach were attached at the hip.

Eimear pulled into the parking lot in front of the welcoming building. Above the doorway was a large, surfboard-shaped sign displaying Surfs Up Grill and Bar. They entered through the doors just to the side, directly into the shop. After looking around, they exited through the rear set of doors and out onto the wooden pier. They walked halfway out the pier, turned, and leaned against the right-side railing. Neither spoke as they inhaled the salty air, looked at the water that lived up to the name, Crystal Coast, and felt the wind coming off the water.

Occasionally, looking further up the pier to their left, they would watch a fish being pulled from the water, the fishing pole bent and jerking as the catch landed on the planks of the pier and was quickly conveyed to an ice-filled cooler. From time to time, a fish taken up almost to the railing would luckily, escape free from the hook at which point, gravity would return them to the safety of the sea.

Philosophically speaking, Spence told Eimear, "I hope that's not what happens to our catch in this case."

"It could be worse," she noted.

"How?"

"Look down the pier. For every fish that's caught, there are scores, if not hundreds, that take the bait from the hook and never get caught."

"You're right."

"That doesn't mean you stop fishing, though, right?"

"Right."

When the pier lights came on, they both turned and headed back through the shop to the truck. The journey back to the DoubleTree was made sans music. The reflective quiet was nice as well.

Arriving at the hotel, Eimear parked the truck in the parking lot and turned off the motor.

"One more thing."

"What's that?"

"You owe me a riddle. It must be one of your own."

"Now?"

"Put up or shut up. And if you're gutsy enough to put up, here's the deal. It will be a blind wager. The victor determines the prize *after* the victory."

"Are you sure that you want to do this?"

"No guts—no glory."

"All right, but just remember, you asked for it. It's longer than your poem."

"Go for it."

Spence paused, took a deep breath, and began, "I had the following dream: I was driving away from the house where my family had previously lived. As I drove away, I noticed someone driving an old flatbed truck coming in the opposite direction. The truck was going slowly, and the driver seemed to be looking around suspiciously. Because the road was a cul-de-sac, I knew the truck would be returning, so I turned off to wait. When the truck came by, I started to follow. The license plate was yellow orange with large black letters, like those seen on European vehicles.

"The driver of the truck noticed that I was following. He began to drive faster. I raced after the truck for a while over dirt and gravel roads. Soon, however, I realized I couldn't overtake the truck, so I decided to drop back and follow from a distance and out of sight.

"After a while, I saw the truck turn off the road, down a rutted path. As all the leaves were off the trees, I could see the truck drive up to a small, unpainted, gray-weathered house. The house had a porch that ran the length of the front of the house with wooden steps in the front center of the porch.

There were no railings on the steps or the porch. The driver parked the truck and quickly went into the house.

"I pulled my vehicle, a white Ford that had belonged to my parents, to the front of the house about fifty yards from the door. I got out of my vehicle and walked toward the house. Somehow this place seemed familiar to me.

"As I approached the steps, the driver came out of the door and on the porch. He was a small man between four and a half and five feet tall. His head and face were thin and narrow. His nose was pointed, and he had dark-brown eyes that were deep set and very close together. His arms and legs were like sticks, and his hand and fingers were like the end of a tree branch in the winter.

"He didn't speak to me but opened the door and led me into the house. The interior of the house was rough and crudely furnished. The floors were wooden. Everything in the house was neat, clean and in its proper place. The front door opened into a room which took up the main portion of the house. On the left side of the room was the cooking and eating area. In the back center of the room was a small closet-like area. Across the doorframe top was a pipe on which hung a blue-gray curtain, which was half open.

"Beyond the curtain, I could see a small, gray plastic cane. The handle of the cane was at an exact ninety-degree angle. Holding the handle was a small, thin, childlike left hand. From behind the curtain I heard a reedy laugh and the voice of one who speaks high in the nasal portion of his mouth. After some awkward and difficult movement on the part of this individual, he came around the curtain and entered the room.

"The miscreant looked and acted as follows: He was short, shorter than the first. His head was extremely large for his body. His hair, though closely cut was receding from the front. His mouth was small and his yellow-brown teeth were like the baby teeth of a young child. Spittle seeped from his mouth down the left side of his chin which he would wipe away from time to time. His head seemed to lean to the right and he never looked straight on but seemed to glance out of the left side of his piercing eyes. When he walked, he limped decidedly to the right. His steps were slow and deliberate and I believe painful.

"Without speaking my name, he seemed to know me. I also felt as if I knew him, knew of him or recognized that which was within him. We talked back and forth, verbally fencing, testing one another, evaluating, and judging. He laughed often, and although his laugh was chilling, I believed he respected and was somehow wary of me. The first individual watched from my left but had not spoken.

"Presently the second, while never taking his eyes off me, said, 'I believe you're now ready to play a game of riddles, the answer of which is yes or no.'

"'Wait! Wait!' shouted the first. From a statue of inactivity, he now became a whirlwind of flailing arms and dancing legs. 'He's not ready! He's not ready!' he shouted even louder. 'You must wait! You must wait!'

"His arms and hands were extended toward the second, his fingers outstretched toward him, although he would only come so close and no farther. With only a glance from the second, the first was silenced.

"Although I was never told, I somehow knew that while there was no reward for guessing the riddle, the consequences of failure were grave.

"Laughingly, the second related the following riddle to me: 'There was once an impoverished man. He and his wife were required to fend for themselves daily. Concern for the needs of life was their constant companion. Wants never had a place in their existence. To them, the only great luxury they knew was a baked potato on rare and special occasions. Normally potatoes were made into watery soup for the both of them.

"'At a time when the man's wife was out scavenging, he occasioned to gain a potato, a potato just the right size and just the right age for baking. Having decided to bake the potato, he set upon the ritual associated with this feast. As is often with the very poor, the joy of preparation and anticipation was as much as part of the ceremony as was the actual eating of the meal.

"'The chipped plate was set just so. The wooden fork was placed on the table and then corrected several times until it was positioned perfectly. The fire was at the most-perfect degree and the valued potato positioned exactly in the correct location therein.

"'Soon the air was full of the aroma of the baking jewel. The man grew anxious. What if his wife smelled the potato when she returned? Or worse yet, what if she should return while the potato was baking or at the point, he was actually eating the potato? He knew she would be hurt and disappointed knowing he thought only of himself and not of her.

"'His thoughts grew more outward and less inward, more kind and less selfish. He thought of the times his wife stayed by him in sickness and hunger. He remembered how hard she worked, her never complaining, the strength he had drawn from her in times that were even more barren than the everyday. She should have the potato! He envisioned the smile that would come to her face, the temporary, brief joy she would have to abandon herself in the moment. For a while, yesterday wouldn't matter and tomorrow wouldn't bother her.

"'But the potato smelled so right, and he was so hungry. Maybe his wife wouldn't return. Perhaps she had left to care for herself—to worry for only one mouth. But he knew in his heart, his faithful would return, bringing what she had found to share with him.

"'He was caught in the vacuum between eating or sharing, the physical as represented by the potato and spiritual as felt by his love of and concern for his wife.

"'And the riddle is, my friend,' said the second, intensifying his sidelong observation of me, 'did the man submit to the physical, or did he persevere for the spiritual? Finally, did he eat the potato or prepare it for his wife?'

"At the exact moment he asked the question, I knew the correct answer. And answering correctly, the first, the second, and the home all vanished, and I awoke from my dream.

"And of course, my reply to him was..."

Without a moment's hesitation, Eimear leaned over and whispered the answer into Spence's ear.

Resignedly, Spence told her, "Let me know what I owe you."

"You can count on that."

Spence got out of the truck and walked around to the driver's window. He leaned in and kissed her. It wasn't a kiss on the cheek. It lasted longer than a three count. And it wasn't a solitary kiss.

CHAPTER TWENTY-FOUR

An Informative Run, a Warning, a Soiree with the Media

S PENCE HAD SET his alarm for three a.m. and was pulling into the sheriff's office parking lot fifty minutes later. As a result of his structured analysis the day before, he had developed an option. Admittedly, it was threadlike, but the case would suffer no adverse impact should this tactic prove to be unproductive. Starting to the left on Craven Street down to Front Street, he began to run the street grid of historical Beaufort. For an investigator to *put themselves into the deceased shoes* was no trite venture. New perspectives can be as impactful on the outcome of a case as the movement of the thumb an eighth inch on the shaft of the golf club.

As he ran, he focused on his surroundings. Sounds, smells, and sights were all processed. After about an hour, he decided to get off the main roads. Back on Craven Street, he turned right onto Middle Lane heading toward Turner Street. Parked next to a white picket fence under the branches of a leafy tree he spotted a battered, multiple decades old, yellow station wagon. Inside, it was filled to the roof with clutter leaving only room for the driver. Spence slowed his pace and mentally took down the tag number. Taking a right on Turner he picked up his pace. He took a right on Broad and a left on

Craven. At the sheriff's office parking lot, he grabbed a pen and paper from his saddle bag and wrote the number down. It wasn't much but sometimes little things can make big differences.

After taking the time to cool down, he set out for the hotel. The ride back was much cooler than he had anticipated. By the time, he got to his room, the first, searching fingers of light were reaching up to grab the horizon. A quick cup of hot coffee and a hot shower and he was ready, for the second time, to meet the day.

He sent a quick text to Rollins asking if he could meet him at the Cox Family Restaurant for breakfast. Shortly, Rollins replied that he would see him there in about thirty minutes. Spence arrived first, got a table, ordered some coffee, and waited. His coffee-based solitude was quickly interrupted.

In the blink of an eye, Linda Compton was sitting directly to his right, leaning directly forward, well within a prescribed comfort zone. Her eyes were narrowed, and she wore what had to be her most emphatic game face. She had positioned her pointed right index finger close to Spence's nose as if she had wanted him to give the finger a close examination.

"I'm gonna tell you something, *Tim*." There was a derogatory emphasis within the pronunciation of *Tim*.

"I figured that rather quickly."

"Listen to me and listen good. You had better not be leading Eimear on." The name Eimear came across in a much softer tone.

"You had better not be *playing* her. Because if that plan is in the back of your pointy little brain, you and me are going to have some serious conflicts. Am I making myself clear?"

By this point, everyone in that section of the restaurant realized they were being treated to breakfast *and* a show. All other table conversation had ceased, and eating utensils were held at half-mast.

It took all the self-control that Spence possessed to keep the smile from his face. Showing Linda the palms of both hands, he told her, "I'm *not* a player, and whatever plans I may have that involve Eimear would have to be her call."

The honesty of his assertion seemed to satisfy Linda. She stood up, smiled, and asked, "What will you have for breakfast?"

"I'll take the combo special."

"Toast or biscuits?"

"Biscuits."

As Linda turned to place the order, Spence endeavored to assure her, "Linda, in time, you'll come to see that I'm *not* a bad guy. I'm betting, one of these days, you and I'll be good friends."

She answered definitively, "Time will tell."

Just as Linda left, Rollins came into restaurant. Noticing that everyone was staring, he wondered aloud, "Did I miss something?"

"Just a friendly good-morning greeting."

Rollins let it go. "There'll be someone joining us. The sheriff has instituted a mentoring program, and I invited the deputy I'm mentoring to join us. I hope that's all right."

"Better than all right. I might need some backup."

Rollins again chose not to pry. He figured if Spence wanted to elaborate, he would.

Another waitress stopped at the table, took Rollins's order and darted away.

"Who are you mentoring?"

"I don't think you've ever met her. She laterally transferred in from another agency. She had previously been a municipal police officer, so we are orienting her to those law enforcement elements that are unique to the sheriff's office—civil, courts and detention. Her name is Barbara Wilson, but everyone calls her BC."

"BC?"

"Bad to Cuss. She went into the navy with an age waiver from her parents and spent four years before her commitment was up. She got out and decided to go into law enforcement. She's a stand-up officer. It's just that she is just a little…salty."

"It never ceases to amaze me how y'all come up with these monikers. I'm surprised you haven't come up with one for me."

"Oh, they came up with one for you some time back."

Surprised, Spence asked, "Really. What is it?"

Before Rollins could answer, up walked the deputy he was responsible for mentoring.

Having no idea that she had just been the topic of discussion, Barbara walked up to the table, put out her right hand in Spence's direction and opened. "Hi, my name is Barbara Wilson."

Standing, Spence shook her hand. "Hello Barbara. I'm Tim. It's nice to meet you. Have a seat."

As she took her seat, Spence knew that he would be more than happy to have her as a backup. Barbara could have easily made a good living performing on the women's professional wrestling circuit.

As Barbara took a seat and settled in, Spence offered, "Barbara, tell me about yourself."

"Well, I'm married. My husband's name is Paul. He is a financial advisor and a bi-vocational pastor."

The incongruity between her nickname and her husband being a pastor provided Spence with a Franz Kafka moment, but he, once more, suppressed what would have been a natural reaction.

"We have two children—a four-year old girl named Lacy and a two-year old boy, Paul Junior, named after his dad. I'm working in patrol right now and happy with what I'm doing. My goal is to someday be a detective."

"I understand. I always enjoy it when I get the opportunity to work patrol as a reserve officer and investigations is a continually learning challenge. Would you like some breakfast?"

"Thanks, but I had breakfast earlier this morning."

Just as the introductions had been concluded, the two meals were placed on the table.

"While the two of you're here, let me ask you a question. Can you tell me who is the mobile hoarder in the Beaufort area?"

Rollins asked, "What's a mobile local hoarder?"

"Someone who fills their car and most probably their home with everything. They hoard everything."

BC chimed in. "Oh, you're talking about Admiral Air Freshener. We call him Double A, for short. Every time he goes into the post office to check his mailbox and leaves, the postmaster has to come out and spray the lobby with air freshener. He's a little...ripe. We used to call him Sergeant Stinky, but then we all had to take this class on *sensitivity* in our annual training requirements, and they told us that was inappropriate, so we promoted him and gave him a better name."

Spence and Rollins exchanged knowing glances at the irony in what Barbara had just shared.

"What's his real name?" Spence asked.

"Something Boone, I think. The word is, he got messed up in a war somehow."

"What war?"

"I don't know that either."

"If it's okay with Rollins, would you please run a check on this tag number?"

Rollins gave an affirming nod, and Spence handed the paper upon which he had written the tag number during his run through the historical district to Barbara.

"I'll step outside and run the plate so no one can hear."

Rollins wondered, "What's going on?"

"I'll tell you later. Right now, I want to know the nickname everyone has placed on me!"

"You sure you want to know?"

"Certainly."

"I don't know if you can handle it or not."

"What's the *name*?"

"All right. It's the Get-Over Man.'"

"The Get-Over Man? How in the world did they come up with that?"

"Because you got over."

"Got over what?"

"Everything. You had a great career with the North Carolina Department of Justice. Y'all came up with the concept of the Academy of Investigative Resources. You're making more money that Scrooge. Don't take it wrong. It's not a derogatory term. Think of it as a tip of the hat. It's just that, other than me, most people just don't see you continually enough to be comfortable with calling you something like that to your face."

Barbara boomed back into her chair. "Okay, his full name is Mark Sessoms Boone. He has no arrest record and no outstanding warrants." She handed the paper with the new information back to Spence.

Spence saw that the details referencing the vehicle matched what he had seen on his early-morning run.

Continuing, Barbara added, "I can tell you this. He lives on hamburgers, French fries, and diet sodas."

Rollins, remembering his mentoring responsibilities, asked, "Okay, Barbara, based upon what has occurred around this table this morning, what can you infer?"

Barbara thought for a minute. "Somehow the admiral is connected to the case you two are working—the two dead lawyers. He might be a suspect or he might be a source. This is the first time that his name has come up in your inquiry."

She pointed at Spence, "Somehow, in your mind, he's a factor for consideration."

Turning her attention to Rollins, "When you sat down at this table you had no idea anything regarding Boone was in play. After I leave, he will bring you up to code about what's on his mind. That's all I've got, and whatever I picked up today regarding Boone, I'll keep to myself."

Rollins made her day. "Not bad. Not bad at all. Thank you for meeting with me this morning. I'll contact you and we'll catch up again soon. In the meantime, if you have any questions, let me know."

"Great. I've got my four-day break starting tomorrow, but if I can help you guys in any way, call me. I'll be at home."

Spence placed his hand out to shake her hand. When she took it, he said, "It's nice to meet you, Officer. I hope to work with you sometime."

"That would be great. I'd welcome the opportunity. Is it okay if I call you Mr. Get-Over?"

Caught by surprise, Spence recovered and replied, "Sure. I've been called worse."

Rollins nearly choked on the food that was making its way halfway down his throat.

Having finished breakfast, the pair decided to make their way to the courthouse. Neither wanted to miss Russell's press conference performance.

The media had herded themselves between the flags and the steps of the redbrick building with the four large, white columns. Cameras and microphones were at the ready. Russell had taken his place halfway up the steps next to the middle of the three white handrails. Well off to the side at the ground base of the right farthermost column stood Spence, Rollins, and Dixie. She was dealing with a tinge of regret for having pushed Rollins into the conference. If everything went south, she feared it would all be on her. Her two companions, on the other hand were eagerly waiting for the show to begin. To them, the further south things went, the more amusing it would all be. Rollins summarized his perspective. "Just because something shouldn't take place, doesn't mean that it can't be funny when it does."

Looking at his watch and waiting until exactly nine o'clock, Russell raised his right hand and demanded quiet. The babble stopped. "Good morning, I'm ADA Bob Russell. Let me tell you how our time together is going to go down. I'm going to read a prepared statement. You may all have a copy of the statement when I'm finished. At that point, I'll take questions. However, I'll not respond to a cacophony of all of you shouting out questions at the same time. If you want to ask a question, you will raise your hand, and when I call on you, you may then ask your question. I'll *not* respond to any questions shouted out. If you persist in talking while I'm answering a properly posed question, I'll turn around and walk up these steps into the courthouse door and leave you here like a bad dream. Have I made myself clear?"

No response.

"Have I made myself *clear*?"

A weak, collective yes followed his second inquiry.

"Thank you so very much. Now, The sheriff's office and the Beaufort Police Department are jointly investigating the deaths of Duke Kacmar and Greg Garrett. It has been determined that these two cases *are* connected to the nationwide series of homicides that have involved members of the legal profession. Investigative-related information from each of the individual state and District of Columbia cases has been and will continue to be forwarded to a national, central nexus. The purpose of the consolidation of information is to identify any patterns, commonalities, or salient discoveries. In turn, that information will be shared with those conducting the various investigations. In that manner, the arrest in any one case may serve as a link to not only resolve the other cases, but to bring to light who or what's responsible for an undertaking of this magnitude. The district attorney's office is fully assisting the sheriff's office and the Beaufort Police Department in the inquiry. Everything that can be done *is* being done. The investigation is a priority for all three agencies. Any information, not capable of compromising the investigations here or nationwide will be made readily available to the media and public. Thank you, I'll now take questions."

Immediately upon his closing, a chorus of questions flooded the air.

Raising his hand, he lamented, "So soon we forget."

A resentful quiet fell. A myriad of hands went up.

Pointing to a raised hand, Russell granted, "You."

"Could you just answer point blank? You say that the investigation is proceeding. Why haven't you asked the feds to assist in the investigation?"

"That's two questions. Which one would you like for me to answer?"

"Why haven't you asked the feds to assist in the investigation?"

"The feds are assisting. As I said in the prepared statement, they are serving as the clearing house and the processing of all available information."

"Another question." He pointed to another hand. "You."

"But don't you think *they* are better prepared to work this case?"

"No. Have they solved any of the homicides involving federal-level attorneys?"

"Not that I know of."

"Then there you go. You were able to answer your own question. Aren't you the one? Let's hear from someone else."

"I want to challenge you on one of the statements you made in your prepared brief. You stated, 'The arrest in any one case will serve as a link to not only resolve the other cases, but to bring to light who or what's responsible for an undertaking of this magnitude.' A recent editorial, stated that with proper investigative procedures, the cases, here in North Carolina, could have already been solved."

"First of all, I read to you very slowly and distinctly in the futile hope that comprehension would take place, 'the arrest in any one case *may* serve as a link to not only resolve the other cases.' I didn't read to you the word *will*. Here's a tip. Make sure you get it right first. Unless, of course, you were trying to put words into my mouth."

"But don't you think there's validity to the assertion within the editorial?"

"No. Let me ask you this, how many homicide investigations has the eminent, print-media editor successfully conducted?"

"In the case of Kacmar, sources have reported that there were no defensive wounds whatsoever. Do you think he was under the influence of some debilitating drug?"

"I can neither confirm nor deny that."

"But reports are that there were no drugs found in his system. Why wouldn't he try and defend himself?"

"I can only speculate here, and I'm only doing that because you somehow managed to stumble upon a good question. But it could be that he was caught by surprise. Or if there was a drug involved, with the passing of time and the walk from his house on Ann Street to the Old Burying Ground, the body may have metabolized the drug. And again, I'm only conjecturing here. Okay, one last question and then we're done."

A media member, reading from a handheld electronic device, announced, "Since studies have shown that climate change can have a profound impact upon the human psyche and that rising temperatures have steadily increased along with violence over the last several decades, how will we be able to mitigate the recurrence of such circumstances as shown by these homicides going into the future?"

"Okay. That's it. If you have any more valid questions, please direct them to Officer Dixie Bell Lee, who is patiently waiting for you over by the column to your right. She will be more than happy to answer any and all questions you may have. She has printed copies of my statement and, as a bonus, a parting gift for each of you."

After Russell's valediction, a chorus of bottled-up questions erupted from the pack of media. He ignored them, turned, walked the remaining way up the courthouse steps, and entered the building. Spence, Rollins, and Lee went straightway to the commandeered conference room that had become their workroom at the sheriff's office.

In the room, Spence called Leigh's personal phone, using his burner phone. After several rings, Leigh answered.

"I'm out of the building so go ahead."

"What were the results of the security sweeps?

"Everything is clear—computers and facilities."

"Great. Then, if you would please, tell everyone to resume normal operation."

"Got it."

"What about the background on the individual that had declined to talk?

"I'll send to you what we've got. It isn't much. But let me tell you: that guy is gone."

"Moved?"

"Nope. Gone. Not a trace. Apartment cleaned out. Office cleaned out. Gone. Leased vehicle left in the driveway—in the breeze."

Spence, thinking out loud, observed, "The dog that didn't bark."

"Dog?"

"Never mind. I was 221B Baker Street for a moment."

"Where?"

"Sorry, if you will, please send to me what you do have on the individual, and I'll take it from there. I'll catch up with you later."

"You've got it. Bye."

Spence ended the call, Dixie asked, "Will you guys need me for the next several hours?"

Rollins answered, "I don't think so."

"Good. I'm going over to the police department, crawl into my uniform, grab some outstanding warrants, and go try and serve them. Russell's press conference made me a nervous wreck and nothing calms my nerves like serving warrants."

With that acknowledgement she was out the door.

As it was just the two of them, Spence read Rollins in on his plan for the evening and the element with the subject that declined to be interviewed. Rollins well understood that, within an investigation, the atypical is worthy of note. Of all the inquiries that had been made, the report of this individual declining to cooperate was informative well beyond the name and background.

Spence opened his laptop and together they read the report on the absconded subject.

Rollins wondered, "Do you think that was his real name?"

"No way of knowing from this report. We could only speculate."

Changing the focus, Spence asked, "Did you ever track down what was behind the release of the investigative documents?"

"They weren't *released*—they were *taken*. And the computer folks have yet to figure out how that happened."

"Your call, but you might want to consider compartmentalizing any further developed information until you're ready for it to be released. You have to assume, after it's placed on the servers, it's *compromised*."

"For sure. I'll back up everything on some external hard drives and take my laptop when I leave the office."

"Good. And as for our plans for tonight, let's keep this inquiry thread between the two of us. What do you think?"

"I'm good with that. Let's just keep things on a need-to-know basis from now on."

"One other thing. Let's get a city map and place it on the board. It might be old school, but I'd like to put some pins on it and see if anything shows up."

"I'll take care of it. Hey since we're going to be 'on the clock tonight,' why don't you come over and we'll grill out?"

"Can't I bring a guest?"

"The more, the merrier."

Spence called Eimear to see if she was up for a cookout.

"That's great. Just tell me where and when, and I'll meet you there. By the way, Linda said she ran into you at breakfast this morning."

"That's right. She did stop by the table, and we chatted for a minute."

"She is really nice, isn't she?

"She is something else."

Rollins's home was located on a six-acre plot on Highway 101—a white three-bedroom, two-bath with a crushed-gravel driveway. The house sat comfortably back from the road fifty feet. The backyard was perfect for a cookout.

The evening was enjoyable and revealing. The setting provided Spence and Eimear with the opportunity to add another dynamic to their developing relationship. They found that they were as compatible in a social setting as they were when it was just the two of them. The conversations and laughter were such that neither Jacqueline or Eimear noticed that Spence and Rollins had chosen to skip the obligatory beers and made do with sodas—sodas with a twist of lemon for effect.

CHAPTER TWENTY-FIVE

A Search, a Request, a Lesson Learned

S PENCE AND ROLLINS left Rollins's home at 10:30 p.m. in the evening. Rollins was driving his unmarked car and Spence was riding shotgun. They made straightway to the fast-food restaurant on Live Oak Street. They arrived just in time to place the last order of the day. At the drive through, Spence ordered two hamburgers, French fries, and a large diet soda. He asked that the hamburgers and fries be wrapped in aluminum foil to help to keep them warm. They had no idea how long their search would take. Beginning on Live Oak they began a slow grid search through the Beaufort Historical District.

Rollins turned onto Broad Street as the two settled in for what they anticipated to be a protracted search. Rollins drove a pattern that allowed them street-view perspectives from various directions. They had been in the search for thirty minutes. As they were again traveling Turner Street, approaching Broad Street, Spence glanced over to his right and there, parked unobtrusively in the courthouse parking lot was Mr. Mark Sessoms Boone—aka Double A.

"There he is, in the parking lot," Spence announced. "He's parked right up at the edge of the lot."

Rollins made his way into the parking lot and with Spence's directions parked directly behind the would-be classic vehicle. Spence grabbed the food bag, the drink, exited the car, and walked directly up to the driver's side to Mr. Boone's open window. Rollins was Spence's shadow all the way up to the door. He was close enough that Spence could hear his breathing.

"I haven't done anything wrong. I'm not breaking any law by parking here."

"No sir, Mr. Boone, you haven't and you're not. First off, I'm here because I have something for you. Secondly, I'm here because I'm asking a favor."

Spence handed the bag and the drink to Mr. Boone who then glanced in the bag and kept it on his lap.

"And why would I want to do a favor for you?"

Spence extended his hand and said, "My name's Tim Spence, Mr. Boone."

As Mark shook his hand, a micro-expression flashed across his face. Spence leaned down and whispered something that only Mark could hear.

In a completely different tone, Mark asked, "What can *I* do for *you*?"

"This conversation has got to stay completely between you and me. My friend Jesse here, who is breathing down my back, and I are working the cases of these two murdered lawyers. I need for you to be my eyes and ears out here through the night until we can get to the bottom of this thing. You don't have to do or go anywhere unusual—just your regular night. That is, if you don't mind. I want to give to you this phone along with a charger. Also, here is my number and the number of your phone. If you see something out of the ordinary, I would appreciate it if you would call me. Call me anytime, day or night. Also, here is another phone, just in case there was a problem with the first phone. The second number is on the back of that piece of paper. And let me assure you, your name will never come up. I give you my word. Will you do this for me?"

"Yes, but can I ask *you* a favor?"

"Absolutely."

Holding up one of the phones, he asked, "Can I call my daughter on this? She lives in California, and I haven't talked to her in a long time." He reached up into the sun visor, pulled out a tattered picture, and handed it to Spence.

"That's her. She's a lot older now and got her own grown kids."

Spence took the picture and used the light of his cell phone to get a good look.

"What a great picture! I'm betting she is a wonderful mom as well as a daughter. I hope that I'll have a daughter someday. Listen you can call your daughter all you want. I've placed a whole lot of talk time on both of the phones. And when they begin to run short, you call me and I'll have some more time put on."

Spence gently handed the picture back. Mark immediately returned the picture to its rightful place.

Spence's daughter assertion caught Rollins by surprise.

"I hope you get to have a daughter too," Mark empathized.

"Thank you. I appreciate your help," Spence offered as he shook Mark's hand once more.

"You'd let me know if you needed anything else, wouldn't you Mr. Boone?"

"I would."

"And I'll let you know if I need anything."

"You do that, Mr. Spence."

With lights off, Rollins drove to another portion of the parking lot, stopped, and cut off the motor.

Looking at Spence, he asked, "So what's the deal?"

"Listen, there are always people that most others never *see*. It's known as *inattentional blindness*. They might be the cleaning crew in a building in the middle of the night, the daytime housekeepers, delivery-service personnel, or in this case, a mobile hoarder. They become part of the landscape—an unnoticed tree in a forest. They just get cognitively filtered out by the majority of those with whom they intersect. But to an investigator, these people can be a valuable source of information. Never summarily preclude someone from an information-seeking, communicative interaction based upon who they are, what they do, or what they don't do. I recovered valuable evidence as a result of information I obtained from an individual that the first investigators on the scene ran off. Just because individuals are ignored by others doesn't mean you have to walk that same path. Even those you arrest can prove to be valuable sources of information if you treat them right."

Rollins filed that away in his mind for future reference.

"Well, what do you want to do now, Spence?"

"Let's just ride around the historical district for a while—see what we see and hear what we hear."

After an hour, Spence said, "Why don't you take me back to your house? I'll get my bike and head for home."

The ride to the hotel helped to clear his head, but there still remained a shading of a cognitive shadow way in the back. He still couldn't shine a light on whatever it was hidden away in a deep, dark recess.

Back in his room, he checked his phone. He saw that it was almost two in the morning and he had one text message: "Please call me, no matter the time. E."

He fixed himself a cup of decaffeinated coffee, took off his shoes, sat in a chair, propped his feet up on the bed, and hit speed dial.

After three rings, a voice still wrapped in sleep answered, "Timmy."

Spence had no issue at all with Eimear's addressing him with the name that had previously been reserved for use only by his mother and sister—no issue at all.

CHAPTER TWENTY-SIX

A Devil's Advocacy, a Message in the Cards, an Understanding

S PENCE AND ROLLINS arrived at the conference room first. Rollins started to place the Beaufort City map onto the corkboard.

"Hey, if you don't mind, wait until it's just the two of us before you put up the map."

"Sure."

Rollins folded the map and returned it in his briefcase. They sat, drank coffee, and savored the quiet, knowing that it wouldn't be long lived. Reverie exited the room at the point Russell and D opened the door and walked in.

Spence made it a point to ask, "Well, how did your warrant-serving therapy go?"

"Served three warrants. I feel like a new woman. I'm ready to take on the world. I've got people lined up for the next four pressers so, unless something dramatic happens, I'm good to go for the next little bit."

Russell glanced at his watch. "And why have we assembled this morning?"

"Jesse and I want to talk through this entire circumstance with you. Our hope is that together, we can develop some additional lines of inquiry. We could use your take on all of this—what we've done, what we have. No one in here is thin-skinned, so don't summarily decline to put something on the table worrying about what someone would think. If, we didn't value your input, we wouldn't have asked you to meet with us. Start us off, please, Jesse."

Jesse spoke as he wrote on the whiteboard.

"We know our two homicides were of the same nature as those across the country. We know all of the victims were lawyers."

With that detail, the three looked at Russell. He dutifully opened his coat and showed them his 45-caliber pistol resting comfortable in a shoulder holster.

Dixie added her two cents. "Good. You had better be careful. You know it would break my heart to find you deader than four o'clock having died in the middle of a magic trick with the bad luck queen of spades turned up in your right hand. Even if there were no media wanting to know or caring about what had happened to you, if that *were* to happen, I would have no reason to go on in this life."

"You and all the other women in the world. You laugh, but as I've often noted, you have no idea how challenging it is being God's gift to women."

"Neither do you," she countered.

Rollins continued. "All of the victims were killed with screwdrivers. None of the homicides involved a firearm."

At that point, D cleared her throat loudly. "Excuse me. I swallowed the wrong way."

With his voice slightly louder, he continued. "There were no defensive wounds on either victim. The nationwide scope of the homicides would seem to preclude the idea of a case-specific connection. The knock and talks have produced nothing. Lakisha sees no connection to regional extremist groups or a specific individual or we would have heard from her. There was nothing substantial on the guy that wouldn't talk."

Russell interrupted the flow. "What guy that wouldn't talk?"

Spence replied, "There was one individual in another state that declined to be interviewed. We ran a background that provided *zilch*, and anyway, whoever he is, he put it into the wind. There's nothing there that we can operationalize into an investigative move."

Russell was preparing to ask another question when Rollins cut him off. "Let's go on before I lose my train of thought. Other than alcohol, there were no discernable traces of drugs in Kacmar's blood. We're waiting on the result of Garrett's autopsy. We haven't found any connection between the two victims. Their practice-focused diversity was such that they wouldn't have crossed swords within a legal setting."

Looking at Spence, Rollins asked, "What have I left out?"

"Right off the top of my head, that sums it up."

Russell jumped in. "There's nothing else?"

Spence fielded the throw. "What else were you expecting?"

After some thought, Russell answered, "Nothing, I guess. I was just hoping for the big piece that would allow me to conduct the prosecution that would make my career. Today, just a lowly state employee, tomorrow, the United States attorney general. And rest assured, I'll not forget all of you little people when I come into my own and receive millions for the publication of my autobiography."

Having declared his assurance of his future grandiosity, he raised his right arm into the air, displayed his open palm into which a crisp, new five-dollar bill suddenly appeared.

Dixie quickly followed suit. "Five dollars! That's four dollars more than you will ever make on anything you write. In fact, I'm certain, I can round up a number of people that will pay good money for you to *not* write a word."

"Don't say that. You know the best chapter in the book will be the one describing the indiscernible love you have for me."

"Somebody hand a screwdriver to *me*!"

Rollins's patience having worn thin, he commanded, "Let's get back to the point at hand."

"First, do you think our two homicides were done by the same person?"

"There was a uniform answer, "Yes."

"Do you think the killer acted alone?"

Spence and Dixie both said, "Yes."

Russell said, "No."

Pointing to the pair, "Why?"

Dixie answered, "Neither of these murders were complex. There were no indications of defensive wounds. Other than getting Kacmar to the Old

Burying Ground, both murders were 'wham-bam-thank you-ma'am.' I think both murders were brilliant in their simplicity."

Now, looking at Russell, "What say you?"

"It seems both of these actions were well planned and executed. That being the case, I think the plan would have included a lookout—a backup. Look, I agree that the actions were simple in the extreme, but I just think someone this meticulous, this precise wouldn't have undertaken to do this singularly. I think there were two of them."

"So, you two think there's only one perp, and you think it involves two?"

Russell added, "You know what they say—'A friend will visit you in jail. A good friend will help you move the body.'"

Rollins answered his own question. "I'm leaning toward a single killer. Secondly, do you think our homicides are connected to the nationwide pattern?"

All of them answered at once. "Yes."

"Okay. Since we agree on that, process the following: if our murders are connected to a larger undertaking, then…"

Dixie said, "There has to be some entity behind it all."

Spence said, "There has to be a reason for the murders."

Russell said, "The reason has to have some kind of validity—at least in somebody's or something's mind."

Spence, "What do you mean *something*?"

"For all we know, it could be some AI entity calling the shots."

Rollins kept pushing. "If, then . . ."

Dixie said, "There could be more homicides in the works?"

Rollins shifted focus. "What about the killer?"

Dixie said, "I think it's a male."

Rollins asked, "Why?"

"Well, as you well know, we ladies do like the poisons. I think if I was going to kill myself a lawyer or two, I'd use poison. It's so much neater, cleaner and usually takes a while to do its job. By the way, Russell, can I go get you something to eat or drink?"

"What about the mental stability of the murderer, assuming it's just one?"

Dixie again spoke up. "Maybe it's a pro—a killer for hire."

Russell said, "That would mean a lot of professional killers across the fruited plain. I think it involves a degree of enjoyment on the part of the individual. The act imagined that accompanies and produces the expectation that comes before the act is always more exciting than the immediate result of the act itself. It's similar to anticipating an event and then finding the anticipation was more enjoyable than the event itself. That's just human nature."

Dixie jumped right back. "Oh, don't give me that philosophical mumbo jumbo. Say, in your family you have a relative who is a murderer serving life in prison and another relative who is a practicing lawyer. Which one would you be more reluctant to tell your new friend about?"

"I'd rather tell them I was related to a lawyer *and* a killer than to have to admit I had a misandrist, gun-toting, knuckle dragging, mouth-breathing, double-X chromosome with a badge somewhere in my family."

"Are you sure you don't want something to drink or eat? I'd be more than happy to get it for you."

Seeing that he was losing momentum quickly, Rollins asked, "Lastly, what investigative steps haven't we taken that we should have taken?"

A heavy silence followed.

Russell filed the vacuum, "I'll tell you in all seriousness, I don't see anything you've missed. Other than going back and retracing your actions, step-by-step, I think you've done all that you can do."

Dixie nodded in agreement.

Spence concluded, "All right, that's it for now. Thank you. If something else comes up, we'll meet again. In the meantime, if *you* think of anything, let us know."

Going out the door, Russell suggested to Dixie, "Let's go get something to eat. I'm starving."

Spence and Rollins allowed themselves a moment to enjoy the quiet.

Finally, Spence broke the spell. "Let's put that map up and stick some pins. Investigative old school 101."

With the map up and pins in, Rollins took out photocopies of the three cards and attached them to the locations where they had been found. Both stood back and contemplated the map.

Spence noted, "I can say without hesitation or mental reservation, this is the most challenging homicide investigation with which I've ever been involved."

"Roger that."

"Other than the first, the cards seem to be predictive. I don't even want to say it out loud, but that third card can be inferring there's going to be another additional hit."

"You think they are going to switch to someone other than lawyers?"

"I don't know. I *do not* know."

"Well, I need to give a briefing to the chief, sheriff, and other stakeholders. It's better when I go to them than them have to come find me. You know, we're fortunate to have a sheriff and chief that will just let people do their job."

"I'm aware of that. Listen, I don't want the information about the cards that we've held back to become problematic for you. If something should hit the fan, we'll play it out as if I had the cards and you knew nothing. At the end of the day, I'm just a reserve officer but you have a wife and two kids. I can ride out the storm. After all, I'm reportedly the Get-Over Man."

"It isn't going to be a problem. And even if it were to become an issue, I can handle it. Worst case scenario, I'd just have to take you up on that job offer—make myself some real money. People would be calling me Get-Over Man Junior."

"I could live with that."

Rollins threw Spence a key.

"I had the locks on this room changed. There are only two keys—one for you and one for me. The cleaning crew can't even get in. Here is a towel. You can pin it up to cover the map. I'm going to brief the brass, get with Russell on the warrant, and search the house. I'm not hopeful that the search will be productive, but we have to try. Somewhere in there I'm going to try and run home for lunch. If something comes up, I'll call you. Does that work for you?"

"Perfectly. I'm going to hang in here for a while and check up on things with my day job."

Calling in, Spence first spoke with all the administrative assistants. Next came the operational personnel that were available. Thirdly came the cadre of section leaders. Lastly, he spoke with the partners. Seeing that there was nothing to add to the efficacy of any of the on-goings, he listened and affirmed. He wrapped up his cycle of conversations with Leigh. She affirmed that the corporate train was on track and that he would do well to engage in activities more suited to that of a vacation.

"I get the point. Call me if you need me, otherwise, I'll check with you later."

Just as he ended the call he received a text from Eimear: "Lunch?"

"Sure, where would you like to eat?"

"Come on over. I'll throw something together."

"On my way."

He stopped by a dollar discount store on Live Oak Street and purchased a number of items. When he got to Eimear's home, he made it up onto the porch before the door opened. There was Eimear with Razor dutifully by her side. Spence extended his right hand, and the dog performed a good-to-see-you-hello sniff.

"I have a chew toy in my back pocket. Is it all right if I give it to him?"

"Do that and he'll be your friend for life. Just know, he'll expect one every time you show up."

Looking back at his bike, Spence noted, "I have a saddlebag full of them."

He handed the chew toy to Razor who took it, turned, and disappeared into the house.

Lunch consisted of tomato soup, a grilled cheese sandwich, crackers, and iced tea.

The conversation floated from topic to topic like a butterfly in a flower garden. As congenial as the dialogue was, Spence could sense that there was something on Eimear's mind. Bringing it out was proving to be difficult.

Never one to beat around the bush, Spence asked, "Have you got something on your mind?"

Eimear paused, looked down at her plate for a moment, and then locked her eyes onto his.

"I *do* have something on my mind."

"Okay, what is it?"

This time there was no pause. "Us." She pointed her right hand back and forth between the two.

"I want to talk. I want to *know* about us. Are we just enjoying one another's company while you're here for the summer, or is it something more? If, for you, it's just a summer thing, I need to know that. And I need to know that now."

Spence put down his half-eaten sandwich, stood up, walked over, placed his hands on each shoulder, and looked her straight in the eye.

"Straight up, I'll tell you what I think about *us*. I think *us* is great. I think about *us* all the time. I know that, for me, *us* is not a summer thing. I know we haven't known each other for very long. I know I learn something new about you every day, and I'm looking forward to learning even more. Sometimes in this life really good things happen in a very short time. For me, this is one of those times. You just have to be smart enough to recognize it and not lose the gift. In this case, I'm that smart. If it were up to me, I'll still be learning new things about you years from now."

Squeezing her shoulders for emphasis, he concluded, "That's what *I* think about *us*. Now, what do *you* think about *us*?"

The passion of her kiss conveyed two things. It demonstrated her commitment to the *us*, and it signaled that whatever uncertainties she may have had before were gone.

Spence put his now-cold grilled cheese sandwich into the microwave for a few seconds, followed by his now-cold tomato soup.

The conversation resumed only now the metacommunication dial had moved to a permanent personal position. The understanding between the two was on a different level altogether.

"I have to go to Washington Saturday morning."

Knowing not to pry, Spence asked, "Any idea how long you'll be gone?"

"Hopefully, no more that forty-eight hours."

"Are you flying out of Jacksonville?"

"Nope—I'm to be picked up via a corporate jet out of Elizabeth City-Pasquotank County Regional Airport."

"Need someone to carry your bags?"

"Thanks anyway. They've got that covered too."

CHAPTER TWENTY-SEVEN

A Telephone Interview, a Kindly No, a Curious Connection

A S EIMEAR WAS preparing for her trip to Washington the next day and Rollins had opted for some much-needed personal time with his family, Spence decided to break his morning into two components. From eight until ten, he would return calls from the list that Leigh had sent to him. From ten until noon, he would fish on the pier. After that, the schedule was up for grabs depending upon whether he heard from Eimear or not. In the case that she was still tied up, a long ride could prove to be a distinct possibility.

His first call was related to a just-hatched, high-priority investigation within which he was taking an assisting secondary role. This case was related to possibly compromised proprietary information involving a security system for a newly constructed luxury hotel. This stakeholder had agreed to be interviewed by telephone. Should this interview prove to be indicative of the possibility of involvement, a follow-up, face-to-face interview would be arranged.

Spence punched in the numbers, and on the second ring, the call was answered.

"This is Gary Franks."

"Good morning, Mr. Franks, my name is Tim Spence. I appreciate you allowing for the scheduling of this call. How are you today?"

"I'm doing okay."

"Is this still a good time for you or would you like to schedule for later today?"

"Now is as good a time as any. This is going to be a noisy day. I can already tell."

"Listen, I've had my share of those kind of days as well. I'll do my best to make our time together as minimal and harmonious as I possibly can—a prelude to your day, not a symphony."

"Now, just so I'm singing off of the right sheet of music, if you would please, tell me about your roll within the organization."

"I've been with the company over ten years. I'm a marketing associate. My primary role is within the bidding process as the company endeavors to obtain contracts. You could say that I'm a rainmaker for the company. I work to sell the company so as to secure the contract."

"I've spoken to a number of people who have shared with me the significant contribution that you make to the organization." So, you're saying that your compensation is enhanced by a percentage of the contracts that you obtain?"

"I wish! Is this conversation being recorded?"

"No, sir, it isn't."

"Whatever gave you that idea?"

"It's just that whenever I think of sales, I automatically think of commissions—you know, like a real estate salesperson. You make a sale and then you're compensated accordingly."

"Well, that isn't how it works here. Not at all. Those above me get bonuses based upon the contracts that I land. I'm just straight salaried here."

"I just find that hard to believe."

"Well, it's true. You can believe it or not."

"I'm just not versed in organizational sales or putting in bids. If you would, explain the process in a way that even I could understand. I could use your help."

"Okay. Let's say like in this case, a new luxury hotel is being built. The hotel must have a security system that's adequate—really more than adequate—for the hotel staff and guests. Security companies like ours take a set of building plans and incorporate, what we believe, is an appropriate security system. We then figure up the costs, add what we believe is a reasonable profit and then submit the bid. On a prescribed date, all of those who have submitted bids will attend a meeting where the bids are opened. Normally, the bid will go to the organization that has the lowest bid—and that's it."

"You say 'normally' the lowest bid will prevail. What's going on when that isn't the case?"

"It could be that the company with the lowest bid has a reputation for less-than-optimal performance. It could be that the company has no track record for successfully completing a contract of the magnitude of the work project. A company does not automatically have to award the contract to the lowest bidder. There are a lot of variables."

"I never knew it could be that complex. So, help me out here. How does someone in a position like yours function within this process?"

"I'm in it from the opening bell until they break the seal on the bids. I have to work with the engineers on the system design, coordinate with purchasing on the related material costs and keep my ear to the ground to hear if any of our competitors are getting out in front of us in the process."

"Out in front?"

"You know—taking the primary decision-makers to fancy dinners, tickets to professional sports, rounds of golf at exclusive courses—greasing the skids."

"So that's how it works, right?"

"You have no idea."

"Knowing that you're putting forth so much effort to secure the contracts yet receiving no subsequent compensation for your success has to produce a certain amount of angst."

"I have a lot of sleepless nights."

"Do you think your sleepless nights are a result of the loss of funds or the lack of loyalty to you on the part of upper management?"

"At the end of the day, I think the lack of loyalty bothers me the most."

"How do you deal with it?"

"I tried to get them to change the protocol so that I would receive some type of related compensation for my success, but they wouldn't buy off on it. I mean, think about it: I'm doing the work, and they're reaping the benefits. To make matters worse, there are others who don't bring in nearly the number of contracts that I do, yet they make the same thing I do—some make even more. I've put out some feelers to other companies, and if something comes through, I'm gone. In the meantime, I just bottle it up."

"I can certainly understand that. Thank you for that lesson on the bidding process and the insight into the compensation—or lack thereof—protocol. I've learned something new. Since you were previously told to expect my call, would you please tell me about your utilization of the security schematic book earlier this week?"

"Well, the day before yesterday around four p.m., went to James's desk to check out book with the security schematics developed for the hotel. Key was not in usual hidden place, asked him to help, and he unlocked cabinet so I could get book. Signed out book and took it to my office. Studied schematic design for the new hotel to try and understand the recent changes that had been made. Needed to have follow-up meeting with construction manager about the system install and need to be better informed on their proposed time for the bidding process to win the contract for installing the hotel security system.

"Later on—I'm not exactly sure of the time but it was dark. Returned to James's desk; he was gone and I was unable to locate the key to the cabinet. Returned book to my office, locked it up in my cabinet, locked office door and went home.

"Around nine thirty yesterday morning, when James arrived at work, unlocked my cabinet and returned the book to him. I can't remember if he unlocked the cabinet and I put the book in its folder or if he did, but I think I did it. That's about it."

"Thank you. Tell me about the security schematic book itself?"

"It's rectangular and has a heavy black cover on the top and bottom. There are two bars for the two-holed, eleven and seven tenths inches by eight and three tenths inches paper. There are about forty sheets in the book each with security schematics drawn onto the building plans. What's this about? Is the book missing?"

"Now, here's the issue as it stands right now. The schematic designs that were recovered from the cabinet were found to be copies, not the originals. It sounds like someone made a copy and inadvertently placed the copies in the book and kept the originals. Why would someone make a copy of the proposed security schematics?"

"I couldn't say."

"How much would those designs be worth to a competitor in actual and opportunity costs?"

"Thousands of dollars, I guess."

"Would you say the designs would be worth more than ten thousand dollars and less than twenty thousand dollars?"

"Well, I guess it would fall somewhere within that range."

"Who could have made a copy of the diagram? I'm not asking for you to speculate as to who did—just who *could*?"

"James, for one."

"Do you think it's possible that someone might be greasing their own skids with the diagrams?"

"I couldn't say."

"Let me tell you this: Persons are in your building as we speak. They are downloading the data from each of the copying machines, including that which was printed and the date and time *of* the printing. Tell me what you think they will find?"

"I couldn't say."

"Gary, if you would like to get out in front of this situation, now is the time to do it. You have a choice to make right now—an important choice. Would you rather talk with someone from corporate ethics or someone with a badge?"

"Corporate ethics."

"Good. There's a Mr. Joe Spivey in corporate ethics waiting to talk with you right now. Give serious thought to cooperating with him fully. What you need to do is to leave your office immediately. There's someone outside your door who will escort you to Mr. Spivey's office. Your computer has been shut down. Leave your corporate phone and keys on the desk. Your personal effects in the office will be provided to you. I'm going to hang up now, Gary. Don't make the situation worse for yourself."

Spence ended the call and immediately called Joe Spivey. "Joe, Mr. Franks should be on his way up to see you right now."

"All right, Spence. As always, thank you."

"Thank you for the confidence and the business. We don't ever take your utilization of our services for granted, and we never will."

"I have you on speed dial. Talk to you soon."

Spence ended the second call. Whatever the disposition of this matter was to be was outside of Spence's need to know. He was aware, however, that, in many cases, the avoidance of adverse publicity for an aggrieved company overrode the involvement of a law enforcement entity and the pursuit of prosecution. Often, after the subject had provided a written admission to include the dollar amount fraudulently appropriated, an IRS Form 1099 would be sent to the individual and the IRS at the end of the year.

Spence made his third phone call to the senior partner that had oversight on this particular case. After the exchange of Southern style phatic communication, Spence briefed her on the disposition of the case.

She concluded the conversation. "All's well that ends well."

"Absolutely. Now, it's time to go fishing."

The next two hours were most satisfying. He was able to chill and give away five, good-sized fish. After his shower he was ready for some lunch. There was still no word from Eimear. A quick bike ride to Swansboro to the Saltwater Grill. There he ate alligator bites, a house salad with ranch dressing, and iced tea. After his meal, he strolled down Front Street across West Corbett Avenue to the Swansboro Bicentennial Park. There he watched the boats on the White Oak River as he mulled over in his mind Rollins's idea of having a boat of his own. Finally, he concluded it would just be something else he would have to maintain.

As it was after three p.m., he decided to do something—anything. He found himself in, what for him, was an undesirable situation—time on his hands with nothing scheduled to do. He concluded, "When in doubt, ride." That phrase being the mantra of the moment, he saddled up and headed out. Soon he was lost in the flow of the motorcycle experience. There was nothing to ponder but the ride. Contemplations were nonexistent and time stood still. By the time awareness caught up with him, it was after five and he realized he was about thirty minutes out from the hotel. The journey from that point to the hotel was not unlike an after-dinner liquor—the satisfying end to a perfect ride.

Back in his room, he placed an order for a cheeseburger, fries, a small salad, and a beer. Not having heard from Eimear, he knew she was maxed out in preparation for her upcoming trip.

The meal, accompanied by the view of the ocean, provided what Spence mistakenly thought to be the end to a perfect day.

Just as he was clearing the table, he received a text from Eimear asking if he wanted to come over. A sixth sense told him that this invitation was politely perfunctory and that she still had a good deal of work to do.

"Give me a rain check. Spent most of the day on the bike—road whipped. Have a safe trip. If you get a chance, text me sometime, when you have access to your phone."

In a few seconds, a sad-faced emoji appeared, which served as an expression of disappointment as well as a thank you for understanding.

The Rollins family had grilled supper in the backyard, and the four were sitting at the wooden picnic playing a card game in which dad seemed to lose every time. As dusk had transitioned into darkness, their table was illuminated by a foursome of mosquito candles on bamboo poles placed at each corner of the table.

Out front, a bicyclist had stopped to perform a simple repair on the chain. The bike and the bicyclist were highlighted by flashing lights. Dressed in a black helmet, black gloves, matching gray short-sleeved shirt and shorts with a small backpack, the rider knelt by the bike and made an adjustment. Pushing the bike twenty feet forward, the rider saw the modification was incomplete and knelt for a second time beside the bike. Finally determining that the necessary adjustments had been made, the biker crossed the road and headed back in the opposite direction.

Shauna Tyler was a divorce lawyer extraordinaire. She utilized her extravagant retainer fee to cull out divorce proceedings that were not worth her time or talent. She had a talent for inconspicuously dragging the cases out seemingly for the benefit of her client. In reality, the more protracted the case, the more she and the opposing attorney were paid. They were known to appear to go at it tooth and nail in court only to share a lunch or dinner after the proceedings were concluded.

To herself only, she labeled her clients as cornucopias. As long as the bounty came forth, the case would proceed. Aside from her legal shrewdness, she could simultaneously milk the client all the while having them believe she was fighting furiously on their behalf. Her undergraduate degree in psychology prior to law school served her well.

Her small, appropriately restored home located just off Pollock Street served as her escape pod from the big city, fast-paced arena of divorce and the very rich. As she sipped her glass of red wine, she wondered what she would do with herself this Friday evening. Her periodic craving for privacy proved to be a double-edged sword. She now had the solitude but lacked the wherewithal to manage it. Anyway, it was a question she need not ask. The evening's activity would be provided to her in a manner completely beyond her capability to manage.

A backyard cookout, a slipped bicycle chain, and an avaricious divorce attorney with time on her hands—how could these three, seemingly independent situations become so interlocked?

CHAPTER TWENTY-EIGHT

A Bottle of Wine, a Diversion, a Rest in the Azaleas

A T TEN P.M. Shauna Tyler heard a soft knock on the door. Sitting in the den, she sat aside the deposition transcript that she had been reading and wondered, "Who could it be at this time of the evening?" She was dressed for bed in matching pink, with blue flowers, trimmed in white, short-sleeved top and pants, size XS. Her matching blue leather moccasin slippers made no sound as she made her way to the door, wine glass secured in her right hand.

She, like a number of lawyers, had become highly cautious, so before she opened the door she asked, "Who is it?"

"It's only me, and I come bearing gifts—a gift to be precise."

She recognized the voice immediately and quickly opened the door.

"Well, I know you aren't here to discuss divorce, so I can only assume we're talking prenup here."

"First of all, I'm here for some help in savoring this." The visitor held up a bottle of expensive cabernet sauvignon. "Secondly, I do need your participation in a small, undertaking in which I'm involved."

"First things first." She stepped aside as a nonverbal invitation to enter the house. "We have got to do this right," she observed. "There's a wine refrigerator in the kitchen. Place the bottle in there. The temperature is already set at sixty-five degrees Fahrenheit. We'll let it cool for twenty minutes, take it out and then uncork the bottle and let it aerate for an hour. After that, we'll partake. I have the perfect glasses. In the meantime, we can finish this off—save the best for last."

"Yes, indeed, save the best for last," repeated the visitor, making their way into the kitchen.

The next eighty minutes were occupied with a variety of conversational topics. At the top of the list were the recent dastardly attacks upon members of the legal profession and the lack of progress across the country. The interlocutors agreed heartily that drastic steps were needed immediately.

Shauna's glass seemed repeatedly to empty quickly while her visitor's glass somehow seemed to continually maintain its volume. She never noticed the inconsistency. She was just happy that the vacuum of her evening had been filled with wine and words.

At eleven thirty, they both agreed that the wine was ready. Shauna ever so carefully made her way to the kitchen, commandeered two appropriate wine glasses, and returned to the den.

"You had better go get the bottle. I don't trust myself to bring it here without spilling half of it."

"No problem," said the visitor, who by now was already in the kitchen, bottle in hand.

After securing the bottle on a sideboard and turning off all but one light, the visitor noted, "Why don't we soften the room a little to match the wine and the ambiance?"

"Good idea," agreed Shauna as she settled into the overstuffed couch. "Good idea."

The minute hand on the antique mantel clock had made two complete journeys as the operative waited for the signal. Shauna, who had fallen dead asleep on the couch, was now dead, lying upon a clear plastic sheet on the floor in the totally darkened den.

Just after two the audible, signals started. It was if every vehicle in the city of Beaufort and Carteret County with a siren turned them on. Ten minutes later a small dark car pulled up to the front of Shauna's house, lights out. Picking up her small frame, plastic sheet and all, along with the backpack recovered from the front porch containing two wine bottles and four glasses presented no problem for the operative. Next, the operative quietly closed the front door behind, crossed the porch, walked down the steps, and made it into the backseat of the EV. There was to be one quick drop off, followed shortly by another drop-off. Within thirty minutes of leaving Shauna's house, the vehicle would be deposited into the bowels of a cargo ship at the Port of Morehead City on its way to the owner, who lived in France and who had recently purchased the vehicle.

Spence was sound asleep when his phone went off shortly after two a.m. "What?"

He heard a calm but emphatic voice. "Spence, this is Dixie. Shots have been fired at Rollins's home. Everyone working tonight is rolling in that direction—lights and siren. I figured you would want to know."

Not taking the time to answer, Spence ended the call.

In ten minutes, Spence was on his bike, throttle wide open, heading in the direction of Rollins's home. He knew that there would be no one to pull him over. With an officer and family in danger, everyone working— police, sheriff, state highway patrol—EMS—was moving that way as if it were magnetic north.

When he arrived, the preponderance of flashing red-and-blue lights were compounded by the morning mist into violet coronas. Dismounting his bike, he could hear the sounds of additional sirens growing louder as the eager to assist continued to arrive. He saw Rollins, the chief, the sheriff, and a bomb tech from the sheriff's office standing near the road.

As he approached the pair, he heard the tech say, "They were like an IED only fused with 38- caliber blanks. Apparently, there were two devices the second timed to go off shortly after the first had run its course. The configuration, at first glance, looks pretty simple. I'll know better after I've gathered up all the parts and reconstruct them in the lab. Apparently, someone was trying to scare you or send a message. That'll be for you suits to figure out. They don't pay me to think. I'm just glad it was no worse than this and you and your family are okay."

Rollins extended his right hand and said, "Thank you. Thank you so much." Just then Spence's burner phone went off. It was Mark Boone.

"Yes, sir?"

Spence listened silently.

"Thank you, sir, I'm most appreciative. Drive away from where you're now. Go to where you park on Middle Lane. I'll catch up with you and talk to you as soon as I can."

Ending the call, Spence looked at the tech and said, "Excuse us for a moment please."

The tech walked away. Spence told the trio this episode wasn't designed to scare you or send a message. It was designed to pull us away from town. There's another body."

"Where?"

"In the azalea bed on Broad Street by the courthouse."

"Who is it?"

"I don't know yet. The body has yet to be discovered."

"What?"

"I'll explain later. There's Dixie. I'll get her to take me there."

"I'll go too."

"Listen, you have a wife and two daughters who are scared out of their wits. Right now, *they* are your main thing. I can't tell you *what* to do, but as your friend, I'll tell you what you *should* do. The chief and sheriff are here to help. When things calm down here, you can catch up. I'll call you if there's something you need to know immediately. Otherwise, I'll keep you in the loop, and you'll make any big-time decisions that need to be made."

"Yeah, you're right. I'll see you later."

Rollins returned to his home and family.

Spence's, phone rang. It was Russell.

"Hey, I just heard. The DA called me. I tried to call Rollins but no answer. What's the status?"

Signaling for Dixie to join him, he quickly explained the situation at Rollins's house to Russell and that, for the most part, all was well.

"There's no need for you to come out here. Everything is under control. As soon as I can, I'll call you and we'll meet up."

"All right."

Turning now to Dixie, "Look there's another body. You and I have got to get there and secure the scene before the world finds out. Can you quickly get me back to town with blue lights only? I'll come back and pick up my bike later."

"Let's go."

The ride back to town was a short blur. At the scene, Spence asked Dixie if she would tape off the area. He looked and saw that Mr. Boone was no longer in the courthouse parking lot. Using Dixie's flashlight, he looked for and found the card he was expecting to see. With his phone, he took several pictures of the card. He picked the card up using a sheet from an inner copy he had removed from Dixie's North Carolina Uniform Citation book. He gently folded the copy around the card and placed it in his shirt pocket. Next, he called Russell and told him where to meet them.

Within fifteen minutes, Russell had joined them. By then Dixie had called the crime scene techs away from Rollins's home and had them enroute.

Shauna Tyler was resting comfortably in the azalea bed under the live oak trees at the corner of Broad Street and Turner Street. The handle of what was taken to be a long screwdriver was pressed upon her chest directly over her heart. The trio stood outside the crime scene tape Dixie had appropriately established.

Spence, turning first to Russell and then to Dixie, said, "I'm making a wild guess here that here lies another attorney, and I'm hoping one or both of you know who she is."

Dixie spoke up, "Her name is Shauna Tyler and she is…was a high-priced divorce attorney. I wanted her to represent me in my divorce while she was in town, but when she told me her retainer fee, I just laughed and walked away. My ex—may he die and go to hell this very day—and I together couldn't have afforded her fee for one of us, much less both."

Turning to Russell, Spence said, "How about you?"

"Oh yes. I know her. Her firm is out of the Virginia–DC area. She offered me a position in her firm, but I wasn't interested. It was for a good deal of money though. I did have to think about it."

Dixie couldn't let it go. "You know if you made substantially more money, it could very well be that a certain type of woman may find you to be not so nauseous. But then again, no woman could ever love you the way that you do."

"I know, and there's the pity."

Raising his voice to recover focus, Spence added, "In any case, we have got to do Jesse a solid and conduct these initial steps appropriately."

Dixie laid his concerns to rest. "The crime scene techs are on their way. I have a patrol officer tracking down her address and posting there until we can have the house searched. I'm sure Russell here will do his best to get the search warrant signed even though we are in the wee hours of the morning. There are no homes or opened businesses in this area so, knock and talks are not viable at the moment."

Looking directly at Spence, she concluded, "Everything that needs to be done is being done—by the numbers. By the way, how did you find out about the body?"

"Anonymous caller."

Dixie could tell by the tone of Spence's voice to dig no further.

"Listen, if you two will, please stay here and keep a lid on things till I get back. I'll not be gone long."

The pair nodded their acknowledgement. Spence made his way down Turner Street and turned left onto Ann Street. Making sure that he wasn't followed, he continued until he turned right onto Craven Street. Eventually, he turned right onto Middle Lane, and there was parked Mr. Boone in the same location as before.

"Mr. Boone, thank you so much for calling me. I owe you big time. Would you tell me please, what did you see?"

"I was parked in *my* spot. I saw a dark car with no lights coming down Broad Street heading toward Turner. Right before they got to Turner, the car stopped and somebody got out of the back and carried something over to the azalea bushes and laid it down. I couldn't tell who it was or if it was a man or woman. After a second or two, they went back to the car and got back into the back seat. Then the car took a right onto Turner and kept going till I couldn't see it no more. I got out of my car and walked over to see what was in the azalea bed. When I saw what it was, I went back to my car and called you, just like you said to. When you told me to leave and come over here, I did."

"Is there anything else you can remember?"

"One thing—the car's motor didn't make no noise."

"Okay, Mr. Boone. Thank you again. Here's some money for your breakfast as soon as some restaurants have opened up."

"I got some money."

"I know you do. You wouldn't want to keep a friend from showing a little appreciation, would you?"

"I guess not."

"Great. When things settle down, you can buy me breakfast. How about that?"

"That would be good."

Shaking Mr. Boone's hand, Spence said, "I'll talk with you soon. Call me if you see something else or need anything."

"I will."

Spence made his way back to Dixie and Russell deviating from the route he had taken previously. Upon arrival, Spence saw that the techs were methodically processing the scene.

"All right, now we can try and get ahead of the curve. Russell, will you get started on the search warrant for Jesse? D, I know your media mob will be descending shortly. If there's anything you need to take care of in advance, now's the time. I can hold down the fort here until the scene is cleared."

Dixie and Russell went their separate ways, onto their individual tasks. Now, Spence had time to think, to process, to infer. Carefully, he removed the wrapped card from his pocket leaving it protected by the sheet from Dixie's ticket book. He then transferred the protected covering and card into a clear evidence bag he had gotten from a tech. This, the fourth, handwritten card, directed that the holder *proceed* to jail. In an epiphany he understood the meaning of the third card. Four cards, each containing a message. Understanding the cards' messages in retrospect was one thing. Understanding a card's message prior to the event was quite another. The darkened corner in the back of Spence's mind brightened ever so slightly.

Rollins arrived just as the body was being taken away for autopsy.

"How's your family?"

"I left them all asleep in one bed. It's going to take some time for the four of us to deal with what happened, but we will. Our pastor came over and spent some time with us and that helped a great deal."

Putting his right arm around Rollins's shoulder, Spence said, "I'm just glad everyone is okay."

"Thank you, me too. Now, please bring me up to date."

Spence detailed everything to include the fourth card and the information Mr. Boone had provided.

He concluded, "This is the first, externally generated break we've had. What say we go to the conference room and process what we have. After that, we'll go get some breakfast—I'll buy. How does that sound?"

When they arrived at the sheriff's office, police lieutenant Bob Brown was there to meet them in the parking lot. Walking over as Spence and Rollins exited the car, Bob said, "Jesse, I just wanted to stop by and tell you personally how thankful I am that you and your family are okay. And if there's anything we can do to assist you, just let us know."

"Thank you. Dixie has been of great assistance and I don't just mean keeping the media at bay. I appreciate the help from all of you with the neighborhood canvassing and everything else."

Turning to Spence, Bob asked, "You think we're ever going to get to go fishing?"

"I believe we're going to go fishing sooner than you think. There comes a time in the commission of a series of crimes when things start to 'go wobbly.' It becomes more difficult to hold it together. I'm sensing we are nearing that point."

"I sure hope so. Okay, I'll wait to hear from you."

Inside the conference room, Jesse asked, "Go wobbly? Go wobbly for whom?"

"That's the question, I was hoping he wouldn't ask. But I'll tell you this, right now, I'm feeling the best about this case that I've felt since we first visited with the late, Duke Kacmar in The Old Burying Ground. We just have to figure out how to 'read the cards' and maybe the pins."

A text message alert sounded on Spence's phone. "Detective Rollins and family okay?—E."

Spence replied. "Everyone and everything, ok. I'll let him know you asked. I'll be glad when you get back."

Rollins wondered aloud, "How'd she know about what happened?"

"That, I can't tell you. Let's take down the cover over the map and put in the next—and hopefully the last—pin."

With the third pin in place, Rollins laid the four cards on the table still contained in their respective evidence bags. "Okay, just so I'm clear, the first card was found on the grave of the little girl buried in a keg of rum. The second card was found in Kacmar's house. The third card was found at the base of the wooden stocks. This fourth card was found in the azalea bed. All of the cards were handwritten."

Tapping the index finger on the third card, Spence observed, "I thought the answer to the question was that the bridegroom would be paying a minister, but now I believe he was meant to be paying a divorce lawyer. What do you think?"

"That take makes sense to me. Each of these cards served as a message and a teaser. In any case, I'm thinking the first three cards are in the past. What's the message—the teaser—hidden in this fourth card? What's meant by 'go to jail'? Maybe if we can answer that, we can solve this case."

They turned back to examine the pins on the map. Rollins noted that the pins, while not perfectly aligned, did denote a jagged, lined pattern.

"Look, the first pin is in the Old Burying Ground—Kacmar. The second pin is below the first at the Beaufort Historical Site—Garrett. The third pin is positioned above the first at the azalea bed near the corner of Broad and Turner Streets—Tyler. If it follows a pattern does that mean another episode somewhere between the Beaufort Historical Site and the water? And if so, how does it relate to jail or someone going to jail?"

"Good point, but maybe we don't have enough data—enough occurrences to discern a pattern. For example, if we take a string of numbers, one, three, and five, we could readily conclude that the next number would be seven. But what if the pattern then involved adding five to each of the three preceding numbers? Then the pattern would follow with six, eight and ten. So, let's imagine that the pattern here reverses. Rather than having the second pin below the first, third pin above the first and fourth pin below the first, what if pattern was for the fourth pin to be *above* the third, where would that be?"

Rollins examined the map closely. "Well, I'll be." He looked at the fourth card. "That's something else!"

"Come on, let's go get some breakfast and flesh this out. I can't think on an empty stomach. Then I'll need for you to run me back to your house to get my bike. After a shower and a shave, I'll be good as new or nearly so."

At breakfast, Miss Compton was so affable to Spence, one would have thought that they were long-lost friends—or maybe even cousins.

CHAPTER TWENTY-NINE

A Theory, a Murderous
Attempt, a Goodbye for Now

S ATURDAY, MIDAFTERNOON, SPENCE and Rollins resumed their deliber-
ations. Rollins noted that they now knew that, in least in the Tyler
murder, there were two participants.

Spence agreed, "Yes, and we've got Mr. Boone to thank for that. Whoever
is doing this has got to be wondering how we knew so quickly that the body
was there. That fact has got to be a kink in the garden hose for them. We had
an element, in this case, on which they had not factored. They have got to be
wondering what else we have up our sleeve. Hopefully, any related anxiety
on their part will result in a hasty decision or act. That's what I meant about
things going wobbly—hopefully, not for us, but rather, for them. I believe
for the first time in almost a month, we have the opportunity to get out in
front of this case."

Rollins walked over to the map. "If there's to be another murder attempt,
and I see no reason to think otherwise, we're thinking it might well be at
the top of the pin line and not at the bottom, right?"

"That's our primary theory, but we do have our alternate theories—it
could take place at the bottom of the pin line or even to the side. But I

think the information provided by this last card strongly points to the top of the line—the courthouse. The target is someone in or associated with the courthouse. The question is 'who?'"

Both went silent in contemplation for a moment before Rollins picked it up. "Every deceased has been an attorney—Kacmar, the patent troll; Garrett, the criminal defense; and Tyler, the divorce lawyer. So, are we thinking the pool consists of lawyers within the courthouse? The courthouse is an anthill for lawyers."

"That's a valid line of reasoning."

"You think they might go after Russell next?"

"No."

"Why?"

"For one thing, the different professional arenas for each of the three deceased, are viewed by society, in a negative light. Lawyers, particularly like these three, along with politicians and the media comprise the major portion of societal bottom feeders in the mind of most people. Conscientious prosecutors, on the other hand are seen as the defenders of the 'good.' Russell doesn't fit the pattern. If there's to be a next victim, it will not be Russell."

"So, the variables are, lawyer—negative assessment—courthouse, right?"

"That's as good a theory as any. Who is your most lenient superior court judge?"

"Walking Wanda."

"Come again?"

"Walking Wanda. Her real name is Wanda Blevins. She is always open to anything as a reason to dismiss a case. And even when there's a conviction, her sentences are as light as she can make them. Defense attorneys will maneuver in any way that they can to make sure their client's case is called when she is holding court."

"Where does she live?"

"Just off of Ann Street. She's close enough that she can walk from home to the courthouse in a short time."

"Okay. Let me run this up the flagpole and you tell me what you think and what you want to do. All of our homicides have occurred in the dark. We—you and I—need to set up surveillance on Wanda's house, starting tonight. I'll rent an older car for us to use. We need to work it so that one of us is awake and the other is grabbing some sleep. We'll trade off so that, while we might be half dead the next day, we can still function. You and I need to keep our same pattern. Everything needs to appear as usual. Your call, but I would only brief the chief and the sheriff as to what we're doing. The more contained this operation is, the better. What do you think?"

"I think anything is better than us sitting here on our hands doing nothing. I'll brief the chief and the sheriff."

"I'll pick you up at your house right after dark. I'm going to hop on my bike and check out the area around her house. Can you get me her address? I'm going to try and figure out, where Mr. Boone would park if he were doing the surveillance."

That night, Rollins took the first shift while Spence slept and then they switched off. In this manner, Rollins could make it to church with his family and hopefully remain awake during the sermon. The night passed slowly and without incident.

The surveillance on Sunday night was just as uneventful. Monday morning as the sun was over the horizon, they made their way to the sheriff's office. Spence headed to the hotel to shower, change clothes, and eat. Rollins went home for the same reason. They reconnected, midmorning in the conference room. Neither were the least bit discouraged by the inactivity of their first two nights. At the very least, no one had been murdered.

The decision was made to put in their conference room time so that all would appear to be normal. After lunch, they walked the azalea bed once more. It *was* possible they could find an overlooked piece of evidence, but more importantly, they wanted to appear to be carrying on the investigation in an optimal manner.

Later, and making sure they were locked securely in the conference room, they catnapped the afternoon away.

In her courthouse chambers, Judge Blevins was preparing to call it a day when someone knocked lightly on her door.

"Come in."

Seeing who the late-in-the-day intruder was, she asked, "And what can I do for *you*?"

"I just have some papers here I need for you to review." Placing the papers on her desk, the visitor said, "Here, let me show you."

As she looked down at the papers, she felt the cold, steel end of a screwdriver placed against the carotid artery on the left side of her throat.

The realization of her predicament flashed through her mind and froze her like a deer in the headlights. Her eyes widened to what she would assume were their absolute limits, her mouth fell open and as the air was escaping her lungs, she could only utter softly, "You." Her second use of the pronoun *you* was dramatically different from the first.

"Me. And if you make one sound or one move, I'll kill you."

Taking a plastic bottle from a small backpack, the operative ordered, "Drink this. It will calm you down."

Wanda took the bottle and hesitated. She felt the sharpened end press ever more forcefully against her neck. She drank the contents of the bottle. With the screwdriver still pressed against her, the operative returned the bottle and the papers to the backpack. Before long, Wanda fell into a deep sleep with her head resting on the top of her desk. The operative locked her chamber doors and turned off the lights and settled into her deep-cushioned, burgundy, leather couch to patiently wait. If patience was a virtue, then the operative was a saint.

After dark, Spence and Rollins had started their Monday night surveillance of Wanda's house together. As her evening activities wore on, the lights would shift from room to room, finally settling on for an extended time in the den. Just after eleven, the light in the den went out and the bedroom light came on. After thirty minutes, it too went out for the evening. Spence crawled into the backseat to grab some sleep while Rollins completed his watch. At one o'clock, they switched—Spence up front and Rollins sleeping in the back seat. The night dragged on until one forty when Spence received a call from Mr. Boone.

"Yes, sir?"

"I just seen a light flicker in the courthouse."

"Like someone turned on a light in a room?"

"No. Like someone was using a flashlight."

"Leave just like you did the other night. Go to the same spot and stay there until it gets light. Go now! We're on our way."

By now, Rollins was wide awake, crawling back into the front seat. "What's going on?"

Starting the car and rapidly pulling away, Spence said, "Man, we were more on the money than we realized. But the fourth murder is not going down here. It's happening at the courthouse right now. And I'm pretty sure, I know who the killer is."

"Who?"

"And spoil the surprise? Let's focus on saving Wanda's judicial robes right now. We're going to have to quietly break in. You got any idea where the best place would be?"

"Ground floor, parking lot side."

Spence kept the vehicle lights off for the short drive and parked away from the courthouse. They ran across the parking lot, found the door, and together, and as quietly as they could, forced the door open. Inside, they quietly made their way through the building, checking rooms and stopping to listen.

Rollins whispered to Spence, "I hear something. It sounds like it's coming from the courtroom on this floor."

Silently, they made their way down the darkened hall, eerily illuminated by red Exit indicators. At the door to the courtroom, they paused. Spence whispered to Rollins, "I hear it too."

Testing, they found the door was locked. Spence told Rollins, "We've got to go, and we've got to go now."

Together, they rammed the door. It gave way slightly. It took less than a second effort to burst through the door. Both heard footsteps running toward the rear doors of the courtroom.

"Find some lights in here. I'll check on Wanda. Put out an alert and have every unit working to set up checkpoints wherever they can. We have only got a short window of opportunity to catch him."

"Catch who?"

"Russell. Russell is the killer."

"What?"

"No time to explain now. Just trust me."

As he ran toward the rear doors of the courtroom, Rollins unhooked his radio and put out a county wide APB. He advised there was an emergency situation at the courthouse needing assistance to include EMS. He then requested dispatch to notify the sheriff offices of the surrounding counties, police departments, and the highway patrol and request their assistance in locating Russell. Out the door, he could only make a guess as to the escape route, Russell had employed. It wasn't long before he was certain Russell was gone. Nevertheless, he would make certain that a complete building search would be conducted as soon as possible.

Spence found Wanda sitting in the spacious chair behind the judicial bench. Her spindly arms were tightly taped to the left and right arms of the chair. Taped in her right hand was a wooden gavel and waiting patiently on top of the bench was a lengthy screwdriver—a screwdriver destined to never making its way "home." As her mouth, too, was taped, she was breathing heavily through her nose. Spence moved forward to remove the tape from her mouth.

Suddenly, the side door of the courtroom flew open as Bad to Cuss Barbara burst into the room. There was a dramatic thud as she bounced her head and the butt of the shotgun on the floor immediately followed by a loud explosion. Spence's long-standing reactions threw him to the floor well before his brain told him that was where he needed to be.

Directly, Spence began to work his way back to his feet. The smell of gunpowder hung in the courtroom like a heavy, velvet curtain. He stood, took a deep breath, and began to assess the situation. Walking Wanda, whose eyes had discovered they were capable of opening even wider, looked up at the newly placed bullet hole in the courthouse ceiling directly above her head. She immediately knew three things: one, the rifled slug would remain there forever; two, the stories about her that would develop around that slug would expand exponentially with the passing of time; and three, every time she looked at it, she would have to remind herself to exercise better bladder control than she had the moment it was placed there. The white bits of plaster that had fallen on her head, looked like the artificial snow utilized by production companies making Christmas movies in the middle of the summer.

Barbara remained on the courtroom floor. Her right arm, shotgun still in hand, stretched out before her like the raised arm of the statue of liberty. It crossed her mind that perhaps she should not have used the same shoulder whose arm and hand death-gripped the shotgun to break through the door. Her mind wanted to get up but her body was just not ready to follow through.

Spence walked over, leaned down, gently took the shotgun from her outstretched hand, cleared the weapon, and laid it on the table utilized by the defense. While walking toward the table and not looking back, he advised, "Maybe you should just stay there a few more minutes until EMS can check you out."

"I think I will," she replied weakly. I thought the door would be harder to bust through. I'm sorry."

"Don't be sorry. You had the guts to bust through the door, not knowing what was waiting for you on the other side. That bravery makes you more than okay in my book. Anybody can trip, but not everybody will go through the door."

Barbara answered with a more encouraged, "Thanks."

Rollins rushed into the courtroom, gun drawn. After assessing the situation, he returned his weapon to his shoulder holster. "I've got to be sure and thank the firearms instructor for preaching to me about target acquisition," he thought as the distinct sound of a metal pistol cradling into leather served to reassure him.

Back again to Wanda and gingerly removing the tape from her mouth, Spence asked, "Can you breathe okay now?" There was not enough data operation remaining in Wanda's brain for her verbalization app to function. Wild eyed and breathing rapidly, she nodded her head slowly up and down.

"Are you hurt?" he continued.

This answer involved her head moving left to right one time just as slowly.

"Okay, I'm going to leave you just as you're so that the medical personnel can get you out of this properly. You may have an injury about which we are not aware." Her response was limited to the slight upturn at the corner of her eyes as she briefly locked her eyes on his.

"Was that a glare?" he wondered as he stepped away. He knew he could have safely freed her but having her remain in that position until the crime scene photographer could possibly preserve her plight for posterity was too great a temptation. In the fullness of time, her courthouse designation would transition to "Wrap 'Em Up Wanda" as her criteria for case dismissal and sentencing would modify dramatically.

Other officers arrived. The courthouse was thoroughly searched. Russell was not to be found there nor by the vehicle check points scattered throughout the county.

Spence smiled as he placed his right hand on Rollins's left shoulder. "My friend, as soon as everyone gets here, you can meet with the sheriff and the chief and bring them up to date on what's happened. I wouldn't want them to be caught flat-footed by the media when this hits the fan."

Spence's burner phone sounded.

"Yes?"

"Spence, I have to say to you and Rollins that was a pretty good piece of investigative reasoning."

"Make it easy on all of us, Bob, and come turn yourself in."

"It would make it easier for y'all, but not so easy for me."

"You know it's just a matter of time."

"That remains to be seen."

"Did the predatory drugs you used come from a court case?"

"Yep. I switched them out in my closing argument—right in front of everyone. It's all about misdirection, you know."

"I'm learning. Who are you working for or with?"

"Even if I knew, I wouldn't tell you. You *know* that."

"Then tell me *why*?"

"Spence, we have so little time. Let's don't waste it in an unproductive philosophical discussion. Let's just leave the why for people with too much time on their hands."

"I'm just curious: How can you justify violating some of the most basic laws of the land?"

"When's the last time you saw the government hold itself subject to the most basic laws of the land? I'm not waiting around for an answer, but you think about this—what are the institutions or bureaucracies in which you put *your* trust? Listen, I don't have much time. Please, tell Rollins that I'm sorry about frightening his family. I couldn't find another option that would produce the effect—misdirection—that I needed. But now *you* tell *me* one thing: How were you able to find Tyler so quickly?"

"I think I'll just keep that card up *my* sleeve. Who knows? I might just need to play it again sometime. Now, as to the cards you left with each body and the one in Kacmar's house, was that you choosing to operate outside the bounds of some protocol?"

"It would all have been so boresome to just take one out and move onto the next. The process is so simple, I had to find a way to make it interesting. The cards did the trick. I just underestimated the two of you figuring out the fourth card. Tell me this: Did the lights at Tyler's house fool you any at all? I had to assume you two would figure who was next and set up a surveillance. So, I set up timers as a misdirection element."

"It did. The timers caught me on my back foot."

"Spence, I've *got* to go. I just have one last question."

"What's that?"

"Are you a friend, or are you a *good* friend?"

Russell didn't wait for an answer. He tossed the burner phone Spence had given to him along with everything else electronic, to include his watch, over the side of the boat into Harlowe Creek. He was navigating toward the Newport River.

"That was Russell?" Rollins asked incredulously.

"That was Russell."

"Anything there we can use as a lead?"

"Not a thing."

An hour later as Spence and Rollins walked out the front door of the courthouse, the first rays of the sun were just starting to finger up and out from the east. Dixie was there to meet them, hoping to join them for breakfast, escape the media and find out everything. As they walked to Spence's rental car, he, Rollins, and Dixie saw Mr. Boone slowly drive by heading toward the water.

"What's Mark doing out here?" Dixie wondered aloud.

Only Spence saw him raise his right hand slightly above the driver's side window ledge of the car, his index and middle fingers forming a V. Only Mr. Boone saw Spence return the salute.

Finally, Rollins asked, "When and how did you suspicion that it was Russell?"

Spence provided his growing suspicion and rationale. Rollins and Dixie both answered in unison, "Wow."

CHAPTER THIRTY

Search within a Search, a Surprise, a Dance on the Beach

ATER THAT SAME morning, Dixie was standing on the courthouse steps. Before her the gaggle of reporters were testing microphones and endeavoring to push away the reporter to their left and right. Now, in the parking lot were many more satellite, media trucks, their antenna pointed skyward. This was the first case, nationwide wherein the killer had been identified. As a result of the discovery, inquiries from various federal entities had been made with offers to come and "assist." Those offers had been respectfully declined by the chief and sheriff. Dixie was preparing to read a statement she and Spence had constructed. Spence wouldn't be at the briefing as he was assisting in the search of the small house Russell had rented.

"Early this morning, the attempted murder of Judge Wanda Blevins was prevented by the cooperative efforts of the Carteret County Sheriff's Office and the Beaufort Police Department. Additionally, surrounding county and municipal police departments have assisted greatly in this investigation and in the rescue of Judge Wanda Blevins. It has been determined that the murders of Duke Kacmar, Greg Garrett, Shauna Tyler, and the attempted murder of Judge Blevins were committed by former assistant district attorney Bob Russell."

The collective intake of air was audible to all in the area. Simultaneously, the members of the herd began asking questions. Dixie held up her hand and paused until it was respectfully quiet.

"A local, state, and nationwide search for Mr. Russel is now underway. Media outlets have been provided with information including photographs and additional related information. Mr. Russell is encouraged to turn himself in to avoid the possibility of an adverse occurrence with his eventual arrest.

"Investigator Jesse David Rollins has and continues to serve as the lead investigator in this case. His investigative undertakings were central in saving the life of Judge Blevins and the identification of Mr. Russell as the perpetrator.

"It should be noted that this breakthrough is the first to occur in this apparent nationwide attack against members of the legal profession. Relevant information will be shared with local and state entities conducting related investigations. Next to speak will be the Carteret County sheriff followed by the Beaufort police chief."

After finishing, Dixie turned and quickly entered the courthouse. Her plan was to go straightway from there to Russell's house to be there during the search. At the house, she found Rollins and Spence fully decked out in crime scene processing gear. Having obtained permission from Rollins to participate, she suited up and entered the house. First, glancing around the den, she then walked down the hall into the single bath. Opening the medicine cabinet and finding it empty, she quickly closed the mirrored door and returned to the hall.

"Has the bathroom been processed yet?" she asked of whoever could hear her.

A collective no reverberated through the house. Having learned that, she returned to the den, grasped her blue, plastic gloved hands behind her back and observed the proceedings until the house was fully processed—inside and out—and the scene cleared.

The search was concluded. Spence, Rollins, and Dixie, now out of crime scene protective gear, stood in the front yard. Rollins had Russell's well-used, now-stripped-of-all-electronics, older car towed to the department for processing within a contained environment.

Rollins ruminated, "He must have seen things beginning to circle the drain. That house is squeaky clean. The only thing left was the furniture that belonged to the house—and even that had been wiped and polished. I don't think there's anything here we can use to move the ball down the field as to who he was working for or where he is headed. And I'll be surprised if his car will provide us with anything viable." Looking at Spence and Dixie, he asked, "Do you think this is it? Was Judge Blevins to be the last victim in any case?"

Spence answered, "I do. I don't know if things are over on a state or national basis, but I think around here, with him most likely gone, that's it. That being said, however, I wouldn't let my guard down."

"What about the second party—supposedly the driver—in the Tyler murder?"

"I'm theorizing here, but I think that's just what that driver was—a secondary party. Whatever this entity is, however, it's well organized and it appears there are participants with different roles—some primary and some secondary. Who knows? Russell was…is an obvious primary contributor. I don't know about you two, but I'm ready for some lunch. Let's meet at the Beaufort Grocery Company." Looking at Rollins, he said, "I want to try the Queen's Club that you were forced to share with Russell when the three of us were there. I'm buying."

As the three sat and enjoyed their meal, Spence looked for an elderly lady playing a crossword puzzle, but she was nowhere to be seen.

Rollins drank the last of his iced tea. "I'm going back to the room. Even though I don't believe it will add anything to the mix, if the autopsy report on Tyler has come in, I'd like to review it."

"I'll go with you. I'd like to see it as well."

Setting his eyes on Dixie, Spence asked, "So, now what's on your plate?"

"Right now, I'm still anchored to the media. I'm going to go ask the chief if I can go back into uniform—back into the real world. If he gives me the thumbs-up, I'm going home, get a little sleep and be ready for third shift, back with my squad."

"Good luck. I hope you make it."

Spence paid the tab with a generous tip, and off they went.

Back in the conference room, Tyler's autopsy report contained no surprises. Spence and Rollins worked methodically to enter the cards appropriately into the chain of evidence. Both felt there would never be a trial in their case, but it always a good idea to go by the book. There were however, no records or reports that referenced Mr. Boone.

A text flashed onto Spence's phone: "I'll have a two-hour access to my phone tonight at seven. Can I call?—E."

"Absolutely," he shot back.

"Russell! Who in the world would have thought that? Later—E. PS— back Thursday."

"This day just keeps getting better and better," Spence said to himself more than to Rollins.

"You know what? We need a break. I'm going to call Lieutenant Brown and see if we can arrange to go fishing tomorrow. Would you like to go?"

"I'm gonna take my family on an outing. I don't know what we'll do or where we'll do it. Anyway, you know, Wednesday night is church. There's a potluck supper before the service and you're welcome to come."

"Let me think about it."

"That was weak, man."

That night by seven, Spence had eaten and was settled in his room well before seven. At the appointed time the phone rang.

"Hey, young lady."

"Timmy, how are you?"

They didn't waste the time they had talking about the Russell case, and Spence wasn't about to ask about her activities. The time was too valuable, too fleeting, too needed. After an hour, which had seemed like moments, she lamented, "I've got to go."

"I know. I'm looking forward to Thursday."

"Me too. Goodnight, Timmy."

"Goodnight."

The next day, Spence and Lieutenant Brown spent the day on the water. The case was never the topic of conversation. Banter was limited to fishing and who would reign triumphant by catching the biggest fish. By late afternoon when they had pulled into the dock, they had forgotten to determine who had the largest catch of the day. The fish were donated to a service that made them available to families in need.

"Thank you for a great time. Let me pay for the gas. "

"Your money is no good here, Spence."

"Then I'll thank of something to repay the favor."

At five thirty, Rollins was making his way down the long set of tables in the fellowship hall of his church. The tables were ladened with aromatic home cooking. There was everything delicious to include homemade cakes and pies. Just as he was reaching for a second scoop of potato salad, he got bumped to the side. Regaining his balance, he saw Spence standing there, plate in hand and smiling from ear to ear.

"Are you going to stay for church?"

"You know me, I'm not one to…eat and run."

Thursday, shortly after lunch, Spence received a text, "Home—come over when you can—E."

Thirty minutes later, Eimear was escorting him into the house. Just as soon as she had closed the door, Spence took her into his arms, kissed her deeply, and held her tightly. Razor took the chew toy from Spence's hand that also held her waist and happily trotted off into another room.

"I've missed you so much."

"I've missed you."

"Timmy, I could use a break. My mind is still on go, and I'm tired of thinking."

"What do you have in mind?"

"Can you dance?"

"Well, not as good as Fred Astaire, but I've been told that I could hold my own. I've got some impressive moves."

"There's a beach-music dance festival at North Myrtle Beach. Let's go."

"Okay. When do you want to go?"

Holding up her helmet she said, "Now, right now. Look, I have my bike-worthy jeans on. Out the door, on your bike, and we're gone. I hate to play this card, but you do owe me for solving your riddle. You game?"

"Now? What about your other clothes and toiletries?"

"I'll buy some when we get there."

"What about Razor?"

"My brother has got it covered."

"What about your computer?"

"I'm not going down there to work."

"Right this minute?"

"Right this *very* minute."

Out the door, on the bike and they were on their way. Traveling south on Highway Seventeen, they crossed the state line into South Carolina. A line from Poe's poem, *Eldorado* came to Eimear,

"Ride, boldly ride,
    The shade replied,—
If you seek for Eldorado!"

She smiled and thought, "Found it!." Having confirmed the fact to herself, she held onto Spence just that much tighter.

Seven Months Later

ITTING OUTSIDE AS the snow fell, waiting for the ordered cheeseburger, fries, and hot coffee was as enjoyable as the meal itself. The fog reaching down to touch the snow gave the Vermont ski lodge and its surroundings a mystical air—otherworldly. Outside the perimeter of the food court, those waiting in the line for the chairlift were enjoying the camaraderie that came with the shared love of skiing.

No sooner had the anticipated meal been placed on the wooden table than a hand was extended and a cheerful voice announced, "Hi there. My name's Mike."

It didn't take the hard-earned medical degree to identify the residual facial swelling and tightness to know that Mike had recently had some facial work done.

"First, I want to congratulate you on completing your objective. I know it has not been easy under the circumstances."

"Excuse me?"

"Completing medical school along with a master's degree in chemistry. Also, holding a college loan large enough to support a small country."

Sitting up straighter now, she said, "And how would you come to know all of that about me?"

"Let's just say it's my job to know about people. You can think of me as a headhunter. I'm a headhunter with the option of paying off your entire educational loan. But first let me ask you a question: How would you like to help make the world a better place?"

"Well, that sounds noble enough."

"Ask yourself this: Could you ever imagine being part of something bigger and more significant than yourself? Lastly, will *normal* be an acceptable descriptor of your life, or would you like for it to be *extraordinary*?"

Before the prospect could answer, Mike asked, "Can we move over to that far table so that we can talk with a bit more privacy?"

Picking up the uneaten meal, the now not-so-hungry interlocutor noticed Mike's feet. *Good Lord*, she thought, *he doesn't have on any socks. His feet must be frozen.*

An hour later, half of the cheeseburger and all of her fries still on her plate, she asked, "It all sounds intriguing, but how do I know I can trust *you*? You might be telling me all of this to lure me away somewhere and harm *me*."

"You've made an excellent point. I would be thinking the same thing. And that's why you will not be leaving with me. There's a female companion to travel with you."

He motioned to a young woman who was mingling with the crowd in the chairlift line. She came over, smiled broadly, and stuck out her hand, "Hi. My name is Annie. I'll be traveling with you should you decide to go." As Annie turned her head, from under her dark-blue woolen cap, her sandy-blond-haired ponytail that hung to the base of her neck danced back and forth across the shoulder of her ski jacket.

The prospect took a deep breath, stood up, and together the trio walked to the parking lot where a black SUV was parked with the motor running quietly.

Shaking her hand, Mike told her, "Very nice to meet you. I enjoyed talking with you."

Returning to the table, he looked at the now, stone-cold, half-eaten cheeseburger and fries waiting patiently on the plate.

No sense letting good food go to waste, he thought as he picked up the remaining portion of cheeseburger and stuffed it into his mouth.

www.ingramcontent.com/pod-product-compliance
Lightning Source LLC
Chambersburg PA
CBHW061026120726
47910CB00006B/2111